Cox

Arizona
Adventure

action-packed true tales
of early Arizona
by
Marshall Trimble

Golden West Publishers

FRONT COVER and maps . . . artwork by Bruce Robert Fischer

BACK COVER . . . photo by Simone Bibeau

INSIDE BACK COVER . . . photo by Kevin Schirmer

Library of Congress Cataloging in Publication Data

Trimble, Marshall.
  Arizona adventure.

  Bibliography.
  Includes index.
  1. Frontier and pioneer life--Arizona--Addresses,
essays, lectures. 2. Arizona--History--Addresses,
essays, lectures. I. Title.
F811.5.T74 1982   979.1   82-11871
ISBN 0-914846-14-0

Printed in the United States of America

Golden West Publishers
4113 N. Longview Ave.
Phoenix, AZ. 85014, USA

DEDICATION

*To my son, Roger Frederick Trimble,
born April 18, 1979.
No honor or event could ever match the total joy
and happiness you have given.*

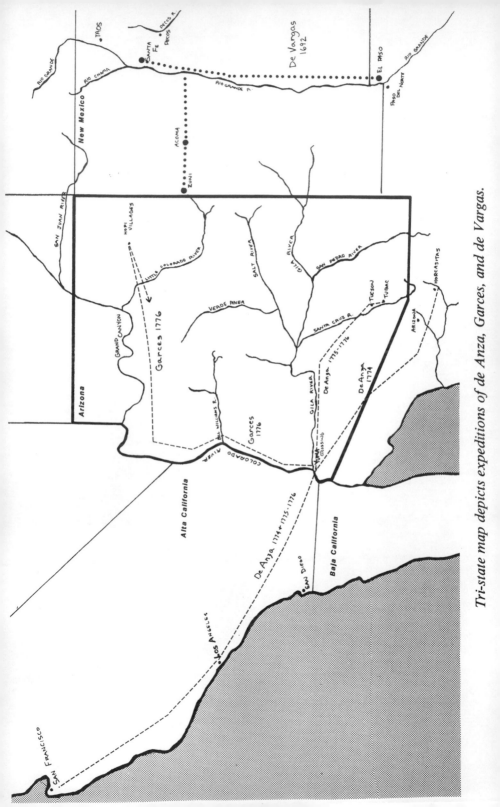

Tri-state map depicts expeditions of de Anza, Garces, and de Vargas.

CONTENTS

MAPS

ARIZONA PLACE NAMES

Early-day settlers Corydon E. Cooley and Marion Clark had been neighbors for a short time, living among the lush, green ponderosa forestland along Arizona's Mogollon Rim. The two became concerned about one encroaching on the other's privacy. Perhaps on a clear day one could see a wisp of smoke rising from the other's chimney. Whatever the reason Cooley and Clark agreed it was getting too crowded and one of the two parties had to move. The issue was to be settled, not by intimidation or gunplay, but with a deck of cards. The game, called Seven-up, where low card wins, was a favorite among frontiersmen. The game reached its climax when Clark said to Cooley as he dealt the last hand "If you can show low, you win." At this point Cooley turned up the deuce of clubs and declared, "Show low it is." Marion Clark moved on down the road a piece and Cooley named the settlement that grew up near his ranch, **"Showlow,"** in honor of the now-famous card game. The main street in thriving Showlow today is called the "Deuce of Clubs" and whenever there is a runoff for mayor the issue is settled by the two political opponents sitting down with a deck of cards. The first to draw the deuce of clubs is mayor for the next term.

Ever since man first set foot in this land called Arizona, he has felt compelled to name every river, waterhole, mountain pass and trail. Inspiration was usually drawn from great natural spectacles and awesome beauty, but not always.

Among Arizona's fabulous mineral laden mountains lie the skeletal remains of storied ghost camps of yesteryear, born in boom and died in dust, the fragile wooden walls, concrete ruins, monuments to hopes and aspirations that didn't always pan out.

These ghostly reminders of the past were generally populated by a variety of boisterous, rough and tumble miners generally characterized as unmarried, unchurched, and unwashed. They named their temporary abodes after former hometowns or countries, girlfriends, local geography, dappled with a liberal touch of tongue-in-cheek humor.

Others came to the land, promptly renamed or corrupted the original name to better suit their own linguistic abilities. **Tucson** gets its name from the dark base of nearby Sentinel Mountain. The Papago Indians usually named their communities for some conspicuous geographical feature and called their village at the foot of the mountain, Chuk-Shon. The Spanish pronounced the name Tuqui-Son, which eventually evolved into Tucson.

When the early Spanish interlopers asked the river people living along the Gila what they called themselves, the response was "Pim," meaning roughly, "I don't understand." The Spanish interpreted "Pim" to be the name of the tribe and the Akimeel Awatam or "River People," became the **Pima.** A similar incident occurred at the confluence of the Gila and Colorado rivers. When the Spanish asked to parley with the "Chief," a young man stepped forward, pounded his chest and replied, "**Yuma,**" which meant "Son of the Chief." These people, who called themselves the Quechan are still more familiarly known as the Yuma Tribe and have a city and county named in their honor.

The Apaches' name for themselves was "Dineh," meaning "the People." **Apache** was a name coined by the Zuni people and popularized by the Europeans. The word means "enemy." **Navajo** comes from similar origins. Closely related to the Apaches, they were dubbed "Apaches de Nabahu," or "Apaches of the cultivated fields."

The Spanish weren't the only ones guilty of misinterpretation. Sometimes lines of communication falter between peoples of the same language. During the 1880's Henry Mortimer Coane became postmaster of a small farming town in the Verde Valley. As was often the case in the birth of a community, the postmaster named the place after himself. In a letter to postal authorities, Mr. Coane suggested the name Coaneville. Somebody in the nation's capital misread the name and officially dubbed the town "**Cornville.**"

Down near Organ Pipe National Monument is a junction in the highway. These junctions are usually referred to as "Y's." In this case, one road led to Tucson, another to Ajo and a third to the Mexican border. When postal authorities asked the folks living at the junction what they wanted to call their community, the response was an emphatic "Y." Something was lost in the translation and with a wisdom known only to the bureaucratic minds of officialdom, the name was approved in Washington giving birth to the town of "**Why,**" Arizona. To which some local wag no doubt responded, "Why Not?"

Eloy is derived from a Syrian word "Eloi," meaning "My God." "My God" is one of those expressions that has many meanings, depending on one's emotional response to a situation. If the Syrian who had decided to settle in the area had stepped down from the train in the middle of August, there is little room for doubt as to the intent of his descriptive response.

There are names that might be categorized in the Department of Redundancy-Redundancy. The Spanish attached descriptive names to the landscape such as **Mesa** and **Picacho.** English speaking people came along and thought the words to be pretty and interesting but not quite descriptive enough. So Mesa became "Table Mesa," and Picacho became "Picacho Peak."

Many of Arizona's communities have misleading names. **Pinetop** was not named for the famous ponderosa that abound in the area, but for a tall bushy-headed bartender who operated a saloon there in the 1890's. **Snowflake** was named for the Mormon Apostle Erastus Snow and early-day colonizer Jacob Flake. "**Fourpaugh,**" "**Poland,**" "**Cowlic,**" "**Hereford,**" "**Land,**" "**Light,**" and "**Love**" were all named after people.

"**Total Wreck,**" in Pima County, came into being in the 1880's when a cowboy named John Dillon discovered a rich ore body of silver. The hill above the ledge on which the mineral was discovered was considered by Dillon to be a "Total Wreck." Today "Total Wreck" is a ghost town, so there is some truth to the town name after all.

"**Lousy Gulch**" earned its name, not because it was a lousy gulch in the common vernacular, but because the prospectors and miners were attacked by pesky lice, thus providing some power of suggestion to naming the town in honor of the dubious happening.

Occasionally, early day name givers displayed a noticeable lack of imagination and creativity such as naming a little green valley near Christopher Creek, "**Little Green Valley.**" The same might be said of such obvious places—names such as "**Hilltop,**" "**Hillside,**" "**Ocotillo,**" "**Cholla,**" "**Cactus,**" "**The Gap,**" "**Seven Springs,**" "**Fish Creek,**" and "**Big Bug.**" There are also some five or six "**Turkey Creeks**" scattered around the state and several "**Rattlesnake**—basins, creeks, hills and canyons.**"

Arizona's best known acronym is the range of mountains in Yuma County called the "Kofas." **Kofa** stands for King of Arizona—an early day gold-mining operation in the region. The state has been called a land of anomalies and tamales, referring to the many different people and diverse landscapes. There are times when Arizona registers the nation's high and low temperatures on the same day. People have been known to snow ski and water ski on the same day. There are anomalies in place-names too. The town of **Pima** is not located in Pima County, but is in Graham County. The town of **Maricopa** is found in Pinal County. To make matters even more confusing, the community of **Navajo** resides in Apache County while **Fort Apache** is in Navajo County.

Patriotism was the motivating factor in the naming of one of northern Arizona's most prominent cities. A party of immigrants bound for California camped at the foot of the San Francisco mountains on July 4, 1876. To honor the nation's centennial, they raised the colors. To celebrate the occasion they called the site "**Flagstaff.**"

A group of miners in Santa Cruz County wanted to call their new town "American Flag," but the idea was nixed in Washington so the folks settled for "**Old Glory.**" In a surge of patriotic fever during World War I residents of a tiny community near **Ajo** wanted to called their town Woodrow to honor the President. Postal authorities refused to allow a town to be named after a living person, so the townspeople compromised and named the town "**Rowood.**"

The coming of the Atlantic and Pacific (Sante Fe) Railroad gave birth to several towns along the mainline in northern Arizona. "**Sanders,**" "**Holbrook,**" "**Winslow,**" "**Seligman,**" and "**Kingman,**" were all named for railroad officials or businessmen with a vested interest. The "billion dollar" copper towns of **Jerome** and **Bisbee** were named for a couple of eastern investors—neither of whom ever took the time to visit his namesake.

Women have played a prominent role in the naming of some Arizona towns and places. When polygamy was outlawed in Utah, those Mormons who wished to continue the practice built a community on the Arizona side of the border. They named their town **"Fredonia."** The free is self-explanatory and "Dona," is Spanish for woman, thus creating a "Free Woman" or "Fredonia," Arizona. **"Sedona"** is named for Sedona M. Schnebly—a member of an early pioneer family in the area.

"Olive City" was a small ferryboat crossing on the Colorado river named to honor Olive Oatman, a young girl taken captive by hostile Indians in the 1850's. Miss Oatman survived her five-year ordeal in the Arizona desert, returned to the white society where she lived a long and productive life. Legend has it the gold-mining boom town of "Oatman," in Mohave County, was also named for Olive.

The town of **"Ruby,"** was named for Lillie Ruby Andrews, who was one of the community's few female residents. Black jack Newman wanted to name the mining community that sprung up near Globe "Mima," after his girlfriend Mima Tune. A group of miners who lived nearby hailed from Miami, Ohio. The names "Mima" and **"Miami"** blended together and eventually the latter won out. **"Mount Lemmon,"** one of the state's highest mountain ranges and America's southernmost skiing area, was named for Sara Plummer Lemmon, who was the first white woman to climb to its summit. She made the trek on her honeymoon and made a return voyage when she was 70 years old.

Arizona's capital city might have been called "Salina," "Stonewall," or even "Pumpkinville," had it not been for a spurious English "Lord" named Darrell Duppa. Duppa was a well-educated world traveler who, it was rumored, was given a substantial allowance by his wealthy English relatives to remain permanently at large.

His raucous lifestyle, highlighted by epic bouts with dipsomania was, no doubt, a source of embarrassment to his relatives and contributed to his banishment to Arizona. It was said "Lord" Duppa was fluent in seven languages. Unfortunately for his listeners, the erudite eccentric spoke all seven in the same paragraph.

Duppa was a member of a committee chosen to select a name for the new settlement on the banks of the Salt River one sunny October day in 1870. An intrepid group of entrepreneurs led by Jack Swilling had cleaned out some pre-historic canals dug by the now-vanished Hohokam people; an irrigation company had been organized and plans were being made to develop farms. Soon the arid valley would grow crops to supply the military post at Fort McDowell and the mining camps throughout the Bradshaw Mountains. Now they decided it was time to give the place a name.

Swilling wanted to call the new settlement "Stonewall," after his hero, the late "Stonewall" Jackson. Another member chose Salina for the Salt River. Still another wanted Pumpkinville for the wild pumpkins growing in the area. When Duppa's turn came, he arose and waxed eloquently on the ancient civilization that had once flourished on the land where they stood. He predicted the rise of another great civilization on the same site. In his inimitable elocutionary style Duppa compared the phenomenon to the mythical **Phoenix** bird in Egypt that lived 500 years, then rose from its own funeral pyre to flourish again. Needless to say, Duppa's proposal carried the day. Soon after "Lord" Duppa gazed wistfully across the Salt River to the mesquite and greasewood-covered desert behind the river crossing at Hayden's Ferry and declared the place reminded him of the beautiful, verdant Vale of Tempe in Greece. The local folks approved of the analogy and the dusty Mexican village of San Pablo became **Tempe.**

The name **Arizona** comes from the Papago "ali-shonak" meaning "small spring." The name became popular following the discovery of rich lodes of silver "so pure you could cut it with a knife," some 25 miles southwest of present-day Nogales in 1736.

The word was ultimately corrupted into "Arizona." The silver didn't last long, but the world now knew of the fabulous "planchas de plata" (sheets of silver) and Arizona. Still, the area was known officially as New Mexico or better yet "Terra Incognita" during the years of Spanish and later Mexican control. New Mexico became a part of the United States following the Treaty of Guadalupe Hidalgo in 1848 and Arizona remained a part of New Mexico. The compromise of 1850 brought New Mexico into the union as a territory. Shortly after the citizens in the western part of New Mexico began clamoring for separate status. Several names were suggested including "Arizona" and "Gadsonia," the latter to honor James Gadsden, the man who had negotiated the purchase of land south of the Gila River in 1853. The name "Arizona" won out and in 1863 there was, at last, a real Arizona.

We Arizonans have inherited a litany of picturesquely, whimsical place names bestowed by cowboys, miners, prospectors and others who arrived in the 19th century and at least one town can lay claim to its existence from the result of a massive hangover. In the spring of 1876, Charlie McMillen and Theodore "Dore" Harris had been on a glorious binge in Globe where the local liquor contained a thousand songs and a hundred fights to the barrel. It was said Charlie was so drunk he couldn't hit the ground with his hat in three tries. The next day, he and Dore were prospecting out north of Globe. Suddenly, Charlie declared he was too ill to proceed and collapsed in deep slumber on the ground. Dore was a prospector true to the code, which was, roughly stated, "Whenever and wherever the opportunity arises, take thy pick and hammer and crush rocks." This he did and somewhere near the body of his sleeping companion he uncovered a rich lode of silver. The fabulous "Stonewall Jackson" mine was born on the spot. Before the boom ended, some two million dollars in silver had been removed. A town sprang up and was called McMillenville in honor of Charlie's "two-million dollar hangover."

The FIRST
AMERICAN REVOLUTION

Francisco Vasquez de Coronado had been the first of the great Conquistadores to come to this land in search of great wealth in the year 1540. Forty-two years later, another fortune seeker, Antonio de Espejo made his entrada. He found silver in Central Arizona's Verde Valley, but had no way to transport it. Besides, the natives were a trifle unfriendly. Next came a wealthy miner named Juan de Onate, who would establish a colony along the Rio Grande and become known as the "Father of New Mexico." He, too, sought fame and more fortune. He found fame and lost a fortune while attempting to locate the fabled Northwest Passage, uncover fabulous mineral lodes and open the region for colonization. In the end, he succumbed to political jealousy, restless natives and defiant colonists.

The Sierra Nevada and Rocky Mountains contained vast hordes of gold and silver, but these lofty ranges kept their secrets safe until American prospectors arrived in the latter half of the 19th century. Had the Spanish explorers discovered the mineral lodes, a rush would have established a permanent center that might have changed the course of American history dramatically.

During the years following the Spanish failure to conquer the vast expanse of dry, inhospitable land that is today's American Southwest, many changes were taking place. For all practical purposes, a military solution was not possible. The nomadic tribes were too intractable and mobile to be permanently located and "reduced," a Spanish term for "civilizing the heathens." The success enjoyed by the missionaries among the rancheria Indians further south was not destined to be duplicated among the tightly-structured Pueblo villages where deep-rooted customs and religious practices made total acceptance of the "Holy Faith" marginal at best. The natives resented the strict discipline and forced labor imposed upon them by all segments of Spanish society, colonists, government and religion. The Spanish colonizers, by and large, looked upon themselves as hidalgos or gentlemen of upper class, not to soil their hands in menial toil. There were no native generals or prime ministers to negotiate for large numbers of people and there was no capital city to conquer. All this, of course, was frustrating to military minds of the period (and still is).

Because of British and Russian threats from the Pacific and French encroachments in the Mississippi Valley, Spain needed a better way to maintain its hold on the northern provinces, the land that includes today's American Southwest. In the early 1600's, Spain proposed to send missionaries to the natives, depending upon the olive branch and a little friendly persuasion rather than a show of power to convert the natives into good Spanish citizens who would defend the entire region from outside invaders. It would be left to the missionaries, especially the members of the Jesuit and Franciscan Orders to root out heathen practices and integrate their own religious activities, and, at the same time, create a loyal native force to hold the land for Spain against outside encroachments.

Unlike the conquistadores who came in search of the *madre del oro* or vast lands to control, the missionaries sought to reap a golden harvest of souls. These were times of the Inquisition and there was an urgent sense of mission to rescue the heathen soul from an infinite tour of duty in hell. It mattered little to the zealous missionaries if they provided a little hell on earth for their charges, as long as the soul found salvation prior to its earthly departure.

Not all this harsh treatment, incidentally, was reserved for the natives alone. A punishment set for Spanish colonists in 1783 read as follows: "Men who consented to prostitution of their wives were to be exposed in public, rubbed in honey, made to wear a fool's cap with a string of garlic and a pair of horns, lashed 100 times and sent to the galleys for a period of ten years,"—all this for the first offense.

During the exploration period (1540-1610), missionaries accompanied expeditions primarily to administer spiritual guidance for the soldiers, keep diaries, map the region and convert natives to Christianity. The years 1610 to 1680 might well be known as the "golden age of the missionaries" in New Mexico.

After permanent Spanish cities such as Santa Fe came into existence (1610), missionaries moved freely among the dozens of pueblos in the region. Operating in groups of ones and twos, guarded at times by only a handful of soldiers, they pushed into the frontier in search of lost souls. During this so-called "golden age," some 250 Franciscan friars worked the pueblos. The crown spent vast amounts of money for humanitarian purposes in New Mexico. More than minimal credit was due to the great persuasive powers of the missionaries in convincing the mother country to spend such great expenditures on an area that provided little monetary return on the investment. All this had a price. The natives would provide the labor force. A system called the *Repartimiento* mobilized the Indians to work in the white man's mines, ranches and farms. In exchange for these efforts, the Spanish sometimes paid a small fee and shared their culture with the aborigines. Another system, the *Encomienda* called for an annual tribute of commodities such as corn and cotton blankets. It didn't amount to much in years of plenty, but during a drought brought great hardship to the natives.

Spanish authorities in the New World found themselves encumbered by an incredible system of bureaucracy. Final decisions on important matters were resolved in Madrid and took months to process. To make matters worse, civil officials, priests, and the military were at odds constantly competing for Indian labor. The Franciscan friars were a law unto themselves in New Mexico. They maintained a separate capital at Santo Domingo and paid little heed to the civil government except in time of strife. The citizen soldiers in the colony resented the fact that the Franciscans, who were pledged to poverty, grazed vast herds of livestock while the citizen soldiers struggled to obtain a few head. They were also obligated to provide protection from hostile Apaches, Comanches and Navajos.

Territorial governors came into Santa Fe and set up sweatshops in the Palace of the Governors, exploiting native labor. Here in a long, low flat-roofed adobe building, captives spent long hours weaving textiles which were sold for personal gain. In an effort to gain more natives for work in the mills, the governors also encouraged slave-hunting expeditions to the Apaches, Comanches and Navajos, something that caused fierce retaliations by these nomadic tribes upon the Spanish citizens. The church protested these practices vehemently, primarily, however, because they wanted the Indians to work at the missions. Priests were sometimes accused by the governors of mistreating and sexually abusing the natives. Physical violence between church and civil authorities was not that uncommon. These quarrels weakened discipline and morale in the colony and were used by native leaders to full advantage to demonstrate the vulnerability of the Spanish system.

The labor force for construction of the churches was provided by local natives. The structures were massive. Tons of adobe brick went into the construction of the thick walls. The great height of the churches was designed to tower over the rest of the village in their midst. No doubt, the natives were awe-struck by these great white cathedrals.

The mission was designed to be the center of community activities. Classes were conducted in Spanish customs, religion, art, Latin, blacksmithing, leatherwork, carpentry, adobe-making, music and drama. Plays were conducted periodically with natives acting out parts which always had a strong religious theme.

The natives seemed quite willing to accept the Christian faith as long as they could integrate it with their native religion, especially the more colorful aspects of Catholic ritual. However, the priests found these practices unacceptable and handed out severe punishment to those guilty of "pagan practices." When they could not prohibit the Indians from reverting to their native religions the priests turned to flogging and hanging. The shamans, whose very authority rested on the maintenance of the ancient native rituals, cared little for the blending of religions. Both sides braced for a showdown.

There was always plenty of work to be done around the missions, enough to keep a small army of natives busy. Workers caught loafing on the job were punished by whipping, the stocks, or having their heads shaved. The loss of hair was a colossal indignity to the Pueblo people. A decree from the viceroy finally prohibited this practice after 1620.

Men were put to work making adobes for construction of the buildings. Among the Pueblo peoples, the division of labor dictated that men performed such functions as hunting, weaving and warfare. In the Pueblo cultural scheme of things, women made adobes and built walls. Native men assigned to perform these tasks were subject to ridicule and jestful remarks by their spouses, sisters and girl friends. The men ran away and had to be forcibly gathered and returned to the mission. The priests seemed to have little awareness or sensitivity for these native customs. In fact, they found these idiosyncrasies downright amusing. It seems, also, they were totally unaware of a deep, smoldering hatred beneath the surface. All that was needed to ignite the spark of rebellion was a catalyst —a leader to unite the Pueblos and drive the Spaniards from their lands.

The Pueblo villages were not interdependent as many would believe. They more closely resembled the city-states of ancient Greece. Even though they shared a common culture, they were a fractious bunch and rarely saw eye to eye on matters, something that made subjugation by the Europeans easier. A great famine and drought in the 1670's had reduced the native population to half of what it had been prior to the coming of the Spanish. Some medicine men in the pueblos saw this as a warning from their gods to throw off the harness of Spanish rule.

The Pueblo culture did not lend itself to individualism. The natives oeprated under a strict code of conformity. A person who sought individual recognition was shunned or censored by the people. For this reason, it was many years before they were driven to accept an individual capable of strong leadership—one who might unite all the Pueblos along the Rio Grande. It was ironic that the man who would lead the Great Pueblo Revolt of 1680 against the Spanish Catholics was named Pope. The insurrection has become known as the "first American Revolution."

Pope was an Indian medicine man from San Juan Pueblo who, along with several others, underwent severe punishment at the whipping post for practicing his native religion. He had been one of forty-seven so called "wizards" rounded up in 1675 after the priests had persuaded the governor to send in soldiers to demolish the ceremonial kivas in several Pueblos.

Prayer sticks had been destroyed and kachinas were burned. Three of the more notorious shamans were hanged while the rest were whipped and imprisoned. In response, a large number of Pueblo warriors gathered at the Governor's Palace and demanded the release of the medicine men. The governor, Antonio de Otermin, backed down and the prisoners were set free. This show of united force by the natives was not lost on the resolute shaman, Pope. The revolt was organized in secrecy at Taos, the northernmost Pueblo, and was planned for early August, 1680. The resolute Pope was so consumed with secrecy that he killed his own son-in-law because he feared the man would betray the revolt. Natives were to rise up in unison on the same day and oust the hated Spaniards from New Mexico and Arizona. Runners were sent as far away as Hopiland, 300 miles to the west, carrying knotted cords. In order to keep track of time, a knot was untied each day. The untying of the last knot indicated the day to strike, August 11. Two messengers were betrayed by Spanish-appointed village governors who refused to go along with the revolt and taken before Spanish authorities. They were able to convince the governor that the revolt was to begin on August 13 instead of the 11th. This caused the Pueblo leaders to move the revolt ahead one day. Believing they had several days to prepare, the Spanish were caught by surprise when the revolt began on August 10.

Twenty-two of the 33 resident priests were subjected to the most brutal indignities before being murdered. In Hopiland, native warriors pulled soldiers and priests from the houses and cut their throats. Churches were left in shambles. At Oraibi, huge beams were pulled down and used to repair the roofs of the kivas. They are still in use today, as are some small church bells which are used for native ceremonies. All remnants of Spanish culture were removed. Names such as Jose, Jesus, and Maria were strictly forbidden.

Europeans were driven from New Mexico leaving behind more than 400 of their countrymen slain by the hordes of warriors who swept down on the hapless settlers. There were some 1,000 Spaniards in Santa Fe of which only about a hundred were trained to fight. All sought refuge inside the walls of the Palace of the Governors. In spite of the odds, the Spanish mounted a counterattack and nearly succeeded in retaking the city. Pueblo reinforcements arrived and cut off the water supply. Within a week, the city was ordered abandoned. The melancholy flight southward down the Rio Grande, through sacked and burned haciendas and churches, still bears the name given it during this turbulent period. It remains the *Jornada del Muerto*—The Journey of Death.

Pope had risen to power by attacking the Spanish system, especially its oppression and high-handed treatment of natives. He promised to repeal the *Encomienda* and *Repartimiento*. Attacks from hostile Apaches, Navajos and Comanches would be curtailed, something the Spanish soldiers had been unable to accomplish. Unhappily, Pope's regime was an oppressive as that of the predecessors. Still, the despotic shaman was able to maintain strict control until his death around 1690.

The Spanish survivors of the great Pueblo Revolt of 1680 had retreated down the Rio Grande to El Paso del Norte (the Pass of the North), or the site of modern-day El Paso/Juarez. The humiliated Spanish didn't give up their province easily. Several attempts were made to reoccupy New Mexico. One expedition went north to the Pueblo of Cochiti, west of Santa Fe, where they were welcomed by the natives. After a great display of repenting, bowing and foot-kissing by the natives, word was sent out that reconciliation with the Spanish was at hand. It was all a shrewd plan to dupe the Spaniards into a false sense of security. The natives planned to have the most beautiful, young Pueblo girls wine and dine the lonesome Spaniards, then lure them off to their boudoir and after an evening of joyous lovemaking, kill them. Fortunately for the Spanish, they learned of the plan in time to gather their forces and hustle back to El Paso del Norte. All efforts to retake New Mexico failed until 1692. At that time a formidable conquistador named Don Diego de Vargas Zapata y Jujan Ponce de Leon y Contreras with 60 soldiers, 100 Indian allies and three friars recaptured Santa Fe. Incidentally, after the revolt the Pueblo people had gone back to their traditional independent ways. Nomadic tribes continued to pillage the Pueblos and many missed the economic benefits of the Spanish system. Old Pueblo rivalries were renewed, thus insuring the eventual success of the Spanish. Still, it took Don Diego de Vargas three years to complete the reconquest of New Mexico. Eventually, all the villages except Oraibi in Hopiland agreed to live peacefully under Spanish rule.

De Vargas was a truly remarkable man for his time. His statesmanship matched that of his military prowess. The conquerer of New Mexico went unescorted to the Pueblos promising the residents that in future dealings their civil liberties would be respected. No longer would they be forced to labor under the harsh controls of politician, colonist or missionary. Raiding and razing the sacred kivas was strictly forbidden. This extending of the olive branch gained much respect for the new governor from the natives but was unpopular with the colonists who wanted to punish the rebels by enslavement in sweatshops, farms and ranches. Phony charges were trumped against de Vargas and he was imprisoned by his peers for three years. In 1703, he was completely exonerated. His political enemies quickly fled the city of Santa Fe. His health ruined, de Vargas ruled New Mexico until his death a few months after his release. A soldier to the end, he died while on a campaign against hostile Apaches near today's Albuquerque.

If Juan de Onate was the "Father of New Mexico," then surely Don Diego de Vargas was its "Savior."

The Spanish learned many lessons from the Great Pueblo Revolt of 1680. Never again was the church so dogmatic in its dealings with the natives, preferring instead to compromise with native religions, something that is strongly characteristic in the Pueblos today. Also, the natives carry on their traditional religions in the kivas as they have for centuries, unhampered by the Catholics. There is little doubt that the Revolt allowed a people to maintain their respect, dignity and above all, their culture. Among the many contributions made by the Spanish to the Pueblo culture, such as the introduction of livestock, merchandise and new crops, something that is often overlooked, was a system of communication. Until Spanish was introduced, many of the Pueblos could not converse because of the difference in language. Spanish became the common language spoken and still is.

The Franciscans had made a little headway with the Hopis during the golden years. In 1629, Fray Francisco Porras led a group of 12 soldiers and three other friars to the Hopi village of Awatovi. They were received "with some coolness" by the natives but when Father Porras baptized, by his own account, 4,000 Indians, these Franciscans named the majestic San Francisco Mountains to the southwest that tower over today's Flagstaff, after the patron saint, Francis of Assisi. The friar's success did not set well with local medicine men at Awatovi and they had him killed in 1633.

Despite the martyring of Father Porras, the Franciscans continued to build missions among the Hopi people. By 1675 there were missions at Awatovi, Oraibi and Shongopavi and visitas at Walpi and Mishongovi.

Harsh penances were imposed upon the Hopi people for various transgressions. In 1655 a trial was held before the Father Custodian on charges accusing Father de la Guerra of punishing Indians by whipping them and smearing their bodies with hot pitch or turpentine. The priest was removed from his post.

According to Hopi legend, another priest, Father Jose de Trujillo, used to send Hopi men with pretty wives on extended trips to distant places so that he might "comfort" the lonely young ladies in his household. The men took their revenge during the Great Pueblo Revolt when they burned the lecherous padre alive.

When de Vargas reconquered New Mexico in 1692, he briefly visited the Hopi villages but left no Spaniards in the area. These villages soon became the "Switzerland" for a large number of refugees from the pueblos along the Rio Grande. The Tewa people occupying the Pueblo of Walpi on First Mesa today are descendants of those who refused to accept Spanish authority. The Hopi pueblos, far from the center of Spanish activity, have retained their culture and traditions and to a degree unequaled among Native Americans.

In 1700 a few inhabitants at the largest Hopi village at Awatovi expressed a willingness to receive missionaries. The old mission was rebuilt and Awatovi became a Christian community. This reconversion was bitterly resented by other Hopi villages and the following year

Awatovi was destroyed. According to Hopi legends, nearly all residents of the village were massacred, most of whom were tortured and dismembered, then buried in a mass grave. A few young survivors were distributed among the various villages and "retrained" in the traditional way of the Hopi. The hostility of the Hopi people towards the missionaries remained adamant. There were at least a dozen attempts to reconvert them, all unsuccessful.

The last occurred during the last days of the Spanish empire when a ubiquitious Franciscan explorer named Francisco Tomas Garces entered the Hopi village of Oraibi from the West. Father Garces was trying to open a trade route between the mission at San Gabriel (near today's Los Angeles) and Santa Fe. His hosts did their best to make him feel unwelcome. They refused to invite him into their homes. Nor would the proud Hopi receive the gift offerings of sea shells and tobacco.

The Hopi remained aloof, eyeing him suspiciously from the rooftops of their stone houses. Only the village dogs approached and they remained only long enough to sniff curiously. They too shunned the priest. That evening Garces cooked a meager meal over a fire of corncobs gathered from the streets. Wrapped in a cloak, he spent the night huddled in a dark corner of the Pueblo. The next morning the friar was awakened by shrill flutes accompanied by the sound of wooden bowls being pounded with sticks. A large party of villagers painted red and bedecked with feathers and other sundry head decorations approached in a menacing manner.

Fearing for his life, Garces called upon them to parley.

"Get thee gone without delay," the leader called, "back to thy land."

The kindly priest tried to no avail, to explain that he had come in peace and that white men and red were all the same in the eyes of God and Jesus Christ.

An old man stepped forward and shouted menacingly for Garces to leave the land of the Hopi.

Wisely, the friar made his final parting. Never again would the Franciscans enter the land of the Hopitu—"the Peaceful People."

As Father Garces made his way down from the mesa, he scribbled a few descriptive notes in his journal, relating events of the past few harrowing hours in Hopiland. He hesitated a moment upon concluding his remarks, then added as a footnote, the date. It was July 4, 1776.

On that fateful day in the distant remote land of the Hopi an issue as old as mankind was debated. The First American Revolution had ended. In another land, far to the east, and just as distant and remote from the Hopi, another was about to begin.

De ANZA and the ROAD TO CALIFORNIA

On July 4, 1776, representatives from the 13 American Colonies met in Philadelphia to declare their independence from imperialist European rule. At the same time, far across the rugged Appalachian mountains, through the verdant Ohio and Mississippi Valleys, beyond the immense wasted reaches of the Great Plains, over the shining Rockies and majestic Sierra Nevadas—*terra incognita,*—the great unknown, another hardy band of colonists were settling on the gentle, grassy slopes of a pristine promised land called Alta (Upper) California. This important chapter of American heritage has been, for the most part, overlooked by American historians who find it difficult to believe that American history could possibly follow any migratory track other than that East to West.

This event—the settlement of Alta California—might have been long-delayed had it not been for a resourceful, intrepid Spaniard named Juan Bautista de Anza, Spain's most illustrious 18th Century soldier.

Juan de Anza was born in 1735 at the Spanish presidio of Fronteras, Sonora, a few miles south of today's international boundary. Both his father and grandfather were officers in the Spanish Army, stationed on the frontier to protect settlers against restive native tribes. Juan's father, also named Juan Bautista de Anza, is credited by many as the first to refer to this region as *"Arizona."* When Juan was only three years old his father was killed in an Apache ambush. The youth chose to follow in his father's footsteps, becoming a soldier at 18. The following year he was commissioned a lieutenant in the Spanish Cavalry.

It didn't take long for de Anza to gain recognition in the frontier cavalry. He bore a soldier's strong sense of fidelity and was utterly fearless in battle. During an inspection of the region, the Marquis de Rubi, a member of King Charles III's high ranking military mission pronounced the zealous young soldier, a "complete officer."

In 1759, de Anza was promoted to captain. He was the youngest in New Spain (Mexico) to hold that rank. With the promotion came the appointment of Commandante of the presidio of Tubac. Tubac, during these years had a population of some 400, including soldiers, their families, a chaplain and other assorted hangers-on. These settlers were called the *gente de razon* (people of reason), a generic term used to describe the people, culturally Hispanic and racially mixed—apart from the Spanish and Indians.

When not in pursuit of hostile Indians, an officer's fringe benefits on the Spanish frontier included sharing and enjoying the companionship of upper-crust society, mingling socially with mine owners, large rancheros and merchants. All were large holders of land—the frontier elite—the gentry.

Although de Anza was among the wealthier landowners in Sonora, he was inundated with the spirit of adventure and exploration. He was relentless in his pursuit of hostile warriors. His soldados de cuera (leather-jacketed soldiers—so called because they wore long, sleeveless jackets—7 thicknesses of cow or deer hide for defense against hostile arrows) considered him tough but fair. To his vanquished foes he was humane, a rare quality on the remote reaches of Spanish authority.

Spanish presidios during de Anza's time were established near missions to protect peaceful natives and colonists from hostile tribes. They were usually spaced no more than 40 leagues (100 miles) apart and were located a discreet distance away from the missions. The presidios were Moorish in design, looking like North African castles. The walls were of adobe, ten to twelve feet high, one entrance, with watchtowers. In the watchtower might be mounted a four-pound bronze cannon. The gun was inaccurate and limited in range, but the noise was intimidating and no doubt considered worth the effect if it frightened the enemy somewhat. The military strength was roughly 50 officers and men along with 10 Indian scouts. Enlistments were for 10 years and the pay was low. The enlisted men lived with their families in huts near the presidio. A few acres of land was given to each family for subsistence farming. It took approximately 400 horses to maintain the outpost; however, the Apaches shifted the balance of power dramatically by sneaking in and running off with the entire caballado (horse herd) from time to time.

Presidios were designed for European-style warfare and were not effective against the guerilla tactics employed by the Apaches who raided incessantly within sight of the watchtower. Even the three-mile trip from Tubac to the mission at Tumacacori required a military escort.

Captain Juan de Anza, the soldier, was also a visionary, a mover and shaker who wanted to accomplish things others had dared not attempt. The Spanish government had long wanted to plant the tri-colors in Alta California. Settlement was essential to thwart the threatening encroachments from Russia and England along the northern Pacific Coast.

In 1769 the first Spanish Missions in Alta California were established at San Diego and Monterey. These missions were supplied solely by sea and since shipping on the rough seas was highly irregular, the colonization project seemed doomed to failure. A zealous padre named Francisco Tomas Garces had been exploring the terrain along the Colorado river and was convinced that an overland road to California was possible. Garces had little trouble persuading de Anza to propose an expedition to the viceroy. De Anza's father had planned a similar effort before his untimely death at the hands of the Apaches more than 30 years earlier. When one considers that most cartographers believed California an island, it is no wonder the soldier was called a visionary—or worse.

Captain de Anza, in the tradition of the old conquistadores, offered to personally fund the expedition to open an overland route across the vast expanse of desert to link Sonora with California.

Because of his near-legendary reputation as a trail blazer, de Anza received quick approval from viceroy of New Spain, Antonio Bucareli.

De Anza's plan was to assemble at the Mission San Xavier, thence go northward through Picacho Pass to the Pima villages and down the Gila river to the Yuma crossing.

However, before the expedition could get under way, hostile Apaches swooped down and made off with the caballado. The Spanish captain then decided to switch routes and follow the dreaded Licheguilla desert to Yuma villages. The road, known as the Camino del Diablo (The Devil's Highway roughly follows today's international boundary), with all its afflictions was considerably safer than the precarious passage through Apacheria.

On January 8, 1774, the expedition, consisting of 20 volunteer soldiers, two Franciscan Friars and a California guide got under way. One of the priests was the tireless explorer Padre Garces. The guide, Juan Valdez, had been called the "Castilian Kit Carson." He skillfully led the party across the wide, arid expanse of unyielding desert.

Upon reaching the Yuma crossing at the confluence of the Colorado and Gila rivers, de Anza quickly won the friendship of Chief Palma, who controlled the crossing. The officer passed out presents and waxed eloquently. Promises were made to build missions and bring Christianity to the natives, an act which they interpreted to mean a cornucopia of gifts from the newcomers. One of the soldiers took out his fiddle, rosined the bow and struck up a tune much to the delight of the natives. The gala event was climaxed when de Anza placed a silver medallion with a bright red ribbon around the Chief's neck. On the surface all seemed friendly. De Anza had adroitly secured use of the strategic river crossing, displaying a flair for statesmanship rare among professional soldiers. Chief Palma's stock rose dramatically among his people as his new allies presented the natives with an assortment of farming tools and other sundry gifts. The natives would come to expect these gifts as part of the diplomatic intercourse between the two cultures.

The Yuma (Quechan) people helped Spanish explorers ford the Colorado river, then bid fond farewell. De Anza left several head of livestock with Chief Palma to be picked up later on the return voyage to Sonora. They crossed the Colorado Desert in Baja California in late winter and arrived at the Mission San Gabriel, near today's Los Angeles on March 22. At long last, the overland route had become reality. Juan Valdez was sent back across the tortuous desert to deliver the report of the successful voyage to an anxious viceroy in Mexico City.

De Anza returned to Tubac by way of the Gila river. News of his exploits had preceded him. A gracious viceroy promoted him to the rank of Lt. Colonel.

Se Fueron con Dios (They Went with God), oil painting of de Anza expedition by Theresa Potter (Courtesy of artist)

De Anza immediately made plans to follow up his initial success with a full scale colonizing expedition. The colonists were assembled at Culiacan. The government outfitted them for the thousand-mile journey with such essentials as tents, camp gear, bolts of cloth. Each woman was issued four pairs of stockings. More than 350 cows and some 700 horses and mules were taken along to be seed stock for the California colony. De Anza included among his trappings three barrels of brandy and a barrel of wine for snake bite, or as the officer stated, "for needs that might arise."

All the men were given military training before the journey to Tubac where more colonists were waiting. Once again, Apaches spoiled the plans by raiding the Presidio corrals. Finally, on October 23, 1775, de Anza was ready to lead his intrepid band of colonists to the promised land. This time they would follow the Gila river to the Yuma crossing. The majority of de Anza's 240 followers were women and children. Only one of the 30 soldiers accompanying the expedition was not married. The official chaplain and diarist was Friar Pedro Font, assisted by Fathers Garces and Tomas Eixarch. The first and only death occurred on the first night out from Tubac when a Senora Felix died while giving birth to her 8th child. The infant was saved and baptized at nearby San Xavier where the mother was given burial services. The resourceful de Anza acted as midwife on the *jornada*, delivering two more babies before reaching San Gabriel.

Father Font found little good to say of the journey through Arizona. As they passed down the dusty trail through Picacho Pass towards the Gila river (today's I-10), somewhere near Eloy, the sardonic diarist gazed scornfully across the desert and wrote: "In all this land . . . I did not see a single thing worthy of praise." He thought the Pimas "smelled a little high" but conceded they did have the decency to clothe themselves which was more than he could say for the Yumas who preferred to go about in the buff.

The crusty Friar didn't spare colleague Garces from his barbed pen. Garces regarded the natives with deep affection. He was happy as a lark when sitting in a circle enjoying their hospitality and food which Font called "as nasty and dirty as the Indians." Garces was more Indian than white, Font concluded and wrote concedingly, "God, in his infinite wisdom, must have created Garces for the place in which he served."

If California was heaven, then the colonists must have felt as if they were going through hell to get there. The choking dust filled their lungs. Cattle strayed into the thickets along the Gila and were lost. Horses died of exhaustion. Through it all, the tireless de Anza prodded his flock of colonists ever westward.

At night families gathered and cooked meals of beans and tortillas. Afterwards there was some socializing under the watchful Father Font who kept a wary eye over the moral character of his charges.

De Anza's diary, in contrast to Font's, is full of optimism, however. Its factual accounts reveal little of the remarkable soldier's personal feelings or emotion. Borderland's historian Herbert Bolton calls the tall, angular cavalry officer, "silent as the desert from which he sprang."

In late November, the expedition arrived at the Yuma villages. The natives extended a hearty welcome to the weary travelers. During the festivities more presents were given. Again promises were made to Chief Palma that soon missions would be established among the Yuma peoples. To the natives, missions meant gift-giving on a regular basis.

De Anza was in a rush to reach California, so after a brief rest stop the party made plans to cross the Colorado river. Native swimmers escorted the colonists and their animals across. Not a single life was lost. The only complainer it seems was Father Font who claimed his baggage had gotten wet.

The most unusual mode of fording was made by the usually intrepid Father Garces who didn't trust horses or river crossings. He stretched out stiff, face up and was floated to the opposite shore by Yuma swimmers.

The epic journey was continued into the arid deserts and mountains of California. Christmas Eve found the expedition camped in a cold desolate canyon. In a valiant effort to raise morale, de Anza broke out the brandy. Soon a holiday spirit prevailed. Naturally, Father Font took exception and used the occasion to reprove the commander for his indulgence.

Their spirits lifted, the colonists continued on what must be regarded as one of the monumental events in Spanish history, reaching San Gabriel on January 3, 1776.

After another brief rest, de Anza led the colonizers up the Camino del Real to Monterey. The officer left his charges in the capable hands of the legendary Father Junipero Serra and hurried on to San Francisco Bay where he had been ordered to select a site for a presidio and mission. At the time, the indefatigable Spaniard had no idea he had laid the foundation for the future city by the Golden Gate.

De Anza covered the trail from Monterey to the Yuma crossing in ten days. He picked up Chief Palma and took the native leader to Mexico City. Palma was ceremoniously baptized by a Catholic and given many promises, none of which were kept it seems. De Anza's suggestions to build missions and presidios at the Yuma crossing immediately went unheeded. The soldier had serious misgivings about the friendliness of the natives at the strategic crossings. His warnings proved ominous. In the summer of 1781, the disgruntled Yumas revolted, closing the overland road to California permanently and killing a large number of Spaniards including the beloved Father Garces. Historians have offered several theories as to why the missins, presidios and gifts were not forthcoming. The Spanish had become involved in helping the American Colonies with their independence; the Spanish tradition of procrastination and Apache warfare diverted energies away from the Yuma crossing.

Perhaps the most significant reason was the transfer of Colonel Juan Bautista de Anza to New Mexico. The continued presence of this soldier-statesman just might have changed the course of Spanish history on the road to California.

De Anza was appointed governor of New Mexico as a result of his successful colonizing expedition to California. The appointment in 1778 was not to be a comfortable retirement post given in gratitude to a noble soldier for a job well done. New Mexico was on the verge of collapse — under siege from all sides by Comanches, Navajos and Apaches.

Once again, de Anza demonstrated his genius as a soldier-statesman. He would defeat the one tribe, form an alliance, then turn the warring tribes against each other. Using brilliant tactics, more akin to Indian warfare, de Anza's army caught the great Comanche leader Cuerna Verde (Green Horn) by complete surprise on the plains of Colorado. Cuerna Verde's warriors were soundly defeated, ending the Comanche menace on the New Mexico frontier forever. A treaty was made between de Anza and the Comanches that lasted long after the Americans arrived and gained possession of the land. It is a significant tribute to the diplomatic ability of de Anza that years later, during the Indian Wars between the American Army and the Comanches (1832-1874), the Comanches still honored their treaty with the New Mexicans. Hispanics could travel the lonely trails of Comancheria unmolested.

Parallels between Colonel Juan Bautista de Anza and American explorers Meriwether Lewis and William Clark are many. The latter duo played a well-deserved and significant role in the opening of the West. It is tragic that the deeds and exploits of de Anza aren't given a footnote in most American history books. Actually, de Anza out-performed his American counterparts. He not only created a trail to the "great and glowing West," he returned to his point of assembly, organized a colonizing party and successfully retraced his path to the promised land.

25

Fulfillment of a Dream, oil painting of de Anza expedition, by Theresa Potter
(Courtesy of artist)

EWING YOUNG
The Southwest's Premier Mountain Man

Mountain men . . . They've been called a peculiar product of the American frontier, a reckless breed of adventurers to whom danger was a daily commonplace; explorers who took tribute of the wilderness and wandered the outerwest with all the freedom of the lonely wind.

These fur trappers and traders, during their brief but exciting heyday between the 1820's and 40's, explored the vast reaches of terra incognita, including the Colorado Basin and Gila River watershed, establishing routes that would eventually become highways for cities and commerce.

The demand for beaver pelts provided the inspiration that made these restless adventurers brave the unknown wilderness in a quest for crafty, fur-bearing critters that provided a world market with hats and other apparel. They alternately traded, lived among and fought with native tribes inhabiting the regions, had deadly encounters with savage grizzly bears who attacked without provocation and faced thirst and starvation in desolate deserts and sometimes left their bleached and forgotten bones in obscure places.

By the time the exuberant cry "Manifest Destiny" caught the imagination of impetuous, but less adventuresome Americans, an advance guard of mountain men had explored every nook and cranny of the far western mountains, rivers and valleys.

Roughhewn mountain men like Kit Carson and Tom Fitzpatrick skillfully guided U.S. soldiers across the rugged unknown terrain during the War with Mexico in the 1840's to capture New Mexico and California. Had these armies relied upon their own limited knowledge of the country, the results might have been costly, altering the course of "Manifest Destiny" and history. Agents representing the aggressive British Empire had aspired to seize California during the interim between the declaration of war between the U.S. and Mexico and the arrival of American troops on the Pacific Coast.

Others, like Jim Bridger and Joe Walker, led wagon trains of immigrants to California and Oregon after their trapping days were over. In the 1860's, the ubiquitous Walker would lead a party of gold prospectors up the Hassayampa River finding rich placer strikes in the Bradshaw Mountains.

By and large, the history of the fur trade in the Southwest regions has been left out of the mainstream of American history. Trappers like Walker, Bridger, Fitzpatrick and especially Carson have become American legends and folk heroes, their fame coming primarily from exploits in the northern Rockies and Sierra Nevada. Contrary to popular myth, the Mexican borderlands had a great impact on industry. During the early 1830's. the heyday of the business, a third of the total furs shipped east came from the Southwest. And when discussing the Southwest fur trade, an obscure individual stands out above the rest. His name was Ewing Young.

He was a tall, strapping carpenter from Tennessee. Like many restive souls of his time, Ewing Young wested to the Missouri froniter and, after an unsuccessful attempt at farming, he formed a partnership with a trader named William Becknell, who would become known as the "Father of the Santa Fe Trail."

In 1822, they led the first wagons west across the plains of New Mexico. Santa Fe at the time was a remote adobe village lined with dirt streets, nestled against the towering Sangre de Cristo Mountains. During more than two centuries of Spanish rule, trade restrictions against foreigners had prevented commerce between the enterprising Americans and the citizens of New Mexico. Following the Mexican Revolution in 1821, Americans like Becknell, who had been out on the Plains trading with Indians, were invited to sell their wares in New Mexico. Thus began the long and mutually profitable Santa Fe Trade.

Like others of his genre, Ewing Young had no aspirations of leading the course of empire, but saw, instead, a business opportunity in the raw, untamed land. Before he quit the region in 1831, he was a central figure in the fur trade in the Southwest. He led one of the first American expeditions into what was to become Arizona, was the first to trap the Salt and Verde Rivers and was the first American to explore the Gila River to its mouth.

Ewing Young is one of the most elusive figures in Southwest history. This quiet Tennessean, who played such an important role in the fur trade, might have gone unknown had it not been for a few letters, documents and journals written by his contemporaries. No photographs or composite drawings exist, and he kept no journal. The uncharted region that some 40 years later was to be called Arizona, was then a part of the Republic of Mexico and only Mexican citizens could trap legally. Therefore, Young's entrepreneuring was shrouded in mystery and remains so today. While many Americans gave up their citizenship to obtain the licenses, Young remained staunchly proud of his and refused to compromise.

Ewing Young began his great adventure on the morning of May 25, 1822, at Boonslick, a rude frontier town near Franklin, Missouri. There, several wagons laden with trade goods, he embarked on an historic journey to Santa Fe in the Mexican Republic.

"Mexico." There was magic in the word, conjuring up visions of breathtaking scenery, romantic pueblos and beautiful, dark-eyed women. And, there was a spectacular profit to be made in the trade. Interest was sparked the previous year when Becknell returned to Franklin and dumped several rawhide bags full of Mexican silver on the street. Keep in mind, at this time the U.S. had not located any of those fabulous gold and silver mines in the Far West.

The thousand-mile journey to Santa Fe was fraught with danger. Most of the travelers were merchants, ill-prepared for the vicissitudes of the trail. One stretch required crossing 60 miles of desert void of watering holes. Rattlesnakes were a constant menace, as were the warlike Plains tribes along the way. Certain necessities, such as water, wood and native range grasses, were vital. Further west, the wood gave way to ever-present buffalo chips, which were used as fuel for cooking.

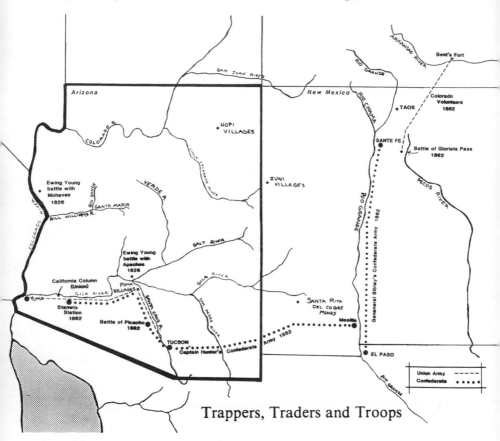

Trappers, Traders and Troops

After completing the journey, which took about ten weeks, the heavy wagons rumbled into the pueblo of Santa Fe to be greeted enthusiastically by the Mexicans with cries of "Los Carros" or "Los Americanos." Since the arrival in late June or early July coincided with the welcome arrival of the summer rains, a myth grew among the simple natives that the Americans were responsible for the rain as well as providing much-needed trade goods.

The picturesque village, located on the slopes of the steep, dark Sangre de Cristo Mountains, was in a delicate enclave of scenic beauty, picture perfect, as if the setting had been placed in position by an artist.

The dusty plaza that marked the "End of the Trail" was the traditional gathering place in the Hispanic Southwest. On the north side stood the ancient Palace of the Governors, a rectangular, flat-roofed adobe structure with a ramada in front and a courtyard in the rear. The rest of the square plaza was lined with characteristic low, adobe buildings consisting of tiendas (shops), cantinas and private dwellings. Bright red strings of chili peppers hung from the cedar vigas to dry in the warm sun. In the evening, the air was filled with the rich, aromatic smell of scented smoke from the pinon wood of the cooking fires.

After going through Mexican customs, the traders sold their goods to eager consumers, packed the Mexican silver coin in wet rawhide bags, then hung them over hot coals to dry. The packs were then slung across pack mules and made ready for the long journey to Missouri.

A few enterprising Americans chose to remain in New Mexico, went into business, married and eventually integrated into the culture. Others saw a lucrative profit in trapping, a business that did not require much capital to start, and headed into the vast wilderness north and west of Santa Fe.

For the next nine years, Ewing Young maintained a base of operations in both New Mexico and St. Louis. He operated a trading post in the slumbering Mexican community of Taos, establishing that region as one of the great staging areas for trappers in the Far West, and himself as a central figure in American trapping, and the fur trade as an important adjunct of the Santa Fe Trade. In Taos, Young also took a common-law wife, who bore him a son.

From Taos, Young's trappers blazed trails into the Colorado Basin and the Gila watershed, traversing vast regions never before seen by whtie men, opening important avenues to California. It is worth noting that Young was the first American to cross both of today's transcontinental routes across Arizona.

Young continued to import from St. Louis essential items ranging from razors and looking-glasses to bright-colored silks and cooking utensils. With profits earned from these, he purchased horses, mules and mule stock (jackasses and jennies) and drove them to the States. There was a "horse famine" on the American frontier at the time, and Young found an eager market for his livestock. Contrary to popular belief, the sturdy, dependable Mexican mules imported to Missouri marked the beginning of the great mule business for which that state was noted on the American frontier.

Following this first venture over the Santa Fe Trail, Young spent the Fall of 1822 trapping beaver around the headwaters of the Pecos River in the Sangre de Cristo Mountains.

The next year he headed west, away from well-established trapping grounds. "I want to get outside of where trappers have ever been," he told a friend. That year he trapped the headwaters of the Colorado River on the rugged western slope of the Rockies, returning with his pack mules loaded with thousands of dollars worth of prime beaver pelts.

A pelt weighed at least 1½ lbs. and sold for an average of four to six dollars each. These "hairy banknotes" were shipped east, some going to American hatters, who removed the fur from the skin and felted it into beaver hats. Other pelts were sent to European fur auctions. The fur business was comparable to giant industries of our time. The only thing that saved the beaver's hide for posterity was the advent of the silk hat in the early 1800's.

The streams of Arizona were an ideal location for finding beaver. In the high country, abundant stands of quaking aspens were a gourmet's delight for the wily, paddle-tailed critters. Further downstream, cottonwood and willows lined the banks of rivers and streams. During this pristine period, prior to giant irrigation projects, tree-cutting and overgrazing, the verdant land was a veritable paradise. With the exception of the hot summer months when the pelts were too thin, beaver could be trapped year around.

Trapping the Arizona wilderness had its grim side. Hostile natives were a constant menace. One trapper recorded only sixteen out of 160 trappers survived a single year in the Gila watershead.

The Southwest never held the annual rendezvous, as was common further north. This trade fair was a peculiar American institution whereby merchants hauled their goods by wagon, at considerable profit margin, to the mountains each summer. There, in some pre-designated setting, trappers sold their furs and purchased what they needed for the next year, and spent the rest on fun and frolic. This barbaric, medieval fair has provided the background for much of the lore and legends of the mountain men. For upwards of a week, they haggled, traded, quarreled, gambled, wenched, drank and fought before returning to the wilderness once more to face another year's toil, danger and hardship.

Although the Southwest had no rendezvous, trappers still found plenty of opportunity for devilment at fortified trading posts like Bent's Fort along the Arkansas River. At Taos, Ewing Young's post was a permanent "rendezvous" for trappers to trade and indulge themselves. Nearby, some enterprising Americans built a whiskey mill which turned out a concoction called "Taos Lightning," guaranteed to peel the hide off a Gila Monster. Taos, because of its proximity to the American border and remoteness—it was some 70 rugged miles north of Sante Fe—became the center of foreign-born residents of New Mexico. These Americans, engaged in smuggling trade goods, could operate freely in the isolated village because there was no customs house and Mexican officials were seldom seen.

In the Spring of 1826, Young sent his partner, William Wolfskill, and a small party of trappers into the Gila watershed, while he went to the States on a trading expedition. Wolfskill's party met with disastrous results. Coyotero Apaches ambushed the group and forced them to return to Taos empty-handed.

About that same time, another party was trapping along the San Francisco, Gila and San Pedro rivers. This band included James Ohio Pattie, whose now-famous *Narrative* provides a written account of the first American expeditions into Arizona. Although Pattie's thrilling adventure story reads something like a western pulp-dime novel, many of the incidents, times and places have been authenticated by other sources. Pattie's group struck paydirt, taking a large number of pelts. After a band of Apaches raided their horse herd, the trappers cached the furs, being careful to conceal all the evidence, and went after more pack animals. In Santa Fe, Pattie re-outfitted and returned to the Gila, only to find that Apaches had found their cache. Once again, a party of American trappers saw an entire season of hard, dangerous work in the Arizona wilderness go for nought!

During the Fall season of 1826, Young was among several Americans licensed to trap the Gila river country. The expedition headed down the Rio Grande river to Socorro, then turned west into the Mogollon Mountains to the legendary Santa Rita del Cobre mines, near today's Silver City. The mine was operated by an American who allowed the trappers use of the facility as a convenient haven before launching off into the Gila wilderness.

Before settling down to trap the Gila watershed, Young's first order of business was to even the score with the Apaches who had routed his expedition the previous spring.

Young was, by this time, a hard-bitten bourgeois ("Captain of Trappers") committed to the trapper's code that the only way white men could go about their work without fear of attack was to take direct and decisive action. The first lesson one learned on the frontier was to never show weakness to the warrior tribes. He led his party of 16 trappers into the lair of the fierce Coyoteros, routing them and inflicting heavy casualties.

Meantime, James Ohio Pattie was back in the Gila county again, this time with a party of French trappers, led by Michel Robidoux. They arrived at a large Indian village at the junction of the Salt and Gila rivers (on the west end of the Salt River Valley).

Pattie maintained it was a "Papago" village, but later-day anthropologists have suggested the Indians were actually Apache or Yavapai. The natives invited the trappers to spend the night in the village, and all but Pattie and a companion accepted the generous offer. Our suspicious hero found a secluded spot a safe distance from the village and made camp. Some time during the night, they were awakened by the sound of bloodletting from the village. The Indians had waited until Robidoux's men were asleep, then launched a bloody massacre. When the dust had settled, all the trappers were dead except Robidoux. He sneaked off into the darkness and joined Pattie, perhaps somewhere around the center of today's Phoenix. The three survivors remained hidden until the next day. That evening they moved through the darkness until they encountered what they took to be an Indian camp. As they crept closer, they heard a couple of men talking in English. Fortunately, the three had stumbled into the camp of Ewing Young. Once again, Captain Young sought vengeance against those who would murder trappers. He led some 30 trappers up a dry arroyo on the outskirts of the village, then had two men act as decoys to lure the warriors into an ambush. The ruse worked perfectly as about 200 warriors took off in pursuit of the two white men. When the Indians were some 20 yards from the arroyo, Young and his men rose and fired their high-caliber rifles killing, according to Pattie, 110 warriors. The rest of the people headed for the nearby hills, except for an elderly, blind and deaf man the trappers left unharmed. Then they set fire to the village and began the unpleasant task of burying the mulitlated bodies of the French trappers. The next day, the village headman called for a parley with the resolute Captain Young and his 33 buckskin-clad mountain men, and in the ensuing discussion, agreed to stop molesting trappers.

From there, Young led his men up the Salt, past today's Scottsdale, to the junction of the Verde, then worked his way up the Verde and back again down the Salt and Gila, trapping sometimes as many as 30 beavers a night, all the way to today's Yuma. This was the first American expedition to follow that river to its mouth and the first American encounter with the Yuma Indians. The meeting seems to have been friendly. Pattie described them as "the stoutest men with the finest forms I ever saw, well proportioned—as straight as an arrow" and "as naked as Adam and Eve in their birthday suits."

Young then led the party up the Colorado river where they had another encounter with natives, this time Mohaves, and it wasn't so cordial. A belligerent headman demanded a horse, and when refused, speared the animal, causing an angry trapper to shoot him dead in his tracks.

The Mohaves backed off and disappeared into the brush, but Young knew their habits and when the natives launched a pre-dawn attack, the trappers were ready. The Mohave weapons were no match for the trapper's guns and 16 warriors were killed in the melee. The fierce Mohaves bided their time, quietly stalking the trappers until the right moment. One evening several days later, they showered Young's camp with poison arrows, killing two and wounding two more. Pattie claimed his blanket alone was pierced by sixteen arrows.

Swearing trapper vengeance, Young pursued the war party and killed several. The bodies of the slain warriors were hung from the limbs of a cottonwood tree as a stern warning to others.

As an added precaution, Young divided his expedition into two groups —one to trap, the other to stand guard. The persistent Mohaves attacked again, this time killing three trappers on the Bill Williams river. When Young found the men, their bodies had been hacked to pieces and were being roasted over a campfire.

Young decided it was time to leave the Colorado river and head to Taos. The 1,000-mile expedition had been profitable, taking some $20,000 in pelts, but he lost a third of his men to hostile Indians.

Young's penchant for wandering had taken him over some of the wildest country in America on this, one of the Southwest's greatest overland expeditions. In spite of the trials and tribulations of the wilderness, Young's troubles weren't over. There had been a changing of the guard in Santa Fe and the friendly governor, Antonio Narbona had been replaced by an "ambitious and turbulent demagogue" named Manuel Armijo.

Once the bureaucratic confusion following the Mexican revolution subsided, the old Spanish policy of strict rules concerning commerce with outsiders was reinstituted. Also, there was the natural suspicion of Norte Americanos, and for good reason. Since the opening of the Santa Fe Trade, Americans had gone to great lengths to avoid paying customs. It was estimated that hundreds of thousands of dollars in contraband furs were being smuggled out of New Mexico each year.

In 1824, Mexico passed a law allowing only Mexican citizens a license or "guia" to trap. However, by some quirk in the law, beaver pelts brought into Mexico were heavily taxed while those taken out were not. Obviously, this only encouraged evasion. Some Americans got around the law by becoming Mexican citizens or secured a proxy permit through one of the locals. Others simply ignored the law because to apply for a license meant exposing oneself to the import tax.

In Taos, American trappers found a friend in the local priest, Father Antonio Jose Martinez. Martinez, for a small fee, arranged things like baptisms and marriages so citizenship could be obtained more easily.

Many Americans entering Mexico from the States had avoided customs by hiding their merchandise in the Sangre de Cristo mountains, then smuggling the goods in after dark. Trappers returning from the wilderness to Santa Fe were doing the same with beaver pelts.

Enforcement of the new law began while Young was still trapping in Arizona. Unsuspecting, he returned to Santa Fe in the Spring of 1827 to find his license was void and the season's catch, worth $20,000, was impounded.

One rambunctious member of Young's party, Milton Sublette, grabbed his furs and ran inside a friendly house occupied by trappers. By the time authorities were able to force their way in, Sublette and his furs had disappeared. The story of Sublette's daring escapade spread and was told and retold around trappers' campfires for years afterwards.

An angry Governor Armijo held Young personally responsible for Sublette's brash action and charges were pressed. He was released from custody a few days later when Armijo could not locate a copy of the Law of 1824. Young's fortune in furs was not returned, however.

Young's 1827-28 expedition into the Gila country was again routed by Apaches. Somewhere near the junction of the Salt and Verde rivers, Apaches ambushed the party, killing 18 of Young's 24 trappers. Despite these occupational trepidations, Young resolved to equip another expedition the following year. This 1828-29 expedition is remembered for the presence of Young's best known protege, a diminutive, bright young man named Christopher "Kit" Carson.

The Mexican authorities had been keeping a careful watch on Young since the 1827 smuggling incident, so he headed north out of Taos some 50 miles towards U.S. Territories, then doubled back across the Jemez mountains to the pueblo of Zuni. From there he went into the White Mountains to the headwaters of the Salt River. With a vengeance, Young sought out the Apaches that had routed his expedition the previous year, whipped them soundly, then trapped his way up the Verde to its headwaters in Chino Valley. On the western slope of Bill Williams Mountain, near today's Ashfork, he divided his party, sending one group laden with furs, back to Taos. Young took 17 men, including Carson, and headed west to California. He had heard much talk about California from other trappers and he wanted a first-hand look. In early 1830, after a near-disastrous journey across the trackless wastes of the Mohave Desert, the expedition reached the Mission San Gabriel.

Ewing Young liked what he saw in California. Beaver were plentiful in the San Joaquin Valley and horses and mules superior to those in New Mexico ran by the thousands in the Central Valley. Young trapped his way into northern California. To avoid carrying the pelts over the dangerous overland trip to New Mexico, he sold them to a Yankee sea captain. At San Jose he purchased a large herd of horses and mules to drive to the States. On their way back, the trappers stopped in Los Angeles where they indulged in a glorious drunken spree. The mannerly Californios were not exactly overjoyed with the increasing number of incorrigible, hairy-faced, buckskin-clad Americanos in their midst. But the winsome young women of Los Angeles, dressed in traditional short skirts, loose-fitting, low-cut blouses, displaying firm un-corseted bosoms, captured the heart of many a lonely American trapper, at least temporarily. The Americans were shocked upon first meeting these liberated Hispanic ladies in the Southwest, but they quickly adjusted. The small-waisted, olive-skinned beauties whirled around the dance floor with great abandon at frequent fandangos. In between dances, they puffed uninhibitedly on cigarillos, just like the men. One observer with Young noted admiringly that the ladies put on "a prodigal display of their charms" for one and all.

The Hispanic men, especially the caballeros (gentlemen horsemen) were even more dazzling in appearance with their traditional low-crowned, flat-brimmed sombreros, banded with oil cloths or tinsel cords, tight-fitting chaquetas, or jackets decorated with elaborate needlework and fancy conchos, and bright-colored sashes wrapped around tight silver-studded calgoneras, or pantaloons. The outer part of the legs were slit up to the knees and decorated with colorful gussets. Embossed leather botas or leggings were worn to protect their ankles. Their spurs were characterized by huge five-inch rowels. A serape saltillero (fancy blanket) usually hung across the pommel of the saddle and was thrown over the shoulders during inclement weather. The rider stuck his head through a slit in the middle of the blanket and the garment hung loosely from the neck. Their elegant style matched the fine-bred horses they rode with considerable pride.

The Californio militia kept a watchful eye on the trappers and perhaps harbored some scheme to place them in custody. Those plans ended abruptly when two of the trappers, an Irishman and an Englishman, exchanged unpleasantries over some frivolous matter and the Irishman nonchalantly stepped down off his mule and shot the Englishman dead. The authorities wisely decided that if the crazy Americanos would shoot each other without provocation, what would they do if somebody outside the group were the antagonist.

Young's party returned to Arizona, trapped up the Gila River, then cached their furs at the friendly Santa Rita Cobre Mine. Young and Carson rode on to Santa Fe where the bourgeois secured a license "to trade with Indians on the Gila." They returned to Santa Rita, picked up some 2,000 pounds in beaver pelts and sold them in Santa Fe. The authorities were, no doubt, surprised at the trappers' uncanny good fortune to have gathered so many pelts in such a short time—quien sabe?

The expedition earned a small fortune for Young, and the word quickly spread about wondrous opportunities in California.

Increasing troubles with Comanches along the Santa Fe Trail, Apaches and Mohaves in Arizona, inspired Young to move his base of operations to California. In the Fall of 1831, he left New Mexico for good.

It has been said that Young's decision to move his operations to the Pacific Coast might have been principally because of mounting problems with authorities in New Mexico who considered him a troublemaker. And there is little doubt those officials were glad to see him leave.

Whichever, Ewing Young's (or "Joaquin Yong" as he was referred to on Mexican records), great Arizona adventure was over. He eventually settled in the Oregon Territory, where he became one of that region's outstanding citizens. Young died prematurely in 1841, years before the "Course of Empire" changed the complexion of the entire Far West region.

As for rugged Arizona, continuing trouble with hostile tribes encouraged trappers to seek safer pastures in California, circumventing the area entirely by using the Old Spanish Trail from Santa Fe across Utah to California.

These trappers and their contemporaries were the embodiment of free spirit and independence. They were rebels against the restraints of society and chose to live their lives in the vast unknown where death could come at any moment in a variety of ways. Many returned to society, only partially, to serve as guides for the immigrant trains that came West in the 1840's and 1850's. Today's super-highways cross deserts and mountains over their trails. It seems ironic that men who sought sanctuary in the West would, in the final analysis, be the ones to lead the society they despised into their final refuge.

"J. GOLDWATER & BROS."
Commerce on the Colorado

"Gold!" The word spread like wildfire. The emotional pitch generated by that single cry sent normally sane men and women scurrying up hundreds of canyons and river beds to wash away nameless mountains—a shovel load at a time—over the riffles of a sluice box.

"Gold!" No other word could stir the souls of men, cause them to abandon fields and families, rent out their church pews and head west to assay out that dream of getting rich without working.

Most of these would-be millionaires were either trying to get something or get away from something. They were, as Bret Harte said, "looking for a fresh deal all around."

Following in the footsteps of the argonauts came the gamblers, tin horn and otherwise, saloonkeepers and shady ladies—all dedicated to that age-old art of "mining the miners."

Among the earliest and most important arrivals to the boom camps were the traveling drummers and merchants. Oftentimes forgotten in the westward rush, the role they played in the opening of the west was significant indeed. Survival in the vast wilderness would not have been possible had it not been for them and their cracker barrel cornucopias.

These all-purpose establishments supplied items ranging from Bibles to whiskey. Inventories included coal oil, calico, coarse wool, cotton cloth, medicine, groceries and hardware. Merchandising goods was not the only requirement of these frontier entrepreneurs. As leading citizens in the community, they were required to perform such civic duties as quasi-judge, i.e., settling local disputes among the raucous miners, and administering a form of informal justice. They were bankers of sorts, extending credit sometimes in the form of a grubstake, and they might be members of the school board.

The all-purpose stores with their fineries of silk and lace provided frontier women a rare touch of beauty to brighten their lives. The mercantile store was to women what the saloon was to men—a place where they could mingle socially and exchange the latest bit of news or medicinal remedy.

One of the most remarkable of these unsung heroes of the raw frontier boom towns was Michael Goldwater. Born into a Jewish family named Goldwasser near Warsaw, Poland, he fled that country in 1847 when the Russian Cossacks invaded. He settled in Paris, but when revolution struck he moved on to London where he met and married Sarah Nathan, daughter of a wealthy importer. At this time he anglicized his name to Goldwater. Mostly through the encouragement of his younger brother Josef, along with a liberal amount of wanderlust, the two set out for the promised land, California, to seek their fortunes.

By 1854 the brothers had formed "J. Goldwater & Bros.," and were dealing in general merchandise in Sonora, California, at the southern end of the Mother Lode.

The store did well until the late 1850's when the gold ran out and the rough and tumble miners evaporated. The brothers closed their doors and moved south to Los Angeles where they started a new business. Around 1860, the enterprising Mike Goldwater bought a wagon, loaded it with essentials and peddled his wares in the desert communities of Southern California and Arizona. The outbreak of the Civil War, along with a severe drought, caused a panic among their creditors in San Francisco and "J. Goldwater & Bros." went under for the second time.

The first of several major gold strikes occurred in Arizona at Gila City in 1858. Before the strike played out, some two million dollars worth of gold nuggets had been plucked from the Gila river bed. The strike was short-lived and by 1864 all that was left of Gila City were "three chimneys and a coyote." In 1862, another rich strike was located near La Paz on the Colorado river by famed scout Pauline Weaver. Another eight million dollars in placer gold was gathered in pans, rockers and sluices. One year later, La Paz came within a few votes of becoming the first capital of the new Arizona Territory. In 1863, the rugged explorer Joe Walker led a party of argonauts up the Hassayampa river into the Bradshaw Mountains where they located rich placer deposits in Lynx, Big Bug and Weaver Creeks. Lynx Creek would prove to be the richest stream bed ever found in Arizona. One member of the Walker party, former Confederate officer and future developer of modern irrigation in the Salt River Valley, Jack Swilling, sent two gold nuggets to General James Carleton, Military Commander of Arizona and New Mexico. These were forwarded to President Lincoln and no doubt played a role in the creation of the Territory of Arizona and the location of the capital at Prescott near the site of the fabulous find.

Following on the bootheels of the Walker party was another group of miners led by A.H. Peeples and guided by the ubiquitous Weaver. In the rugged mountains, at the foot of Yarnell hill, members of the Weaver-Peeples party found gold in the saddle of a steep-sided mountain which came to be known as Rich Hill. Within weeks, some $250,000 in nuggets had been picked up by the eager miners, making Rich Hill the biggest single placer gold strike in Arizona history.

About the same time, Henry Wickenburg located what was to become the richest deposit of gold ore in Arizona, about 10 miles southwest of the town that bears his name. Records reveal that Wickenburg's Vulture Mine produced some 17 million dollars in gold and was known locally as the "Comstock of Arizona." The total worth of the mine will never be known, as millions more were stolen by highgraders.

Nineteen men were hung from a large tree in the middle of Vulture City, mute testimony to the violence in the boisterous mining camps.

Morris Goldwater, Mayor of Prescott
(Arizona State Lib.)

Michael Goldwater, Arizona merchant
(Arizona State Lib.)

The rich strikes of gold and silver opened the new territory to settlement. Almost immediately, wagons loaded with freight rumbled down the Bradshaw road from San Bernardino to the settlements on the Colorado. Among the first to arrive were the enterprising Goldwater brothers. "J. Goldwater & Bros." were back in business, this time at La Paz on the Colorado. La Paz was a boom town of some 1,500 living in tents and brush or adobe houses. After the gold played out, La Paz became an important river port for the steamboats hauling cargo up the Colorado. The Goldwaters hauled goods into the Bradshaw Mountains, supplying both miners and military.

Wickenburg's mine, called the Vulture, was located several miles from the Hassayampa river. Since water is essential to the reduction process, ore was hauled overland to the river. Mike Goldwater grubstaked the miners $35,000 to build a mill to crush the ore, and when the company ran into production difficulties, he took over the operation until it was running on a profitable basis and the note was repaid.

In 1868, the fickle Colorado river changed its course, leaving the port city of La Paz high and dry. Mike and Joe packed up their goods and located a suitable port on the river's edge six miles downstream. They called the new town Ehrenberg, in honor of German engineer Herman Ehrenberg, one of the first white men to locate rich minerals within the boundaries of the new American acquisition.

Ehrenberg was a hot, dusty town of some 300 inhabitants, one meandering street, a row of adobe houses facing the river and a boat landing.

It was from these humble, dreary beginnings that the merchant dynasty of Goldwater got its start. Over the next few years, the family would open stores in Prescott, Parker, Tombstone, Bisbee, Contention, Seymour, Fairbank, Crittenden, Lynx Creek, Benson and Phoenix.

The Goldwaters arrived in Arizona during the peak of Indian hostilities. On one occasion, not far from Prescott, Joe and Mike were attacked by a band of Mohave-Apaches. In a running gun battle, reminiscent of some Hollywood western, Joe was severely wounded and spent three weeks in a makeshift army hospital at Camp Date Creek, recovering from the bullet wounds.

He had one of the bullets made into a watch fob as a souvenir of his harrowing escape. He carried it the rest of his life. Hostile Indians were not the only culprits. A few years later, a store operated in Bisbee by Joe Goldwater and Jose Castaneda was robbed by five gunmen. On their way out, the thieves shot and killed four citizens. The five perpetrators of the so-called Bisbee Massacre were later legally hanged in Tombstone with rope generously supplied by Messrs. Goldwater and Castaneda.

During those turbulent years on the Arizona scene the Goldwater wives maintained residences in the refined city of San Francisco. Neither woman cared for the harsh vicissitudes of a frontier existence. Mike and Joe made periodic visits often enough to keep the family flourishing with offspring. Several of Mike's eight children would eventually enter into the business in Arizona. Most notably were sons Morris and Baron.

In 1872 Mike decided to open a store in the new farming settlement on the banks of the Salt River, now called Phoenix. Morris, 20, a young, energetic, resourceful entrepreneur was selected to manage the operation.

Morris Goldwater deserves credit for bringing the first telegraph to the town. The line was being installed by the military and was planning to bypass Phoenix. Morris (ably armed with a bottle of premium John Barleycorn) was able to convince the soldiers that Phoenix should have a telegraph. He even offered to let them install an office in the Goldwater store and promised to act as telegrapher, all for free. Morris' entrepreneurship notwithstanding, fledgling Phoenix was not quite ready to support a large mercantile business and the store closed its doors three years later.

Prescott became the main mercantile center for the Goldwater brothers after the Southern Pacific railroad stretched its ribbons of steel across the territory in the early 1880's. Up to that time, most of the cargo came by way of steamboats on the Colorado to Ehrenberg and was hauled to the interior by freight wagons.

Goldwaters laid their wares out in a two-story brick building across the street from today's Yavapai County Courthouse. Morris, popular, dapper, and sporting a handlebar moustache, was by this time taking an active role in running the business. He was also the most public-spirited of the family. He firmly believed it was a man's moral duty to repay the community for his monetary enrichment by serving that community. He quickly became one of Prescott's leading citizens, serving in the territorial assembly (he was president of the 20th Territorial Council) and vice president of the Constitutional Convention in 1910. He organized the first volunteer fire company in Prescott, helped organize the Democratic Party in Arizona and served as Mayor of Prescott for 22 years.

Several years before, in Ehrenberg, Joe was given an unusual opportunity to demonstrate his public spirit. The community hired its first school teacher only to discover that she couldn't speak Spanish and none of her pupils could speak English. The problem was remedied when Joe agreed to come to class and act as interpreter for the remainder of the term. No doubt many a youngster of Mexican descent learned to speak English with a thick Polish accent, thanks to Joe.

Mike ventured into the political ring once and that was enough for the rough and rugged merchant. At the urging of his son, Morris, he ran for mayor of Prescott and won. Mike lacked his son's finesse and affable nature. Besides, he was a strong-willed product of the harsh frontier, with neither the patience nor tolerance required to deal with petty politics and molly-coddling greenhorns. He resigned before his term expired and semi-retired, rejoining his wife in San Francisco. Earlier, Joe had sold out his interest and went partners in a store in Bisbee with the aforementioned Jose Castaneda. He died in Tombstone in 1889. The operation was now in the hands of the second generation of Goldwaters.

Mike's youngest son Baron finished school and came to Arizona in 1882. He hired out as a clerk in the Prescott store, learning the business from the ground up. Baron was a hard-working fastidious man. He learned quickly and was rewarded 10 years later when his brothers voted him a full partnership. At that time he was charged with opening a store in Phoenix. The earlier effort had failed, but much had happened during the interim. Phoenix had been made the permanent capital in 1889. A spur linking the capital with the Southern Pacific at Maricopa had been completed two years earlier, and by 1895 the Santa Fe would link Phoenix to Prescott, Ashfork and the northern transcontinental line from Chicago to Los Angeles. Frontier Arizona had officially closed. A century was born and a century had died. Soon Arizona would take her long awaited place as a full-fledged member of the union of states. Born with the territory, "Goldwater's" would prosper and grow, reaching maturity in statehood, becoming one of the Southwest's leading department stores. The business remained in the family until it was sold to a large eastern corporation in 1962.

Michael and Josef Goldwater had been among the first white men to arrive in the raw, lonesome land. They came—not just to take from the land its rich minerals—but to build. They remained and helped carve out a frontier society in the wilderness. Pioneers in the truest sense of the word, they and their legacies have served Arizona and the nation well.

THE BATTLE OF PICACHO

Picacho is a steepsided titanic altar of ancient volcanic remnants, rising several hundred feet into the air some fifty miles northwest of Tucson. Through the ages, it has stood gaunt and grim above the desert floor, acting as a beacon to weary travelers—much the same as Chimney Rock and Independence Rock were for the wagon trains bound for California and Oregon.

Pre-historic Hohokam travelers stopped off on their way to and from commerce dealings further south. Their modern-day descendants, the Pima and Papago, did the same. Spanish missionaries, on their way to christianize natives along the rivers to the west and north, quenched their thirst at one of several springs near the base of the mountains. The Mormon Battalion built the first wagon road across the Southwest in 1846. They, too, stopped to rest at Picacho, a Spanish word meaning "peak." Anglos, in their eagerness to apply easily understood descriptive place names to the lands they traversed, gave it redundant Picacho Peak —or simply "Peak Peak." In the 1850's, the Butterfield-Overland Stageline had a station in the pass. Today, Interstate 10 and the steel rails of the Southern Pacific railroad run through the pass connecting Phoenix and Tucson with the rest of the outside world. Lengthy winter rains transform the harsh grey-buff desert in the foothills near Picacho into one of nature's finest tapestries of variegated colors, as galaxies of wild flowers carpet the earth, heralding the coming of Spring.

It was in the Spring of the year in 1862 when two American military units clashed briefly at the foot of the ancient picacho. That skirmish is generally referred to as the westernmost battle of the Civil War.

At the outbreak of hostilities between the North and South in 1861, large numbers of Southern-born officers in the Federal Army resigned their commissions and went home to fight for the Confederate cause.

One of these, a tall, bewhiskered, swashbuckling, ex-major named Henry Hopkins Sibley went immediately to the Confederate capital, Richmond, Virginia, and presented President Jefferson Davis a grandiose plan for making the upstart Confederacy an ocean-to-ocean power. Sibley, who had campaigned extensively in the Southwest, proposed a territorial conquest that included New Mexico, Arizona, California and the northern state of Mexico. If successful, the rich gold and silver bullion being produced in the West would fall into Confederate hands. Thousands of new recruits would be enlisted for the Southern cause. A transcontinental railroad line would link the southern states with the west coast and the Mexican and California seaports would be in Confederate hands.

It would be impossible for the Union Navy to impose an effective blockade over such a vast area. President Davis had to agree; the plan was pregnant with possibilities. The conquest and its amenities would likely bring support from European countries, something the Confederates needed desperately. Its success could guarantee the secession of the eleven Southern states.

The campaign began in July, 1861, when Lt. Colonel John R. Baylor, a hard-bitten, frontier Indian fighter, led three hundred Texas Mounted Rifles into New Mexico and occupied Mesilla, near present-day Las Cruces. The Texans received an enthusiastic welcome from the Anglo population of the bustling community who were mostly Southern sympathizers from Texas. One of Baylor's first acts as leader of the army of occupation was the creation of a new territory which was called Arizona. This new territory did not have the same boundaries that Arizonans would later come to know, but consisted of all lands in the New Mexico territory south of the 34th parallel and ranged from the Colorado River on the west to the 103rd meridian on the east.

There were fewer than 2,500 federal troops in New Mexico. The men hadn't been paid for several months and morale was low. The commander of the New Mexico forces, Colonel E.R.S. Canby was determined to consolidate his troops along the Rio Grande to meet the expected entrada of Texans.

He ordered the troops stationed in Arizona to destroy what supplies they couldn't carry and march to the Rio Grande to reinforce his demoralized army.

These orders caused a great deal of resentment among the residents of Arizona who accused the federals in Santa Fe of leaving them to the mercy of hostile Apaches, especially the Chiricahuas under Cochise who had been on the warpath for the past several months. The Arizonans had been clamoring for separate territoral status for several years, claiming their needs had been largely ignored by territorial officials in Santa Fe. Removal of federal troops from the area was the last straw.

In late January, 1862, General Sibley invaded New Mexico with an army of 2,600 men. He immediately ordered Captain Sherod Hunter to take a company of 54 mounted riflemen and occupy Tucson. Hunter's arrival in Tucson was a welcome sight to the local citizenry, as the Apaches had pretty much created a reservation for whites at the "Old Pueblo." The locals didn't care whether the soldiers wore blue or grey, as long as they offered protection from the hostile tribes.

Sibley's grand scheme to take the Southwest was two-pronged. One force would march north and occupy Santa Fe; the other, Hunter's, would join with the Californians. One of Sibley's assumptions was that secessionists in southern California would gain control and open the entire West for the Confederacy.

Captain Hunter's tactics in Arizona were to create the illusion of a much larger force than he actually had on hand. Using friendly Tucson as his base of operations, the vigorous Confederate officer dispatched troops along the Old Butterfield-Overland trail to Yuma, destroying supplies gathered for the pending invasion of the California Column. His deception was successful. Union spies reported at least eight hundred Confederates in the Tucson area.

Meanwhile, the threat of a Confederate invasion of California had prompted Secretary of War, Simon Cameron, to authorize the raising of volunteers in that state. A flinty-eyed, hard-core regular army officer, Colonel James Carleton was selected to lead this "California Column" of some 2,000 volunteers across the harsh, inhospitable desert and reconquer Arizona and New Mexico. For the next several months, Carleton, a professional who left nothing to chance, concentrated his men and supplies at Fort Yuma, in preparation for the long journey across the Arizona desert.

Colonel Carleton dispatched Captain William McCleave and nine men up the Gila River to the Pima villages near today's Sacaton, where he was to select a defensible site to store supplies for the Californians. A Union sympathizer named Ammi White owned a mill in the area and McCleave's orders were to locate a storehouse nearby. The officer was then to take his force on to Tucson where, under cover of darkness, he was to capture or destroy the Confederate garrison.

Before McCleave's patrol arrived, the resourceful Captain Hunter had occupied Ammi White's mill, taken the owner prisoner, and since he had no wagons to carry the large supplies of flour and wheat back to Tucson, distributed them among the Pimas. When Hunter learned that 50 wagons were coming up the trail from Yuma to pick up supplies, he decided to hang around White's mill and capture the wagon train. These plans went awry when Hunter's scouts noted the approach of Captain McCleave's tiny force riding in advance of the wagon train. Hunter quickly changed into civilian clothes and assumed the role of Ammi White.

McCleave unwittingly stumbled into a Confederate trap. When he asked the disguised Southern officer if he knew the whereabouts of a Mr. Jones, Hunter replied he didn't know any "Mr. Jones," but wondered where the rest of McCleave's troopers were. When informed that there were no more Union soldiers nearby, Hunter pulled his revolver and informed the surprised officer that he was now a prisoner of the Confederacy. At that instant, several Texas soldiers stepped out of the brush with rifles aimed and ready.

McCleave was so angered by the ruse that he challenged Hunter and his men to a bareknuckle, winner-go-free, fist fight—Californians against Texans. Even though Texans outnumbered the Californians nearly 2 to 1, Hunter politely refused the offer and ordered Lt. Jack Swilling to take the feisty Union officer and his men to Mesilla. Swilling later deserted the Confederate Cause, became a Union scout, then joined Joe Walker's band of argonauts prospecting for gold in the Bradshaw Mountains. Later he cleaned out some old Hohokam canals in the Salt River Valley and established an irrigation company, becoming known as the "Father

Jack Swilling, adventurer, Confederate officer, Union scout, and "father of irrigation in the Salt River Valley" (Arizona Historical Foundation)

of Irrigation" in that area. It has been written that Swilling was in charge of the Confederate troops that fought at Picacho. This was not true, as he was escorting prisoners to Mesilla at the time of the battle. However, Swilling enjoyed a good tale and seems to have contributed to the myth. It was due to his proclivity for telling tales that led to his undoing. While on a glorious drinking spree, he jokingly boasted of his role in a holdup. His enemies seized the opportunity to press charges against the colorful frontiersman. He died several years later in the Yuma Territorial prison, while serving a sentence for a crime he didn't commit.

A few days later, while scouting the California Column at Stanwix Station, some eighty miles east of Yuma, Hunter's troops fired upon some Union pickets, wounding Private William Semmilrogge. The skirmish confirmed Hunter's suspicions of a large army approaching. He made a hasty march back across the Butterfield-Overland trail towards Tucson. At Picacho, he left Sergeant Henry Holmes and nine men at the pass to keep him posted on Union activities.

When Colonel Carleton learned of McCleave's capture, his ire was raised. Determined to rid himself once and for all of the troublesome Rebels, he ordered Captain William Calloway to take a force of 272 men to drive the Confederates out of Tucson. At the same time, they were to attempt to rescue McCleave and his men before they could be taken to New Mexico. Furthermore, on personal orders from Carleton, they were to capture "Mr. Hunter and his band of renegades and traitors."

In his haste to engage in combat with the Rebel force, the ever-cautious Calloway spent a couple of leisurely days at the Pima villages recuperating from his desert ordeal. After being informed by his Pima scouts of the presence of Confederate soldiers at Picacho, Calloway ordered Lieutenants James Barrett and Ephraim Baldwin to take a detachment to the pass. Barrett was to take 12 men and circle around behind the Confederate pickets and wait, while Baldwin would advance on the pass from the west. Calloway's main force would follow Baldwin.

The route of march was up the old Butterfield-Overland road, roughly following today's Interstate 10, southbound towards Tucson.

Sometime around noon on April 15, 1862, Barrett, a brave but reckless young officer, located the Confederate encampment in a dense thicket and attacked without waiting for support. He took three prisoners including Sgt. Henry Holmes. Although several shots were fired, there were no casualties in the first encounter. The rest of Holmes' troopers, alerted by the gunfire, had retreated further into the thick brush and taken up defensive positions. At this point, Barrett's scout, J.W. Jones, suggested they dismount his troops and enter the thicket afoot. Barrett disregarded the advice and charged single file, headlong into the regrouped Texans. A fierce volley of rifle fire greeted Barrett from the thicket and, when the smoke had cleared, four Union saddles had been emptied. Barrett rallied his small command and this time charged the thicket on foot. The furious battle lasted some 90 minutes and when it was ended, the brash young lieutenant and two enlisted men lay dead on the ground along with three wounded. At this point, the Californians broke off the fight, gathered their wounded along with the three prisoners and retreated back towards the Gila. The dead were left in the field where they had fallen. One soldier, Bill Tobin, could thank the brass ornament on his hat for saving his life. He suffered a serious, but not fatal, head wound, when a lead ball ricocheted off the metal.

The Confederates suffered two casualities in the skirmish, both of whom would die from their wounds. Casualities were high—of the 24 soldiers involved, eleven were killed or wounded. After the battle, the Texans took their wounded, and rode to Tucson to warn Captain Hunter of the approach of Calloway's large force.

For reasons never fully explained, Calloway took his command, along with the three captives, and retreated all the way back to the Pima villages. Although it is only a footnote among the vast volumes of Civil War history, the Battle at Picacho Pass is considered to be the westernmost battle of the war.

After a series of dramatic victories in New Mexico, the Confederate bubble burst in late March at a place called Glorietta Pass, just east of Santa Fe, New Mexico. Sibley's once-conquering army left New Mexico in complete disarray. This event coincided with the entrada of the California Column from the West, thus ending the southern dream of a continental conquest.

On May 4, 1862, Captain Hunter lowered the Confederate colors at old Tucson and retreated towards Mesilla. The day after they left Tucson, the beleaguered Texans clashed with another family foe. A large band of Apaches attached Dragoon Springs, near present-day Benson, killing four soldiers, and running off nearly 60 horses and mules.

Arizona's brief stint as a separate territory had ended. Within two years, the rich mineral-laden region would gain official territorial status from the Union and would begin the long road to statehood.

After the battle, the three Union soldiers were buried and a cross was erected where they had fallen. The site is some 20 feet from where the tracks of the Southern Pacific Railroad runs today. The graves remained undisturbed until 1892 when a detachment from Fort Lowell, near Tucson, was sent to remove the remains and rebury them at the Presidio, in San Francisco. The burial detail recovered the bodies of the two enlisted men. Pvts. George Johnson and Wm. Leonard, but were unable to locate Lt. Barrett. They left the cross in place and the incident, along with the dashing young cavalry officer, were nearly forgotten.

Many years later, in the early 1920's, a group of concerned citizens and history buffs decided to erect a bronze plaque commemorating the site. During construction of the monument, workers discovered a human skeleton wrapped in an old army blanket. At long last, the body of James Barrett had been located. The fragmented blanket was taken to the Arizona Historical Society and the remains of Lt. James Barrett, Co. A. 1st Cavalry Volunteers, lies buried, on the field of battle where he so gallantly gave his life.

Re-creation of Picacho Peak Battle (1979) at battle site (Photo by author)

THE LAST CAMPAIGN of Lt. HOWARD CUSHING

The hot desert sun bore down relentlessly on Lt. Howard Cushing and his small cavalry troop as they wound their way towards the precipice of a rocky, cactus-studded mesa in central Arizona's Pinal Mountains.

When the soldiers reached the top, Cushing turned and quietly called a halt and ordered the troops to dismount. The tired soldiers loosened their saddle cinches and reached for canteens. Cushing's Apache scout, Manuel Duran, motioned him towards the opposite side of the table-topped mountain. The scout pointed towards what looked, at first, like a tiny dust devil about a mile and a half down the slope among a maze of boulder-choked side canyons. "That Apache campfire," Manuel said in his guttural English. Cushing gazed for several moments at the faint wisp of smoke ascending far below. Manuel's keen senses detected the smell of mescal baking in the Apache camp. Certain that the hostiles were unaware of his presence, Cushing posted Manuel and two soldiers as lookouts and moved the rest of his troop back down the southeastern side of the slope and waited for darkness.

The hostile band were a mixed group of bronco Aravaipa, Pinal and White Mountain Apaches under the leadership of a chief named Azul. A few days earlier, they had ambushed a small wagon train on the road between Tucson and Camp Grant. The wagons were hauling merchandise for a store located near the post, owned by Newton Israel and Hugh Kennedy. Among the members of the ill-fated party were two women, several children and twenty-one men. Unwittingly, they carried only four weapons. Cushing's cavalry troop at the small army post at the confluence of the Aravaipa and San Pedro Rivers was alerted when one of the survivors staggered into the post. Sergeant John Mott of F Company quickly rallied the men and rode to the scene of the ambush to find the charred and mutilated remains of 17 bodies. A short distance from the massacre, they found the leader of the party, Hugh Kennedy, mortally wounded. He was barely conscious from loss of blood, but was able to describe the ordeal. He had cut one of the mules loose and tried to ride through the crowd, but his bold dash for freedom was thwarted when an arrow struck his chest. Still, he almost made good his escape when a wild shot struck the mule in the rear and it bucked him off. He crawled into a narrow crevasse about 25 yards from the road and escaped detection. The Apaches spent little time searching for Kennedy, as their attention was diverted to several boxes of patent medicine, which they took to be whiskey. After plundering the wagons, they set fire to what remained. Captain John G. Bourke, in his memorable book, ***On The Border With***

Crook, vividly described the grisly scene.

> There were hot embers of the new wagons, the scattered fragments of broken boxes, barrels, and packages of all sorts; copper shells, arrows, bows, one or two broken rifles, torn and burned clothing. There lay all that was mortal of poor Israel, stripped of clothing, a small piece cut from the crown of the head, but thrown back upon the corpse—the Apaches do not care much for scalping—his heart cut out, but also thrown back near the corpse, which had been dragged to the fire of the burning wagons and partly consumed; a lance wound in the back, one or two arrow wounds, a severe contusion under the left eye, where he had been hit perhaps with a stock of a rifle or carbine, and the death wound from ear to ear, through which the brain had oozed. The face was as calm and resolute in death as Israel had been in life.

Lieutenant Howard Cushing of the 3rd Cavalry had only recently arrived in Arizona after previous campaigns in Texas and New Mexico. Cushing's reputation for bravery and relentless pursuit of the enemy had preceded him. Early on, the popular young officer earned the respect and admiration of his fellow officers in a trade that was often wrought with politics and petty jealousy. The troopers in his command idolized him. Cushing had come from a family of warriors. He and his brothers, Alonzo and William, had all gained national recognition for bravery during the Civil War. After the war, he transferred from artillery to the cavalry and headed west where his notoriety as an Indian fighter made the name Cushing a household word on the southwest frontier.

Cushing's first major scout upon his arrival at Camp Grant was to track down and punish the Apaches who perpetrated the Kennedy-Israel wagon train massacre.

The trail wasn't hard to follow at first, as it was lined with empty bottles of patent medicine. Cushing and his men tracked the hostile Apaches into the narrow steep-sided gorge of Aravaipa Canyon, then northeast across the Gila River. Several times the wily Apaches set fire to the countryside to destroy their tracks, but each time, Cushing's eagle-eyed Apache scout, Manuel, picked up the trail. Next, Azul and his band doubled back to within a few miles of Camp Grant and then headed over the Dripping Springs range and into the Pinal Mountains. Feeling safe and secure, they made camp on the western slope not far from where Miami is today. It was at this location that Manuel spotted the camp fire smoke.

Cushing waited until midnight, then gathered his troops and, after posting guards around the horses, began a tortuous night march through the seemingly impenetrable maze of rocks and cactus towards the rancheria. The soldiers reached the hostiles' camp just before dawn. He divided the command into two parties. Cushing led one group down the train towards the rancheria and sent another around to hit the Apache camp on the flank.

At the first light of dawn Cushing and his men charged the camp with rifles and pistols blazing. Azul's men, caught unaware, grabbed their Springfield breechloaders and Spencer carbines and returned the fire, but the disorganized resistance was no match for Cushing's energetic and

Lt. Howard Cushing, killed by Apaches

aggressive soldiers. Those Apaches who survived the first volley of fire broke and ran, but were cut down by the well-deployed soldiers who seemed to be everywhere at once. When the smoke and dust cleared, Cushing counted thirty dead warriors in the immediate vicinity of the camp. Cushing's men had suffered no casualties in the attack. Captive Apache women and children told the soldiers that the band had been returning from a raid in Sonora when they came upon the Kennedy-Israel wagon train.

The hardy band of soldiers that manned the lonely, dusty military posts and policed the frontier during the days following the Civil War performed a remarkable task that even today is not fully appreciated. The remote posts were nearly always undermanned and the companies under-strength. Disease killed far more than combat.

The task assigned the army by a government in Washington that could never seem to make up its mind about how to deal with the "Indian question" was a mission impossible. While the War Department, Department of Interior, advocates for Indian rights and Indian-haters played politics, the Army was given the thankless job of trying to appease all parties concerned. Often they were caught in the unpopular role as peacemaker between warring tribes. If they pursued and destroyed a hostile band, certain parties accused them of being "warmongers" and "exterminators of the noble red man." When they acted as humanitarians, others accused them of "mollycoddling the murdering savages."

The Indian wars were not of a conventional nature. There was no native general or prime minister to surrender and no capital city to conquer. The easiest and most likely place to locate the hostile natives was in the villages or rancherias, which were also occupied by women and children. Also, no Indian rules of warfare exempted women and children from participating in the melee, as many veterans could attest. Oftentimes it was difficult to tell the "good" Indians from the "bad" ones, as both resided in the same environs. Each side considered their own attacks justified, while the other was determined to be wanton and murderous.

The Apaches, made up of several groups and sub-groups, had occupied the brawny mountainous regions of central and southern Arizona for some four hundred years. They had a long history as raiders and plunderers to sedentary tribes like the Pima and Pueblo peoples, as well as the Mexicans. The arrival of the Anglos to the area, in the years following the Treaty of Guadalupe Hidalgo in 1848 and the Gadsden Purchase five years later, opened up all kinds of new markets for the Apaches.

The Army began establishing military posts in Arizona in the 1850's when miners began digging silver out of the hills of southern Arizona, but these were abandoned when the Civil War broke out in 1861. For the next few years, few dared venture outside the walls of Tucson after dark. After the war, and the opening of rich mining areas, the Army was again called upon to protect the new settlements.

Apaches continued their warlike ways into the 1870's. Unlike many of the warrior tribes in the west who engaged in battle on the open plains, the Apaches were masters of stealth and cunning. They usually fought when and where it suited them, and on their own terms. The army in Arizona succeeded in turning the tables by energetic and relentless pursuit; by well-organized and trained pack-supply trains that enabled the troops to stay in the field for weeks, even months; and most important, Apache scouts led soldiers into the hidden and remote canyons that the Apaches had always considered impregnable sanctuaries.

Arizona presented the frontier army with its greatest challenge. Its rugged terrain was as intractable and formidable as the hostile tribes who occupied its vast regions—danger lurked everywhere. Everything in the desert either stabbed, stuck or stung. Boots had to be shaken out before being pulled on to rid them of some pesky scorpion. Rattlesnakes thick as a muleskinner's wrists slithered in and out of camp. Water was as scarce as horseflies in December. Soldiers on a scout might find themselves sweltering in the blazing heat one day and waist-deep in snow the next. Some of the canyons and mountains were so steep that a mountain goat had to shut his eyes and walk sideways.

Quite naturally, the Apaches lived in harmony with this inhospitable land. U.S. soldiers, those long-suffering unsung heroes of the American West, were expected to locate the enemy, defeat him in battle on his own terrain—all for $13 a month.

The successful pursuit and destruction of Azul's band enhanced Cushing's reputation as the southwest's most energetic and enterprising young officer. Over the next few months, he led several other scouts into heretofore Apache strongholds where few army officers had dared to venture. Cushing loved hard campaigning. He remained in the field throughout most of 1870 and early 1871, but despite the heroic efforts of his small command, Apache warriors grew bolder.

In the fall of 1870, while in pursuit of a band that had attacked an army paymaster, mounted Apaches struck Cushing's camp, killing two soldiers and wounding three. The soldiers fought back, tenaciously recapturing some stolen cattle in the donnybrook. Just as things quieted down, the Apaches swooped down and retrieved their plunder and made a successful getaway. A week later, Cushing was chasing the band that had stolen a herd of mules on the outskirts of Tucson.

In the spring of 1871, Cushing and his command were ordered to take to the field and engage hostile Apaches whenever he saw fit. The situation in Arizona had grown so desperate that even territorial Governor A.P.K. Safford was riding at the head of the company of volunteers.

Cushing believed the Chiricahua chieftain Cochise was at the bottom of most of the Indian depredations in southern Arizona and the dashing lieutenant of F Troop, 3rd Cavalry, became obsessed with capturing or killing the famous Apache.

Cochise had been at war with the army since February, 1861, when he was wrongly accused by Lt. George Bascom of kidnapping a child near Camp Crittenden on Sonoita Creek. During the unhappy incident that has come to be known as the Bascom Affair, several of Cochise's relatives were ordered to be held hostage until he returned the child. Cochise retaliated by seizing and killing three employees at the Butterfield stage station at nearby Apache Pass. Lt. Bascom countered by hanging his Apache hostages. Since that time, Cochise waged a long and deadly war against the army.

Today, some call Cochise a noble leader who was wronged by the Army, while others have called him a "lying, thieving rogue." Cochise was an Apache, a man caught up in the turbulence of his time, a product of his environment, a leader who reacted instinctively to a situation that was as natural to him as a wild animal defending its young.

In short, Cochise and Lt. Bascom, Lt. Cushing and Azul all were figures caught in the dramatic, inevitable clash of two diverse cultures thrown together in a land that couldn't sustain both.

Cushing determined that the only way to get Cochise was to lead his command into the Apache-infested mountainous islands that had been a bastion for the past ten years.

Cushing left Fort Lowell, near Tucson, on April 27, 1871, with 17 soldiers and one packer to scour the Sonoita, Santa Cruz and San Pedro River valleys along the Mexican border. The command traveled southeast along Pantano Wash, spending the first night at Cienega ranch, a Butterfield Stage station some thirty miles east of Tucson. The following day Cushing and his men rode south to Camp Crittenden on Sonoita Creek, near today's Patagonia, where they procured fresh mounts. After laying over an extra day, they rode in a southwesterly direction to noted Indian fighter Pete Kitchen's ranch at Potrero, a few miles north of today's Nogales. Kitchen volunteered to guide the soldiers up the Santa

Apache scouts prepare for service

Cruz River into Mexico and through the Patagonia Mountains. After passing over the Patagonias, the soldiers rode across the beautiful grass-carpeted, oak-clustered woodlands and rolling hills that separates the Patagonia range from the Huachucas. On the afternoon of May 1, Kitchen, his work completed, rode back towards his ranch. He hadn't traveled far when he noted a party of some 30 Apaches stalking the soldiers. Kitchen set fire to the range grass to warn Cushing of the impending danger. Cushing and his second-in-command, Sergeant John Mott, saw the fire and concluded that the Apaches had started the blaze.

Unaware of the danger, the soldiers rode on to the Mexican village at Santa Cruz where they made camp. When informed by the Mexican commandant at Santa Cruz that a band of Apaches had been spotted in the Huachuca Mountains, Cushing headed eastward and by the evening of May 2 pitched camp on the east side of the Huachucas. The next day, the troop headed north to the vicinity of today's Sierra Vista. They camped in a canyon on the eastern slope of the Huachucas where they spotted fresh signs. The following day, the troop rode north over rough country to Alisos Canyon. Forage for the horses was scarce, as the Apaches had been up to their old tricks of setting fire to the range grass.

On the morning of May 5, the soldiers left camp early and headed in a northwesterly direction towards old Camp Wallen on the Babocomari River. The abandoned post had been located on the site of an old Mexican rancho that overlooked the river. Again, the grass had been set afire, forcing Cushing and his men to move north to Bear Spring in the Mustang Mountains. About two miles north of Camp Wallen, they spotted the tracks of a woman and pony heading towards the spring. Cushing sent Sgt. Mott and three men in pursuit of the woman, while he led the rest of the troop up the main trail. Sgt. Mott followed the trail for nearly a mile. The tracks were so easy to follow that Mott, a seasoned veteran, became suspicious. The trail led into a deep arroyo that had several smaller arroyos running perpendicular into the main gorge. There he caught sight of the woman taking great pains to leave a trail. Mott, certain they were being led into a trap, climbed out of the gulley for a better view. His suspicions were confirmed when he saw some 15 Apaches waiting in ambush in a side canyon. Mott sent one soldier back to warn Cushing, while he and the other two prepared to make a stand. At that moment Mott spotted a larger party of Apaches moving towards his rear. The sergeant and his men jumped on their horses and prepared to make a run for it when an Apache bullet hit one soldier and another struck a horse. The Apaches, armed with breechloaders and revolvers, were closing in on the trio trying to capture them alive, when Cushing arrived with the main body.

Cushing and his men, numbering eleven, charged into battle pouring heavy fire into the Apaches who fled into the hills nearby leaving five dead warriors behind. Even though outnumbered 15 to 1, Cushing, his strength down to eight men, prepared to attack the Apaches, who had taken cover on higher ground. Sergeant Mott and the civilian packer, Simpson, advised Cushing against charging the Apache's position, but the lieutenant was convinced he could still destroy the band. The soldiers charged and the first volley of fire dropped Simpson with a bullet through the head. Cushing dispatched a soldier to the aid of the fallen man and when the Apaches saw the chargers numbered only six, they attacked. Sergeant Mott's report described the action: (In order to preserve the flavor of the times, Sgt. Mott's report is re-printed exactly as he submitted it.)

When the Indians seeing our party so small, rushed down from all sides (it seemed as if every rock and bush became an Indian). I was at that time about five yards in advance of Lieut. Cushing, and hearing the words, "Sergeant, Sergt., I am killed, take me out, take me out," turned and saw Lieut. Cushing face towards the horses, clasp his hands across his breast, and fall to the ground; calling to Fichter to assist me, I seized the Lieut. by the right arm, Fichter taking the left, and started for the rear followed by Green who I noticed was very lame. The other two men started to get out the horses. We carried the Lieut. about ten or twelve paces, when he was again shot through the head and fell dead in our arms; we continued to drag the body until we caught up with Yount and Mr Simpson, when the latter was again shot through the body, killing him instantly. Looking behind me I saw the enemy within thirty or forty yards of me firing as he advanced. Dropping the body of Lieut. Cushing, Fichter and myself turned to sell our lives as dearly as possible, causing the Indians to pause, thus enabling Privates Green and Yount to mount. Acting Corporal Kilmartin now open fire with his party, thus enabling Fichter and myself to mount, but scarcely had we done so when both horses were shot, two balls striking Fichter's horse in the flank, a third mine in the fore leg, and a fourth killing Private Green. Immediately mounting Lieut. Cushing's horse I detached part of my command (now reduced to 14 effective men) to move out with the pack train. I keeping the remainder with me to cover the retreat, then commenced a running fight for about a mile until finding I had drawn the enemy from under cover I halted to offer him battle (hoping I could flank him and recover the bodies.) He halted also but declined the gage, evidently having had enough of that kind of fighting, preferring to cut off and ambush me on the trail to Crittenden, which passed the foot hills within one and one-half miles of his position. I, having to go around the mountains, could strike it in about four miles. Seeing through their design, I crossed the Rio Barbacoma four miles above old Camp Wallen, and continued my retreat over the mesas thus placing the swampy head of the Barbacoma and a half mile of ground between me and the place of ambush and the trail; I had scarcely arrived opposite this place when the Indians uttered yells of savage rage and disappointment, but were powerless to molest me. It was becoming dark, or about 7 o'clock P.M. I continued my route to Camp Crittenden at which place I arrived about one o'clock A.M, on the 6th of May. Four of the pack mules being very weak and poor owing to the scarcity of grass (the country along our route having been burned off by Indians) I had to abandon in my retreat. I succeeded however in carrying off Lieut. Cushing's pistols and Mr. Simpson's Henry rifle.

The Indians were well handled by their chief, a thick, heavy set man who never dismounted from a small brown horse during the fight. They were not noisy or boisterous as Indians generally are, but paid great attention to their chief, whose designs I could guess as he delivered his instructions by gestures. I believe I am stating truth when I set down the number of the enemy killed at thirteen (13); it may be more, but that number was seen to fall.

No one is certain today if the band of Apaches who stalked Lt. Cushing and his command were led by the notorious Cochise or by another noted Chiricahua chieftain named Juh. The latter seems to fit Mott's description. What is certain is the Apaches were able to skillfully lure Cushing and his small troop into a battle on their terms and the results were disastrous.

Cushing, the army's gallant, *beau sabreur,* had gone on to that Valhalla for warriors. It is easy to understand why the hard-riding young officer wanted to ride hell-for-leather into the midst of the Apaches. These tactics had served him well on previous campaigns and a few well-trained soldiers could nearly always rout a superior number of undisciplined native warriors in an open confrontation. The same might have been true on this occasion had the Apaches not been led by a man of capable leadership qualities. In retrospect, one wonders why Cushing did not have a dependable Apache scout with his command to warn him of impending danger that day on the western slope of the Whetstones. Any frontier officer of his experience fighting hostile Indians would have assuredly realized the value of the scout in Apache country. Perhaps his spectacular success against the Apaches had created illusions of immortality on the field of battle. Cushing would certainly not be the first soldier since the dawn of mankind to suffer from the effects of that affliction.

Like so many bold, brave men and women who helped tame the Arizona frontier, the name of Lt. Howard B. Cushing is known to but a few today. There is a street in Fort Huachuca named in his honor and there used to be one in Tucson, but in the name of progress and efficiency, it has been changed to 14th Street.

A few months after Cushing's death, a group of Tucson citizens outraged over Apache depredations, attacked a band of Aravaipa Apaches near Camp Grant. Although the citizens were welcomed as heroes upon their return home, Pres. U.S. Grant called the attack "murder" and ordered the perpetrators of the so-called "Camp Grant Massacre" brought to trial. A trial was held and the verdict was "not guilty." No jury on the frontier would convict a white man of killing an Apache. If the roles were reversed, it is doubtful if any Apache jury would have found a fellow Apache guilty of killing a non-Apache.

Pres. Grant then sent an emissary named Vincent Colyer to Arizona to arrange a treaty with the Apaches. When Colyer's mission failed, he ordered Gen. Oliver Howard to extend the olive branch to the various groups of Apaches. He, too, failed with the Apaches in the Central Mountains, but remarkably, the general met with Cochise in the latter's stronghold and arranged a treaty. The long, bloody war with the Chiricahua had at last ended.

Grant's next move was to unleash the hard-riding Gen. George Crook on the hostile Apache and Yavapai bands in the Central Mountains. For hundreds of years, these Indians had used the rugged terrain as a sanctuary, following their raids along the river valleys and into Mexico. With a brilliant display of perseverance and tenacity seldom seen by the Apaches, General Crook's columns took to the field guided by Apache scouts and scoured the remote canyons and mountains. Within a few months, nearly all hostile Apache and Yavapai bands had surrendered.

During the 1870's, the tribes were located on reservations. Crook, the Army's most successful Indian-fighting general, was transferred out of Arizona. He was a man the Apaches dreaded in war but respected, trusted in peace. During Crook's absence, malcontents such as Geronimo, gained influence among the disgruntled Apaches. In the latter 1870's and early 1880's the Army was in the field in pursuit of small bands who had bolted the reservation and gone raiding.

In 1882, Crook was transferred back to Arizona to restore order. This time, the general's campaign was hobbled by politics, something the old campaigner had little use for. Still, he waged a successful campaign against Geronimo and others until the spring of 1886 when the "experts" in Washington replaced him with Gen. Nelson Miles. Miles continued Crook's basic tactics and within a few months, Geronimo agreed to terms and for all practical purposes the Apache Wars ended.

55

Geronimo and his Apache warriors. (Photo by C.S. Fly, 1886)

BOOM TOWNS
and mineral mania

The gold and silver rushes, more than anything else, provided the inspiration for people to give up relative comforts in the east and come west. Opportunity to get rich quick is a uniquely American article of faith and was virtually born in the west. With a single lucky break, one could instantly make more money than he could lend, spend in a lifetime.

So, it was "off to Californey, Coloradie, or Arizonie with my wash pan on my knee," looking for, as Bret Harte said, "a fresh deal all around." Most were either trying to get something or get away from something. It was called the "greatest mass migration of greenhorns since the children of Israel set out in search of Canaan."

Gold's out there everywhere and everybody is a millionaire. "If you stumble on a rock, don't cuss it, cash it," "Window curtains assay out at $10 a ton after a dust storm in Wickenburg," and "If you wash your face in the Hassayampa you can pan four ounces of gold from your whiskers." Rumors, and each one sends hundreds of would-be millionaires scurrying up countless streams, washing away nameless mountains of dirt, a shovel load at a time, over the riffles of a sluice box.

It was Lynx Creek or bust, Rich Hill or bust, Tombstone or bust. Far away from home, the miners were generally unchurched, unmarried and unwashed. Wherever there was a rumor or a hole-in-the-ground, they built a camp around it. They christened their towns Old Glory, Oro Belle, and Columbia. Each one claimed to have been built right smack on top of the mother lode and its streets would be cobbled with golden nuggets.

Few lasted longer than the mineral. "When the gold ran out, so did the miners," someone said. Today, all that's left of these storied ghost camps are a few melted mounds of adobe, remnants of rusted machinery and the skeletal remains of some weathered old headframes. Born in boom and died in adobe dust, those names are epitaphs for places that passed on.

Arizona was one of the last regions to be tapped by those incurable jackass prospectors of the 19th century. Its history is chock full of stories of lost treasures and bonanzas. They came from all points of the globe in search of the golden boulders of the *madre del oro* or lost mines like the Phantom Peralta, the Mislaid Peg Leg and the Lost Dutchman.

Arizona, like the rest of the West, was opened for settlement by the jackass prospector. Whenever a prospector made a rich strike, other enterprising persons were sure to follow. The first place of business and social gathering place was usually a saloon. This might consist of two whiskey barrels with a plank stretched in between for a bar. There was, by rough estimate, one saloon for every 100 persons. Next, a merchant would arrive and set up a crude store selling anything from tobacco and horse liniment to shirts and shovels.

Arizona hardrock miners in the early 1900's

These were soon followed by the soiled doves and gamblers, tin horn and otherwise, and speculators. If the camp possessed any staying power, and the mineral deposits held out, it would soon become a small bustling town. In time, a railroad company might see fit to run a line to and through the town, thus insuring many years of prosperity.

These overnight boom towns bore a litany of picturesquely whimsical names like Total Wreck, Bumble Bee, Lousy Gulch, and Timbuctu. These names give insight to the colorful nature and personality of the people who inhabited them. The new camps were populated by a ramshackle collection of boisterous, dirty, devil-may-care reprobates. Some struck it rich, but most of those who did were the ones who came in, not to pull the rich ore from the earth, but to remove it from the pockets of the lucky miners or prospectors. It was called "mining the miners."

Down on the old tenderloin district one might have a short term love affair with such excessively soiled doves as "Lizette-the-Flying-Nymph," "Peg-Leg Annie" and "Little-Gertie-the-Gold-Dollar," who were always ready to fulfill the romantic illusions and pluck the pockets of the unwary prospector. Card sharks and tin horn gamblers such as "Jack-the-Dude," "Coil-Oil-Georgie," and "Senator Few Clothes" took what was left and sent the prospector scurrying off to the hills in search of more yellow dust.

Living conditions in these towns was deplorable. There never was enough room for everybody. Miners in towns like Bisbee and Jerome slept in shifts. Old timers say the men in Jerome kept warm on cold winter nights by walking the four-mile road down Mingus Mountain to Clarkdale and back. It is also said the jail had spikes on the floor, rendering a night's sleep impossible. This discouraged one from getting himself thrown in jail just to have a place to sleep.

Conditions of the streets during inclement weather were another problem. The avenues became seas of mud, and people and animals were thought to drown or disappear in them. Drunks were thought to be especially susceptible. During the wet season, streets were not only impassable, they were not even jackassable.

Many of Arizona's mining towns were built on mountainsides right next to the mineral lode, on slopes so steep it was said, that if you spit tobacco juice out your front window, it would land on your neighbor's back porch. Mothers were warned to tether their children by rope when they were out playing in the yard, lest they fall onto their neighbor's rooftop.

The communities were male-dominated and when payday rolled around once a month, the miners rendezvoused at the local gin mills and parlor houses such as one might find at Bisbee's famous Brewery Gulch. The elevation of the town was 5,000 feet and "that's about as close to heaven as any of 'um ever got," one said. Mark Twain said of one such city, "It was no place for a Presbyterian." He quickly followed with, "So, therefore, I did not remain one for very long."

A Tucson newspaper published a letter from a Tombstone resident extolling the social virtues of the boisterous new frontier metropolis of Tombstone in the 1880's. It read: "The town is not altogether lost, even if there is a population of 1,500 people, with 2 dance houses, a dozen gambling places, over 20 saloons and more than 500 gamblers. Still, there is hope; for I know of two Bibles in town."

Placer gold, the kind you could mine with a jackknife or the toe of your boot, soon played out and the day of the fabled jackass prospector faded into the realm of romance.

Mining was big business and the man who did the digging did so for wages. They labored six days a week, ten hours a day, for $3. Glory holes had to be deepened in what became known as the world's deepest underground lunatic asylum. Never before in history had men worked so hard to get rich without working. Professional hardrock miners were imported from Mexico, Germany, Wales and Cornwall to extract the rich mineral from the earth.

Men voluntarily went thousands of feet into the earth in the employ of a company that overlooked safety standards, believing that "men were cheaper than timbers." Single-jackers and double-jackers, drillers, muckers and power men gouged out the drifts and slopes, gutting the mountains, extracting the ore, leaving the tailings piled high just outside the mine. These leached-out, man-made mountains were so sterile that nothing would ever grow on them.

Timbers were removed to make charcoal and to shore up the mines. What vegetation remained was killed by the fumes of the corrosive sulphuric chemicals used to roast the ore.

These reeking mineral factories do not paint a pretty picture of life in the mining camps, yet unemployed immigrants waited in line for work. A miner not pulling his weight or making his quota was fired at the end of the shift and another sent down in his place the next day. They called it the era of the three-shift miner. One man was down in the mine, a second was going down the road after being fired and a third was standing in line waiting for a job. They also called it the time of the 10-day miner. It was said a man could only stand 10 days of work before his body would give out. At 2,300 feet, the temperature was 120 degrees. At the 3,000 foot level, the temperature increased five degrees for every 100 feet. The air was so stagnant that the men could only work 15 minutes out of every hour. Wooden pick handles were so hot the men had to wear gloves. The heat and the pressure gave a man stomach knots, cramps so disabling that he would only work a few days at a time. Miners lived in constant terror of being crushed in a cave-in, scalded by an underground cavern of hot water, a thousand foot fall into a water-filled sump or atomized by misfired explosives. A man never knew when he came on shift whether or at what turn of the tunnel he'd come face-to-face with death.

Labor-saving equipment, such as the steam drill, was introduced in the latter part of the 19th century. This made it possible to go even deeper into the earth and did eliminate some hazards; however, it created another. The dust kicked up by the drill got into the miners' lungs. This silicosis of the lungs killed so many that the miners dubbed the machine the "widowmaker."

The ones who really suffered were those who waited at home, the families of those miners who perished in line of duty. There were no benefits. A collection was taken up for the widow and children, but that was a small pittance. The widow usually had to seek employment in the community as a domestic.

Hard times fell on Arizona in the early 1890's. Silver was demonetized by the Republicans in 1893 and almost every silver mine in Arizona had shut down. One old timer spoke for the majority when he said, "Anyone who called himself a Republican out here was either a newcomer or a damned fool."

Still, with indomitable spirit and inexhaustible fortitude, people survived. They always will. They built churches, schools and raised families. Some of their children would become city, county and state leaders in the coming years.

ED SCHIEFFELIN
finds his tombstone

The tall, lanky prospector brushed back his thick, matted, unkempt hair and looked out across a jumble of high mesa hills, scanning the rough terrain on the east side of the San Pedro valley. Somewhere out there, he was convinced, lay the vast riches he had long sought.

The region he searched was virtually uninhabited except for the soldiers who had recently established a military post at the foot of the Huachuca Mountains and the roving bands of bronco Chiricahua Apaches who had stubbornly refused to take up residence on the San Carlos reservation. It was the latter group that was chiefly responsible for the lack of population in the fertile, mineral-rich valley.

It was a well-known fact that this area, some 60 miles southeast of Tucson, was rich with minerals. Several bold men had died trying to pull the vast riches from the soil, something that added to the mystique of the San Pedro Valley. The first was Frederic Brunchow, a Russian-German mineralogist, who set up operations on the east side of the San Pedro River in 1858. He and some of his men met an untimely death at the hands of Mexican employees who robbed and pillaged the place before heading for Sonora. Others, including Arizona's first U.S. Marshal, Milton Duffield, would take up residence in the adobe buildings erected by Brunchow. Each ended in tragedy at the ill-fated site on the banks of the San Pedro.

The San Pedro Valley, located in southeastern Arizona in today's Cochise County, was part of the last territorial acquisition that makes up continental Untied States.

James Gadsden worked out a treaty with the Republic of Mexico in 1853 that settled a land dispute that had been a source of irritation to both countries since the end of the U.S.-Mexican War in 1848. With the stroke of a pen and the sum of 10 million dollars, the U.S. acquired the vast territory that ranged from the Gila River to today's international border. Whether or not to purchase the land was a hotly-contested issue in the U.S. Congress, mostly for political reasons. Northerners didn't want any new territory in the southern part of the U.S., fearing the expansion of slavery. Also, many thought the land to be a worthless piece of desert inhabited by rattlesnakes, Apaches and Sonoran bandits.

The Southerners wanted the territory to finalize their dream of building a southern right of way for an all-weather railroad to the Pacific.

In the end, the treaty was ratified and the Gadsden Purchase became a reality. Through compromises, the amount of land purchased was cut down considerably, eliminating the possibility of Arizona having a seaport on the Sea of Cortez.

Perhaps of greater significance, and something beyond the wildest dreams of those who sought the new lands, were the vast riches within the rugged, brawny mountains of southern Arizona. During the next few years, rich lodes of gold, silver and copper would make the region the nation's leading producer.

It is one of the ironies of man's existence in the southwest that when Francisco Vasquez de Coronado made his historic trek in search of the fabled cities of gold in 1540, the expedition passed across these same lands, giving it an incurious glance, never realizing the fabulous fortunes that lay beneath the soil and within the craggy rock formations.

More than 300 years later, when other regions of the West began relinquishing their hoards of gold and silver to 19th Century argonauts, the mountains of southeast Arizona kept their riches a secret, chiefly because the region was also the stamping grounds of the wily Chiricahua Apaches, the last of the tribes in the Far West to surrender to the U.S. Army.

It was this hostile land that Ed Schieffelin ventured into in the spring of 1877.

Schieffelin was not yet thirty years old, but looked well past forty at the time. The hard toil and the harsh desert sun had taken its toil on the incurable prospector. His long, dark, unkempt hair hung well past his shoulders, and his full beard was a tangle of knots. Tall and lean, the thick-chested and broadshouldered Schieffelin had taken up prospecting in Oregon with his father before reaching his teens. That was all the education he was to receive. By the time he was seventeen, Ed was on his own, wading waist-deep into the chilly mountain streams, eking out a meager living off the placer gold that he panned. By the time he reached twenty, Ed had been in most of the West's gold camps. He never really worked at any other occupation other than to earn another grubstake to continue prospecting. He once wrote that at one time he held a job for a year and a half, but quit, saying he was "no better off than I was prospecting and not half so well satisfied."

Once, he returned to his parents' home in Oregon to find that most of his friends had taken up farming and business and had become prosperous. He wasn't envious. Ed loved the life of a prospector and held fast a passionate faith that someday he would make his lucky strike.

Like most confirmed prospectors who turn their backs on society, Ed became more of a recluse, coming out of the wilderness just long enough to earn enough money and then return, alone, in search of the sourdough's elusive dream.

At the age of 24, Schieffelin had nothing to show for his years of toil but a few dollars which he promptly spent to outfit himself for a venture into the wilds of Arizona. He arrived in the territory in early 1877, prospecting around the Grand Canyon for a spell. As usual, his luck ran from bad to worse. He'd heard stories about the unexplored mountains of southeast Arizona and when he learned that a troop of cavalry was

Ed Schieffelin, the discoverer of Tombstone mines

headed to the San Pedro Valley to campaign against Victorio's Apaches, he decided to ride along. When they reached the Huachuca Mountains, on the west side of the San Pedro, Schieffelin decided to strike out on his own. The soldiers joshed the prospector, who seemed to them, a comic, ne'er-do-well, saying the only thing he would find in the Apache-infested hills would be his own tombstone.

Ed took a job at the old Brunchow Mine, standing guard for two men hired to do assessment work by the current owners of the property. His lookout post was atop a high knoll. From this vantage point he was able to examine closely the surrounding hills through field glasses. Off to the east, the rolling, grass-carpeted mesas on the north end of Mule Mountains caught his well-trained eye. There was strong evidence of a prospector's delight; a geologic upheaval had exposed ledges of grey-granite ore-bearing rock. These upheavals caused rich minerals to be found near the surface. The mineral belt appeared to extend some eight miles, running east and west. The dominant rock protruding up through a thin layer of limestone was porphyry, a formation where large bodies of ore are known to occur. Schieffelin could not have known it at the time, but deep into the porphyry the limestone vanished and in its place were large amounts of rich silver-bearing quartzite.

Ed could not be sure, but instincts garnered from a lifetime of prospecting told him that the drab, greyish mantle was masquerading one of the West's richest treasures.

Ed could not take his eyes off the interesting outcroppings of rocks on the table-like mountains a few mules east of the Brunchow. He decided to have a closer look. Moving along the arroyos that led away from the river, he worked his way eastward. On the way, he found pieces of float, or ore that had broken away from the mother lode and washed downstream. Although he found nothing that promised great riches, Ed was convinced that he was on to something big.

He spent the summer of 1877 scouring the hills east of the San Pedro River, gathering old specimens. Remembering the soldiers' sage advice, he named the site Tombstone.

By the end of the summer of 1877, Ed's grubstake was running out, so he gathered his few belongings and ore specimens and headed for Tucson where he recorded his claim. The local response to his request for financial backing was less than enthusiastic. Those who saw his ore samples proclaimed them worthless. Undaunted, Ed returned to the San Pedro Valley to gather more ore. He arrived to find that moving bands of Victorio's Apaches had driven most of the ranchers and prospectors out. Driven by passionate faith, he worked the grey-granite ledges again. Upon returning to Tucson he was again turned down. By this time his clothes were threadbare, his shapeless old hat patched with pieces of rabbit skin.

Steadfastly holding to his belief that those mountains held great wealth, Ed decided to ride over to Globe where his brother Al was working in the mines. When he arrived in the mining camp on the northeast end of the Pinal Mountains, he learned that Al had moved on and was working at the McCracken Mine in Mohave County more than 250 miles to the northwest. Ed had but 30 cents in his tattered pockets which he spent on a plug of tobacco, his only vice incidentally, as Ed neither smoked, drank nor swore.

Ed received only a lukewarm reception when he finally located his brother in the mining camp on the Bill Williams River. Al was the practical one of the two, not given to romantic pursuits of elusive mother lodes. He took a look at Ed's ore samples and was unimpressed. He suggested Ed throw the rocks away and go to work at a regular job. Al considered himself a prosperous miner, earning four dollars a day.

At this point, fate intervened on Ed's behalf. Richard Gird, an assayer and mining engineer of renown, was working at the McCracken Mine. By chance, he got a look at a few of Ed's ore specimens and ran an assay. The samples assayed out at $2,000 to the ton. That evening, the three men formed a verbal partnership. This partnership was to sustain them for many years. It stands out as a hallmark of honesty and trust during a time when lawsuits and litigation were commonplace among others of the same profession.

The trio had to literally sneak out of the McCracken camp. Such was Gird's reputation as a knowledgeable mining man that his sudden disappearance was a sure sign that he was on to something big. Despite their surreptitious exit, others did follow.

They journeyed down to Wickenburg on the Hassayampa River and from there to the small settlement now being called Phoenix. From there, they crossed the Salt River on Judge Charles T. Hayden's ferry and headed south to Maricopa, where they picked up the old Butterfield Overland Trail down through Picacho to Tucson. They didn't remain in the Old Pueblo long, heading east into Apache country. At the Pantano stage station they saw the bullet scars on the adobe walls of a recent Apache attack. A few miles further, they discovered the shallow graves of a couple of unlucky travelers who had been waylaid by Victorio's warriors. At the tiny Mormon settlement of St. David they turned south, following the San Pedro River some 20 miles up to a place called the Narrows, where the river cut between several high knolls. It was here that the Mormon Battalion fought its famous battle with wild bulls in 1846.

After passing through the narrow defile, the prospectors turned off to the left and rode over to the Brunchow Mine. They set up housekeeping in the three-room adobe house. Gird built a crude assay furnace out of one of the two fireplaces and the three would-be millionaires were ready for business.

Hard luck struck again. The glory hole turned out to be a rich, but shallow pocket. To bestow honor on their buried aspirations, the claim was named the Graveyard.

The latest turn of hard luck caused Gird and Al to suggest pulling up stakes, and they might have left then and there except for the persistence of Ed to try again.

They divided up the chores, Ed continued picking up ore specimens, Gird did the assaying, while Al provided the groceries with his hunting rifle.

A few days later, Ed uncovered a ledge of ore-bearing granite from a deep running vein of almost pure silver, so soft that when a coin was pressed against it, an imprint was visible. Gird ran a test and the ore assayed out at $15,000 to the ton silver, and 12 to 15 hundred dollars to the ton in gold. Gird looked up from the final results of his assay and exclaimed prophetically, "Ed, you are a lucky cuss, you have hit it."

Ed's long-waited dream had finally come true. Faith and perserverance had paid off handsomely. He named the claim the "Lucky Cuss." No longer would he be the subject of amusement and ridicule to the soldiers patroling the San Pedro valley or the citizens of Tucson. Now, people would seek his company and hang on his every word of wisdom as befitting a man of achievement. Such are the vicissitudes of human nature.

Ed Schieffelin's great discovery had far greater implications than merely vaulting him into the realm of respectability. The strike would have a far greater impact on the economy of Arizona than anything previous.

Other prospectors, lured by Gird's reputation, were snooping around the camp and the partners knew they must act quickly before the johnny-come-latelies staked claims on Ed's discovery. Ed began tracking the ledges around the rich site. One particular outcropping, rich in horn

Tombstone 1882

silver, was hard to follow because part of it ran underground. Because of this tricky faulting, Ed called the claim the Tough Nut.

Meantime, another argonaut named Hank Williams had begun prospecting in the area. He worked a deal whereby he would share with the partners in exchange for Gird's assay work. Williams hit a rich vein and when he tried to renege on the deal, the partners went to his camp and argued for their rightful share. Williams, who had named his claim, the Grand Central, backed down and gave them a share. Because of the dispute, the partners called it the Contention.

At this point, Ed said they had "all they needed." A swarm of prospectors would converge upon what was now being called the Tombstone district. Some would prosper; however, the richest strikes had already been claimed. None of the others would come close to producing the silver and gold of the Grand Central, Contention, and Lucky Cuss.

It is one thing to locate a rich vein of silver and quite another to raise the vast amounts of capital necessary to extricate the mineral from the site. Some prospectors locate a strike then sell the claim to capitalists, who in turn, develop the property. The original locator or prospector earns hundreds, perhaps a few thousand dollars for his efforts, while the high rollers earn millions, or lose fortunes, depending on lady luck and how deep the vein runs and, heaven forbid, they didn't get hoodwinked into buying a "salted" mine.

The partners decided to secure the financial backing to develop the property themselves. They took in as partners ex-territorial governor A.P.K. Safford, who raised the capital to build a mill which they called the Tombstone Mining and Milling Company.

The townsite of Tombstone was established nearby and soon became the major city in Arizona. Like most boomtowns, Tombstone established a quick reputation as a place to get-rich-quick, attracting the wide gamut of frontier society.

Ed reaped a fortune from his rich silver strike and subsequent sale to eastern capitalists. Through it all, he remained a kindly, generous man, always ready, honest and reliable as a railroader's timepiece. Ed represented the best features in every jackass prospector who ever turned over a piece of rock or flipped a flapjack. He built a mansion in San Francisco, married and traveled extensively in the east, where his rags to riches, Arizona adventure story had by now become a part of the romantic lore of the Old West.

Once more, the call of the wild beckoned. He missed the solitary life in the wilderness, the smell of bacon sizzling in the pan and coffee boiling in the pot over an open campfire. Most of all, he missed the sensational feeling gleaned from discovering another rich lode. He had all the money he could spend in a lifetime, but that did not fulfill the need to go looking for another glory hole.

Once again, he donned his red flannel shirt, floppy hat and tucked his corduroy pants into a pair of hob-nailed boots and set out prospecting.

He spent his remaining days searching for that proverbial rainbow. His body was found in a lonely cabin on May 12, 1897. His last written words were perhaps his greatest epitaph, or those of any incurable prospector:

> I am getting restless here in Oregon and wish to go somewhere that has wealth for the digging of it. I like the excitement of being right up against the earth, trying to coax her gold away and scatter it.

In honoring his last request, Ed was dressed in prospector's garb along with his canteen and pick and taken to Tombstone for burial. His tombstone was a huge, rugged stone monument, the kind prospectors use to mark their claim, erected, fittingly, near the site of his fabulous discovery.

Ed Schieffelin Monument, Tombstone, Arizona

WYATT EARP and the COCHISE COUNTY WAR:
reconstruction of a myth

On a crisp, blustery afternoon in late October, 1881, in Tombstone, Arizona Territory, four tall, well-dressed men walked two abreast down Fourth Street towards Fremont. At the corner of 4th and Fremont, they turned and headed west. The men moved at a quick, determined pace, their stern faces were expressionless. Three of the men bore a striking resemblance, lean, square-jawed with reddish blond hair and handlebar mustaches. The fourth was perhaps a couple of inches shorter with sunny, blond hair and sweeping mustache. Without a word being spoken, they fanned out in the middle of the street, still walking four abreast.

Further down, standing between two buildings on the south side of Fremont Street were five men dressed in the attire of cowboys—wide-brimmed hats, loosely-tied silk neckerchiefs, tight-fitting trousers tucked into expensive boots.

Another man stepped onto the street and said a few words to the men in business suits. They quickly brushed past him and walked towards the cowboys. When they were only a few feet apart, one of the men spoke sharply. "You men are under arrest. Throw up your hands," he commanded.

There was blurred movement, shots rang out, and in the space of a few furious seconds, three men were hurled into eternity and the West's most celebrated gunfight was history.

Since that day, historians, writers and self-styled "silver-maned old timers on the scene" have attempted to piece together the conflicting and complicated events that led to that classic confrontation on the streets of Tombstone that day. Even more controversial is the enigmatic man at the center stage of that event, Wyatt Berry Stapp Earp.

Was Wyatt Earp saint or sinner? Historians and afficionados still debate the virtues and vices of the legendary gunfighter. To some, he was a noble defender of law and order, to others, a ruthless highwayman who used his badge as a shield to cover his nefarious schemes.

Wyatt Earp has represented through the years, best and worst of the Western man. He emerged as a winged knight in dusty leather through the writings of Walter Noble Burns and Stuart Lake. This image was perpetuated by several Hollywood films and capped with a long-running television series.

Primarily, because of such "cowboy classics" as Burns' *Tombstone,* and Lake's *Wyatt Earp: Frontier Marshal,* fate and the luck of the deal selected Wyatt for immortality as one of the great, glorified paladins of the "great and glowing west." Today he is accepted as a full-fledged folk hero. In reality, the tall, handsome, laconic, steely-eyed blond with the handlebar mustache was a mining and real estate speculator, entrepreneur, perennial prospector and gambler. Earp personified the breed of restless adventurers who roamed the frontier in search of fortune during those tumultuous years following the Civil War.

Unlike many of his contemporaries who "Wested" briefly to establish reputations as gunfighters, then dictated their embellished escapades to some pulp writer who sold the story to an adoring eastern audience, Wyatt had "won his spurs" as a bona fide man of the West at an early age. As a youth, he crossed the continent to California. By his late teens, the venturesome lad was on the Plains hunting buffalo, and after that, a peace officer in several Kansas cowtowns.

Wyatt outlived most of his contemporaries, dying in 1929, long after trail dust had settled. The day of the gunfighter had passed from reality into the realm of romance. The ex-lawman lived long enough to see his breed portrayed on the silver screen by such sagebrush saviours as William S. Hart and Tom Mix. While most of the other western figures had gone over the great divide, some glorified, some passed over by history, Wyatt was around to tell his story and a nation hungry for heroes was eager to listen.

A quiet, reserved man, Wyatt would be amused and perhaps bewildered by all the fuss. Unlike many of his contemporaries, Wyatt was a reluctant storyteller. During the late 1920's, in an effort to set the story straight, he consented to be interviewed by both Lake and Burns. Displaying epic imaginations, both authors disregarded Wyatt's story as given and created the larger-than-life legend of Wyatt Earp. Lake, a master storyteller and thorough researcher, his interpretations and insight remarkable, admittedly over-dramatized much of Wyatt's story. Had the old gunfighter lived long enough to see his fictive lifestory in print, there might have been one more shootout—Burns and Lake being the likely targets.

Over the years, other self-styled authorities, such as Frank Waters and Ed Bartholomew, published erroneous accounts of his storybook life. These yarns included contributions from a few of Wyatt's arch enemies such as Billy Breakenridge and perjurious testimony given during a hearing by a known outlaw, Ike Clanton, and the newspaper files of the *Tombstone Nugget,* a paper owned and operated by a ring of deceitful politicians in Cochise County.

The raucous, bibulous silver camp on Goose Flat that folks were beginning to call Tombstone, was just beginning to feel its oats when the real estate boom began in early 1880. The town, located on a mesa a few miles east of the San Pedro River, some 75 miles southeast of Tucson, was experiencing prosperity unsurpassed in the history of Arizona. The great strike was cause for talk of creating a new state, and the territory's fastest growing metropolis was being touted as the next capital. Some 2,000 boisterous, devil-may-care, would-be millionaires pitched tents, wicki-

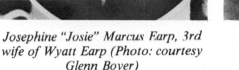

Josephine "Josie" Marcus Earp, 3rd wife of Wyatt Earp (Photo: courtesy Glenn Boyer)

Wyatt Earp, Pima County deputy sheriff, U.S. deputy marshal, Wells Fargo undercover agent

ups, shanties and set about the business of getting rich without working. Unbeknown to most, the best mining properties had already been claimed and developed. Still, there were other ways to become wealthy. One could always "mine the miners." The saloons and gambling halls on Allen Street were wide open for business 24 hours a day. The capacious multi-story homes that typified other western mining towns failed to materialize in this remote district in the southeast corner of the territory. The boom wouldn't last long enough for such indulgences. In spite of its reputation for lawlessness, however, the community was not found lacking in schools, churches, fine restaurants, hotels and cultural programs.

Tombstone was, perhaps, the last of its kind—raw and untamed! Great gold and silver strikes would occur in other regions of the West, but times were changing. With the dawning of the 20th Century, mining towns would owe their existence and allegiance to a patriarchal benefactor known simply as "The Company."

Wild and wooly, Tombstone became not only the gathering place for mining entrepreneurs and business speculators, but attracted some of the West's most notorious figures representing both sides of the law.

Events that occurred during the early 1880's attracted national attention and caused a U.S. President to threaten to declare martial law have been generally referred to as the "Earp-Clanton Feud," the Earp-Cowboy War, and most notably, the "Gunfight at the OK Corral." It would be more accurate to call it the Cochise County War, as the strife was of greater scope. Simplistic movie themes have failed to scratch the surface of this fascinating period of Arizona history, and the complexities and issues of this controversy continue to be debated.

The Earp brothers James, Virgil, Wyatt, and Morgan, arrived in

Tombstone in December, 1879, and began investing in mining claims, water rights and town lots. Another brother, Warren, arrived later. The opportunistic Earp brothers were a clannish bunch and didn't make friends easily, but one man who did penetrate the brotherhood was a tall, lean, ash blond, ex-dentist with a witty, but sardonic personality and a penchant for getting into trouble when drunk, named John Henry "Doc" Holliday.

Virgil Earp had been a peace officer in Prescott for a couple of years prior to his moving to Tombstone, and in an effort to maintain law and order in the region, U.S. Territorial Marshal Crawley P. Dake swore him in as a U.S. Deputy Marshal. Several months later, in July 1880, Pima County Sheriff, Charlie Shibell, appointed Wyatt a deputy for the Tombstone district (until January 1881, Tombstone was still a part of Pima County). Since there were no courts or judges in Tombstone at the time, enforcement of the law was somewhat ineffective. It is likely Shibell and his political cronies in Tucson sought Wyatt's services more as tax collector in the rich mining district, since at that time, the county sheriff also served as tax collector. Shibell, for his part, received 10% of the collections, something that could increase his meager sheriff's salary tenfold. Wyatt saw his job as more than mere tax collector and put the word out to the lawless element in the eastern part of old Pima County that law and order would be maintained. The rustlers, as if to take up the challenge, stole Wyatt'e favorite horse.

The southeast corner of Arizona became a favorite stamping ground for bandits, driven to the region as civilization and the law moved west. The rugged terrain near the Mexican border was an ideal place to hide stolen cattle. Cattle ranchers on both sides of the border were victimized by a large, loosely-organized band of renegades under the leadership of a hard-bitten rascal known as Newman Haynes "Old Man" Clanton. Gang members Tom and Frank McLaury posed as honest ranchers, using their ranch in the Sulphur Springs Valley as a clearing house for stolen cattle. Others in the gang that numbered more than a hundred included Clanton's sons, Phin, Ike and Billy, along with Johnny Ringo, Frank Stilwell and the notorious William Brocius Graham, alias Curly Bill Brocius. Curly Bill was a tall, bushy-haired fellow with coarse, ugly features but gregarious-natured and a popular figure in Cochise County. Beneath that sunny disposition was a cold-blooded desperado. Called "the most famous outlaw of Arizona," he had assumed the leadership of the Clanton gang in August, 1881, after "Old Man" Clanton had been killed in an ambush.

Cattle rustling wasn't their only stock in trade. Mexican smugglers along the border were another prey as were stagecoaches rumbling along the lonely roads leading to and from Tombstone loaded with payroll or bullion from the mines.

The outlawry was so widespread, the thieves so brazen, that cattle were being stolen in broad daylight. The name "cowboy" became synonymous with rustlers. The rush of population to Tombstone had created a beef bonanza. Meat contractors and butchers couldn't care less whose beef they were buying, something that made disposal of stolen cattle easier.

Soon after Wyatt was appointed deputy for the Tombstone district, he was visited by a Captain Hurst of Fort Rucker, a military post in the southern part of the Chiricahua Mountains. Hurst was upset over the theft of some army mules. Wyatt, Virgil, and Morgan Earp, along with the officer and four soldiers, tracked the missing animals to a ranch southeast of the Dragoon Mountains, owned by Tom and Frank McLaury, well-known members of the so-called Clanton gang. Word was passed to Captain Hurst that the mules would be returned only if the Earps removed themselves from the scene. Reluctantly, Wyatt and his brothers departed and the McLaury's told Hurst to inform Wyatt that "if you and your brothers interfere with them again, they'll shoot you on sight."

"Tell 'em they'll have their chance," Wyatt replied tersely. A few weeks later, Wyatt met Tom and Frank McLaury on the streets nearby Charleston, a mill town in the San Pedro River. "That army official give you our message?" they asked. "He did," Wyatt answered, "but in case you didn't get my answer, I'll repeat it." The McLaurys turned and walked away, making threatening remarks as they departed.

This was the first of many hostile exchanges between the Earps and gang members before the climactic gunfight. The army mules were never recovered. A few days later in a local paper, Captain Hurst publicly accused the McLaurys of stealing government property. An indignant Frank McLaury published his own retaliation, accusing the officer of stealing the mules.

Several months later, Wyatt, acting on a tip, went to Charleston to recover his stolen horse. Sitting astraddle the animal was young Billy Clanton. Clanton made a feeble attempt to run Earp down but thought better of it when Wyatt put the palm of his hand on the butt of his revolver. Billy surrendered the horse and his guns, threatening to "get" Wyatt all the while.

Trouble erupted again between city police and the rustlers on a late October evening in 1880, when Tombstone's first marshal, Fred White, was shot to death while trying to arrest Curly Bill. Wyatt had run to White's assistance as soon as he heard gunfire, which initially had been a bunch of "cowboys" shooting at the moon in violation of a local gun ordinance. He arrived, pistol in hand, just as White was shot, and knocked Curly Bill cold with a blow of the pistol barrel, a maneuver termed "Buffaloing" in that time and place. A few of Curly Bill's friends, including the Clanton and McLaury brothers expressed their displeasure, as Wyatt dragged the outlaw chieftain off to jail, by snapping off a few poorly-aimed pistol shots at the deputy. Later that evening, one by one, each was knocked cold by the barrel of Wyatt's Smith-and-Wesson and thrown into the cell with Curly Bill. Surprisingly, Marshal White's death was ruled an accident.

Wyatt's quick action stirred the ire of the cowboys. He had opened a war on two fronts—the cowboys regarded him as an antagonist and a threat to their free rein in the county—and the County Ring wanted him out of the way for political reasons. An uneasy truce was in effect during the next few months, as opposing factions sized up one another.

Wyatt did not remain Shibell's deputy in Tombstone long. When the Democrat ran for re-election, Wyatt resigned and threw his support behind Republican law and order candidate Bob Paul. Shibell appointed Johnny Behan to fill the vacancy. Shibell seemed to have won the election when it was learned that a large party of rustlers at San Simon went to the polls and voted again and again for the incumbent. After an investigation, Paul was named the winner and became Sheriff of Pima County.

PART II

The get-rich-quick schemes and political skullduggery that were to take place over the next few years in Tombstone had ties not only in local politics but extended to county and territorial levels. Pristine Tombstone, as yet, had no social conscience, an affliction that bred corruption on a grand scale.

The first major scandal developed in late 1880, while Tombstone was still a tent city. Part of the town site had been laid out over some existing mining claims, thereby putting a cloud over clear title and creating a feud between businessmen and miners. Mayor Alder Randall and a few of his political croinies decided to take advantage of the confusion to feather their speculative nests. They organized a town lot company to which the mayor transferred the titles of 2,394 lots to his friends. The schemers then attempted to resell the lots, causing an uproar among the local citizenry.

The plot was foiled when the fiery editor of the *Epitaph,* John Clum, obtained an injunction to prevent the transactions. Clum's actions led to the formation of a vigilante group calling themselves the Citizens Safety Committee. When talk began to circulate about a necktie party, ex-mayor Randall left for other parts. They substituted the editor's name as mayor on the ticket and Clum was elected by a landslide.

The Citizens Safety Committee shared many common interests including business, politics (Republican), real estate, and mining speculation. This committee would rely heavily on the Earp brothers, in the coming months, to act as enforcers causing their rivals to refer to them deridingly as the "company men."

The other political faction had its beginnings in some of the highest offices in the territorial government. Tombstone's residents would be called upon to line up on one side or the other in the coming fight for political control.

When John C. Fremont was appointed territorial governor in 1878, he was somewhere near the end of the trail of a checkered military and political career. The old "Pathfinder's" appointment was the result of an old political debt owed for services rendered. He considered the position in Arizona banishment rather than reward and spent most of his tenure in absentia promoting various mining schemes in the east. The day-to-day operations were left to his underlings, many of whom were raking in the dough throughout the territory by shady dealings in local government and politics. A few politicos in the territorial assembly cast greedy eyes on the rich Tombstone mining district. Their ringleader in Tombstone was a jovial, political hack named John Behan. Earlier, in 1879, Behan had served in the territorial legislature where he made an acquaintance of one Artemus Emmett Fay, a Tucson editor. Fay and Behan were to lay the cornerstone of a political machine that was to become known as the County Ring and would be responsible for much of the violence that would take place over the next few years. Their first order of business was to engineer an enabling act to create a new county out of the eastern part of Pima County which would be called Cochise. Others in the coalition were territorial delegates Hugo Richards of Prescott, who aspired to be territorial delegate to Washington or governor; Harry Woods, who ram-rodded the measure through the House, creating Cochise County, and Thomas and John Dunbar, the former also a territorial delegate.

The Dunbar brothers had been close friends back in their home state of Maine with the powerful Republican Senator James G. Blaine. Senator Blaine had little trouble persuading Governor Fremont to appoint Johnny Behan sheriff, the most important office in Cochise County. The creation of a new county would create new problems for the Citizens Safety Committee. Tombstone would be the new county seat, meaning an entourage of county officials would set up offices in the town. Natur-ally, this would create a degree of overlapping of authority, especially between county and city peace officers. Tombstone residents would be called upon to line up on the side of one or the other political factions in the power struggle.

It is interesting to note that besides wheeling and dealing to create Woods (a new county), Richards, Fay and John Dunbar all played an important part in the origin of a newspaper, the *"Tombstone Nugget,"* to act as their official organ.

In the Spring of 1881, a legislative deal was struck, establishing Cochise County from the eastern part of Pima County. John Behan was appointed sheriff and became the political kingpin for the County Ring. Behan's business partner in a Tombstone livery stable, John Dunbar, brother of a territorial delegate, was named treasurer and Harry Woods, a territorial delegate, who had promoted the formation of Cochise County, became undersheriff. A couple of others, Frank Stilwell and Billy Breakenridge, went to work for Behan. Stilwell, a known outlaw in the area, was made a deputy. (It was said of highwayman Stilwell that the stagecoach horses were so familiar with his voice, they responded better than to their own driver to his command to "Halt"). Breakenridge lived long enough to

John H. "Doc" Holliday

Virgil Earp, Tombstone City marshal,
victim of vendetta

gain some respectability in 20th Century Arizona, even to the point of being called "Colonel." The self-proclaimed deputy had a book ghosted for him by Wm. McLeod Raine, *Helldorado,* glorifying his alleged role. Such are the advantages of outliving (and outtalking) your contemporaries. In reality, Billy was an errand boy for sheriff Behan. His most notable talents were his chummy relations with the rustlers in Cochise County. The sheriff sustained a non-interference policy towards the rustlers, a pursuit that had its parallels in the 1920's with bootleg liquor. At the same time, the sheriff's office became the rendezvous point for the County Ring.

As the feuding between county and city politicos heated up, Mayor John Clum's *Epitaph* became the clarion of the Citizens Safety Committee, while Behan's undersheriff, Harry Woods and his *Tombstone Nugget* was the official organ of the County Ring. Interestingly, Woods defended the rustlers as a "mythical horde" of misunderstood young boys just out having a little fun. Since the cowboys spent a good deal of their ill-gotten money in the town saloons, brothels and gaming tables, many locals agreed and resented the efforts of the Citizens Safety Committee to restore order.

PART III

Even though Johnny Behan had been named sheriff of Cochise County, the appointment was only temporary until popular elections could be held. Wyatt had planned to run but withdrew his name after Behan promised to make him undersheriff.

However, Behan reneged on his promise, saying that "something" changed his mind. That "something" was really something—a beautiful dark-eyed lady named Josie Marcus.

Josephine Sarah Marcus was the daughter of a wealthy San Francisco merchant. She first met Johnny Behan near Prescott while traveling with a theatrical troupe performing the popular stage play, "Pinafore on Wheels." Johnny was smitten by Josie's beauty and followed her home to San Francisco where he applied the same smooth-talking modus operandi that had won him political favor in the smoke-filled rooms of Arizona. Josie, only eighteen at the time, was charmed into returning to Tombstone under promise of matrimony. She even hocked her jewelry to purchase a house for her and gentleman Johnny. Johnny, a perennial woman-chaser, was up to his old tricks soon after he and Josie set up housekeeping in Tombstone, and Josie was not the type to take this sort of thing lying down. One day she encountered tall, quiet and mannerly Wyatt on the streets of Tombstone, and for both, it must have been love at first sight. Much to the displeasure of sheriff Behan, the handsome couple were soon living together. Behan developed a lasting hatred over the Josie affair. From that time on, the sheriff stopped at nothing to even the score. This blind thirst for revenge would eventually lead to his political downfall.

It should be mentioned that, despite this illicit beginning, Wyatt and Josie remained "till death do us part." Josie was loyal to Wyatt's memory long after he was dead and the mythmakers and debunkers started taking their licks.

Josie, as paramour of antagonists Behan and Wyatt, had a unique role in the drama. As Behan's fiancee, she was privy to much of the skullduggery going on in county politics. She was also a close confidante of Marietta Spence, wife of Pete Spence, one of the outlaws. Unfortunately for history, her affair with Behan ended just as things were getting interesting. Her recently published memoirs, *I Married Wyatt Earp,* edited by Glenn Boyer, shed much light on events in Cochise County in the early 1880's. More important, we are able to gain insight into Wyatt Earp from a woman's perspective.

The event leading directly to the famous shootout near the OK Corral occurred on March 15, 1881, when the Benson stage carrying several thousand dollars in silver bullion was fired upon by four masked men. The driver, Bud Philpot, fell from the stage mortally wounded. Shotgun messenger Bob Paul quickly grabbed the reins when Bud was shot and sped from the scene, foiling the robbery attempt. One of the hail of bullets, fired after the stage, killed passenger Pete Roerig. Twenty empty cartridge cases were later found at the scene. When word reached Tombstone, Wyatt, Virgil and Wells Fargo agent, Marshall Williams, formed a posse and went out to pick up the trail of the bandits. They tracked one of the outlaws, Luther King, to a ranch where he was captured without a fight. The frightened prisoner identified his accomplices as Bill Leonard, Jim Crane, and Harry Head. All were well-known members of the "cowboy" gang. King was turned over to Sheriff Behan, who turned him over to undersheriff Harry Woods, who turned him loose. Woods, doubling as editor of the *Nugget*, insisted the prisoner escaped while he and John Dunbar, Behan's partner in a livery stable, were making out a bill of sale for King's horse. Actually, King just walked out of jail, where a fresh horse was conveniently waiting, and headed for Mexico. In an effort to cover his own misdeed, Woods tried to shift blame for the robbery by publishing a version of the attempted holdup implying that one of the participants was none other than Doc Holliday. Bill Leonard, one of the gunmen, was an old crony of Doc's from earlier days. Doc, a quondam dentist, who still practiced when his consumptive cough didn't interfere, was something of an enigma. Moody and morose on occasion (and witty on others), his friendship with the Earp brothers dated back to their days in the Kansas cowtowns.

The County Ring took advantage of the friendship between Wyatt and Doc to make a clever strategic move using Doc's dubious reputation to discredit and politically embarrass Wyatt in his quest to become sheriff of Cochise County.

Seeds of public distrust had been planted wisely by those seeking, for political reasons, to paint a tarnished image of the Earps. The citizens of Tombstone were openly divided on the issue. On one side was the "Law and Order" Citizens Safety Committee, supported by many of the town's leading businessmen, professionals and entrepreneurs. On the other side, the County Ring politicos continued to propagandize the high-handed activities of the Committee and its enforcers, the Earps.

Also, since the cowboys were free-spenders, a large number of locals resented efforts by the Earps to suppress their activities. Doc responded to the robbery charges with wry indignation at the reflection on his ability, protesting that, if he had pulled the job, they would have gotten the loot. Town gossip was the only thing connecting Doc with the robbery-murder, until Doc's inamorata, Big Nose Kate Elder, started talking. Kate, for whatever reason, probably in a drunken stupor, was persuaded by Behan to sign an affidavit stating that Doc was one of the bandits.

A warrant was issued and Doc was arrested for murder. Wyatt and Virgil reacted quickly to the turn of events, the former posted bail while the latter sobered Kate up enough so she could testify at the hearing. Kate admitted she signed something she hadn't understood and the charges were *nole prossed* by the DA. Doc gave Kate $500 to get off his back. With this she went to Globe and made a down payment on a small hotel.

The accusation against Doc was an embarrassment to the Earps' law-and-order policy. Wyatt decided the best way to vindicate Holliday would be to capture the robbers himself. By so doing, he would also enhance his chances of winning the race for sheriff. To expedite his plans, he sought out Ike Clanton to be his Judas. Ike was well-known as a leaky-mouth with a penchant for getting others in trouble.

Meeting in secret, Wyatt offered Ike the Wells Fargo reward money if he would lure the bandits to a prearranged site where they could be arrested. Ike agreed on the condition that he could include Frank McLaury and Joe Hill in on the deal.

Unfortunately, in the interim, the three robbers, Jim Crane, Harry Head, and Bill Leonard all met violent ends in unrelated gunfights, leaving Wyatt empty-handed and Ike minus the blood money.

The secret deal between Wyatt and Ike was exposed, accidentally, soon after by Marshall Williams, the Wells Fargo agent. Williams, who was not privy to the plot, either figured out what had transpired or made a lucky guess. Whichever, he had a few drinks too many one night and chided Ike for betraying his comrades. Ike, who had also been drinking heavily, confronted Wyatt and charged him with letting Williams in on the secret. When Wyatt denied the accusations, Ike complained that Wyatt must have told Holliday. Again Wyatt issued a strong denial. The confrontation took place in front of several witnesses, so Ike's concerns over secrecy became inane. Morgan Earp was sent to Tucson to fetch Doc, not because Wyatt wanted to convince Ike especially, but because the Earps had been warned the showdown was coming. Having Doc tell Ike that Wyatt hadn't blabbed probably took place as a last-minute maneuver to head off serious trouble the Earps didn't want. Doc placed a lot on loyalty, regardless of which side one represented. He angrily rebuked Ike for his treachery. Heated words were exchanged and Doc challenged Ike to get his gun and commence. The confrontation had to be broken up by Wyatt and Virgil. The Earps did not want to let matters get out of hand. Later that evening, the drunken outlaw threatened Wyatt, who told him to "go sleep it off." As the saying goes, the fat was in the fire. The Earp brothers and the Clantons were on a collision course. For Ike, the only way he could vindicate himself to the other outlaws was to eliminate the Earps.

Ike Clanton's situation was getting desperate. His attempted double-cross was out in the open and he was as good as dead, unless he could twist the story enough to satisfy Curly Bill and the others. Ike's explanation to gang leaders that Wyatt had deliberately lied to get him in trouble was accepted, with reservations. To clear himself, they said, Ike must force a showdown with the Earps. Ike, a man more of words than action (for example, when he said fight was his racket, Mrs. Earp later observed, he should have said, racket was his fight) made several public threats against the Earps over the next several days, growing more brazen with each shot of whiskey. Not surprisingly, all his bravado was displayed while going around unarmed. A few days before the fight, he and brother Billy, along with Tom and Frank McLaury, had gone to Charleston and obtained the release of another rustler, Billy Claiborne. Claiborne, a brash young self-proclaimed "Billy the Kid," had been in jail for killing a man in a barroom brawl. Meanwhile, Curly Bill, Ringo and friends had gathered in Tombstone, spreading word up and down Allen Street that the Earps' days were numbered. Interestingly, by the afternoon of the 25th, most had left town.

On the morning of October 26, Ike was again threatening to kill the Earps and Doc on sight, this time armed with a pistol and rifle. He was joined by Billy, Frank and Tom McLaury and Billy Claiborne.

Virgil, hearing Ike was on the prod and looking for the Earps or Doc, approached Ike from behind. As the outlaw swung his rifle around, he tranquilized him with a pistol barrel. Ike was hauled before the local magistrate, fined $25 for violating the gun ordinances and released. A few minutes later, Wyatt and Tom McLaury met on the street and exchanged hot words. Wyatt "buffaloed" him when he wouldn't go after his own pistol. Soon after, Wyatt chastised Frank McLaury for violating another city ordinance, that of letting his horse walk on the boardwalk. Again, a heated exchange took place between the adversaries. The outlaws retreated to a gun shop where they armed themselves, then headed for Behan's and Dunbar's livery stable where they were joined by an accomplice, West Fuller. The Earps were gathered in Hafford's Saloon, awaiting further developments, when Sheriff Behan walked in and warned them of the impending danger. Virgil advised the sheriff to arrest the cowboys, but was told it was none of his business. Behan returned to the rustler's lair, no doubt gave warning that the city police were armed and ready for action.

The three Earp brothers left Hafford's Saloon at about half past 2 p.m. Virgil decided to make an arrest when friends informed him the cowboys were on the street armed. Prior, they'd been in the livery stables, which was evidence they might be leaving town. It was legal to carry arms *coming* or *going,* but not in town. The fight occurred when it did because Doc was living at Fly's Boarding House on Fremont Street between 3rd and 4th. It is likely the "cowboys" were laying for Doc, hoping to catch him alone.

PART IV

The handsome Earp brothers were all over six feet, and from a distance it was impossible to tell them apart. Anyone witnessing the scene could not miss the sense of drama as the Earps' faces, frozen in grim determination, went forth to keep a rendezvous with destiny. Holliday joined the party as they walked north on 4th Street. Doc was carrying a cane which he traded to Virgil for a Wells Fargo shotgun. Virgil and Wyatt took the lead, Morgan and Doc close behind. Wyatt had on a canvas mackinaw, designed for riding, with a built-in pistol pocket. Doc had on a buffalo overcoat of a decided albino hue. Virgil and Morgan were dressed in plain street clothes such as any businessman, not the gambler rigs seen so often in movies. When the party reached Fremont and turned west, they spread out in line and moved into the middle of the street. Sheriff Behan approached and informed Virgil he had disarmed the cowboys. The city marshal then asked if the cowboys had been arrested. when Behan said

"No," Virgil quickly brushed past and moved towards the cowboys.

Wes Fuller wanted no part of the action and beat a hasty retreat. He was quickly followed by Billy Claiborne. The others, Tom and Frank McLaury, Billy and Ike Clanton stood facing the Earps. The two positions were less than 15 feet apart, when Virgil called on the cowboys to surrender their weapons.

No one is sure who fired first, but it is commonly believed that either Doc or Morgan got in the opening round.

When the smoke had cleared, some 30 shots had been exchanged in a span of a half minute. Morgan and Virgil both suffered gunshot wounds, Doc had a slight crease across his left hip and only Wyatt came through without a scratch on the Earp side. The cowboys didn't fare so well. Billy Clanton, Tom and Frank McLaury lay dead. Ike showed his true colors at first fire by running forward and claiming he didn't want to fight. Wyatt told him to get to fighting or get out. Ike considered discretion the better part of valor and ran away, leaving the others to finish his fight. There is a good chance that Ike was expecting Curly Bill, Ringo, Stilwell and the others to back his play. When they didn't show, he lost his nerve.

The Citizens Safety Committee under Colonel Herring, perhaps 50 to 100 strong, arrived, almost in military formation, within seconds of the end of the fight. Officials placed the slain men on planks in Behan's livery stable and convened a coroner's jury to view them. The officials were Behan and coroner Matthews. Later, they were dressed in suits and placed in the window of Ritter & Evans funeral parlor. Next to the bodies, friends placed a sign which read "Murdered on the Streets of Tombstone."

Ike Clanton swore out warrants for the arrests of the Earps and Holliday. During the lengthy hearing, witnesses and friends testified before Judge Wells Spicer. The testimony of Sheriff Behan and Ike was damaging to the Earps case, and for a time it looked like the Earps and Holliday would face murder charges. Ike played the role of martyr, portraying him and his friends as harmless, unarmed cowboys at the mercy of the ruthless city police. Ike accused the Earps of "piping off" from Wells Fargo, using murder and robbery to cover up their transgressions. He had been well coached and his story sounded convincing on the surface. According to Ike's sworn statement, the Earps had planned the robbery of the Benson stage. Their cohorts, Head, Crane and Leonard knew too much and Wyatt wanted them dead. Wyatt also had to execute Ike and Frank McLaury, as they also knew too much. (Wyatt had a chance to shoot Ike point blank at the street fight, but didn't when the latter refused to draw his weapon.) Ike's tearjerking testimony, no doubt, sought vengeance for the killing of his brother, but more important, he needed an alibi to cover up his planned betrayal of the stage robbers. Ike's cowardly act during the gunfight no doubt lowered his esteem with the gang and everyone else, and his absurd allegations were the last-ditch effort of a desperate man.

Ike's self-righteous, garbled testimony was laden with errors and in the end, the court ruled the Earps acted in the line of duty.

The illogical accusations made by Ike Clanton during the hearing have served, down through the years, as a source of primary evidence used by 20th century debunkers who sought to portray the Earps as stage robbers. In reality, during the period in question there were four stage robberies. In each there is overwhelming evidence to prove the Earps could not have been involved. Also, Wells Fargo had several undercover agents working around Tombstone. These agents were cooperatives of the Earps. It is highly unlikely these agents would be providing information to the Earps if there was the remotest suspicion of them being stage robbers.

PART V

To get a better understanding of some related events, it is necessary to backtrack a few months to August, 1881, when Curly Bill Brocius and some friends robbed a Mexican smuggler train of some $4,000 in bullion. The Mexicans were all slain, their bodies left where they had fallen. The place is known today as Skeleton Canyon and is best remembered as the site where Geronimo surrendered in 1886.

A few days later, "Old Man" Clanton and four companions were ambushed, most accounts say, by Mexicans, seeking vengeance for the robbery-murder in Skeleton Canyon. Another theory offered as a motive for the showdown was that some people around Tombstone were saying that it was the Earps, not a party of vengeful Mexicans who bushwacked "Old Man" Clanton and his gang. This could have occurred, (inadvertently), when they tried to follow Joe Hill, an outlaw brought in by Ike as a part of the deal cooked up between him and Wyatt. Hill had gone to entice stage robbers Leonard, Head and Crane into a trap and the Earps and Holliday had trailed him to the Guadalupe Mountains. In the ensuing trap laid down by the Earps, "Old Man" Clanton, Crane and some others decided to fight and were killed. There is a strong possibility that young Warren Earp and Doc were both wounded in this fracas. It explains why Doc was using a cane at the "Street Fight," when he had never done so previously.

On September 8, 1881, two masked men robbed the Bisbee Stage. A posse led by the Earps went in pursuit and captured Frank Stilwell and Pete Spence. Stilwell was, at the time, a deputy for John Behan. The two were taken to Tucson for a hearing before a U.S. Commissioner and released a few days later.

On the night of December 14th, some six weeks after the "Street Fight," Mayor Clum narrowly escaped death when the stage he was riding was held up. The coach was carrying no money and remarks made at the scene indicated the outlaws planned to assassinate the mayor. The plot was foiled when the horses panicked and the coach rambled off down the road. The outlaws brought the stage to a halt when one of them accidentally shot the lead horse. A bullion wagon coming behind driven by one "whistling Dick" was hit. Clum wisely slipped out into the darkness and walked back to town. The outlaws were later identified. Among their number were Ike Clanton, Curly Bill, Frank Stilwell and Johnny Ringo. The Bisbee-Tombstone stage was robbed again on January 6, 1882. Stilwell and Spence, still out on bail, were identified as the bandits. Curly Bill and Ike Clanton were also accused.

Wyatt's pursuit was unsuccessful, as the "cowboys" in Cochise County were too well organized. Fresh horses were readily available at rustler lairs throughout the vast region.

The enforcers for the Citizens Safety Committee were dealt a serious blow on the evening of December 28, 1881, when Virgil Earp was hit with a shotgun blast as he walked along Allen Street. Virgil was permanently crippled in the attack, ending his fighting days in Tombstone. The prime suspects in the shooting included Curly Bill, Frank Stilwell and Ike Clanton. Warrants were issued for their arrests, but at the hearing several witnesses swore they were miles away and the case was dismissed.

The new city marshal, Dave Neagle, was honest but not forceful. Gun ordinances imposed by Virgil were ignored and Tombstone reverted to an armed camp as the cowboys returned in full force. The only thing in their way were a few stalwarts on the Citizens Safety Committee and a number of intrepid gunmen sporting colorful names like Sherman McMasters, Texas Jack Vermilion and Turkey Creek Jack Johnson who remained loyal to the Earps.

Curly Bill was making himself scarce in Tombstone these days. Filling in for the outlaw chieftain was the overrated Johnny Ringo. Ringo was, in reality, a drunken bum, who was pumped up by Billy Breakenridge in *Helldorado,* probably to spite Wyatt, then yet living. A sullen, brooding man, he was reputed to be the "brains of the outfit," a dangerous gunfighter and a scholar. Actually he was a high school dropout and there is no evidence that he ever shot a man in a fair fight.

The outlawry in the county reached such a state that acting governor John Gosper (Fremont had resigned) proposed special appropriations to offer large rewards for the capture of Curly Bill and his associates. U.S. Marshal Crawley Dake recommended Wyatt to head the federal posse. Sheriff Behan took steps to abort the project by reopening the "Street Fight" case, persuading a local justice in Contention City to oblige. Warrants were issued on Wyatt, Morgan and Doc Holliday for the murder of Tom and Frank McLaury and Billy Clanton. The Citizens Safety Committee, fearing the Earps and Holliday would be assassinated, intervened at this point and demanded they be allowed to provide the escort. At Contention City, the judge quickly sizing up the tense situation, refused to hear the case.

The second tragedy struck the Earp family on the evening of March 18, 1882, when Morgan was shot to death by assassins in Bob Hatch's pool hall. Another bullet narrowly missed Wyatt. Morgan lived just long enough for brothers Jim and Warren to assist Virgil to the scene.

Witnesses testified before a coroner's jury, naming the killers as Pete Spence, Frank Stilwell, Florentino Cruz and Hank Swilling. Curly Bill and Ringo were also seen near the crime. Evidence indicates Will McLaury, a Texas attorney, and brother to the slain cowboys, financed the killing. There is further evidence to indicate that Johnny Behan was involved. Sometime earlier, Morgan had chivalrously intervened during an argument between Josie and her erstwhile paramour. When the dust had settled, Johnny had taken a severe beating and had reason to harbor a deep hatred for another Earp brother. Johnny was not the type to gun a man down, but he certainly wasn't above having somebody else do his dirty work. Wyatt knew his brother's killers would never be brought to justice in Cochise County. Even if they were, alibis would be provided by other members of the gang and the killers would go free. Wyatt decided to become his brother's avenger, acting as judge, jury and executioner.

The first to pay the price was Frank Stilwell. On the evening of the second day following Morgan's murder, he, Ike, Pete Spence and Hank Swilling had ridden to Tucson to await the train carrying Morgan's body to California for burial. Wyatt and Doc escorted the body, along with Virgil, who was still ailing from gunshot wounds, as far as Tucson. Wyatt had suspected correctly that an attempt might be made on his helpless brother's life. A few minutes before the train was scheduled to pull out of Tucson, he bid his brother farewell. As he was preparing to leave the train, he caught sight of the assassins lurking in the train yard. He jumped from the rail car and rushed towards the gunmen who broke and ran into the darkness. When the headlights of a steam engine outlined a shadowy figure moving across the tracks, Wyatt caught up with the man who turned and faced him. It was Frank Stilwell. The outlaw looked at the tall, slender figure with the sweeping mustache. A strange, frightened look appeared on his face. "Morg," he hesitated then said again, "Morg." Wyatt stared coldly at Stilwell for a brief moment then pulled both barrels of his Wells Fargo sawed-off shotgun.

Wyatt later claimed he'd "often wondered what made him say that." Many people couldn't tell the three brothers apart in broad daylight. Frank Stilwell lost what edge he might have had in the fight when he thought Wyatt to be the ghost of Morgan Earp standing in the steam cloud of a passing locomotive.

The next victim was Florentino Cruz, who acted as lookout for the assassins. Wyatt found him at Pete Spence's place. After listening to Cruz's confession, Wyatt gave him a chance to go for his gun. Cruz was no match for Wyatt. A coroner's jury ruled the killing justified.

Wyatt next encountered Curly Bill and eight members of the gang at Mescal Springs, in the Whetstone Mountains, about 35 miles west of Tombstone, and killed the outlaw in a blazing shotgun duel. Wyatt left Arizona for a spell only to return in July. At Turkey Creek in the Chiricahua Mountains, he shot and killed Johnny Ringo. By this time, most of the others responsible for the shootings of Virgil and Morgan had left the county.

In the feud's aftermath, Warren Earp was shot to death at Willcox in July, 1900, motive uncertain. Morgan was dead and Virgil a cripple. The Earp brotherhood had paid a high price for its role as enforcers for the Citizens Safety Committee. Large scale outlawry in Cochise County subsided for a while due to the fact that the Earps killed the leaders and enough of the followers to scare the rest out of the country. Wyatt planned to return to Tombstone and run for sheriff, but eventually changed his mind. No doubt, too many unpleasant memories haunted his mind.

For those who regard the Earps as murderers, and there have been many accounts by reputable writers who have done so, one needs only to check the facts. All the Earp victims had holes in the front. The Earps, in every case, were the victims of backshooters and hidden assassins.

John Behan, the "good ole boy" perennial office holder, continued on the government payroll, becoming assistant superintendent of the Territorial Prison at Yuma. Behan never achieved his former stature with the Democratic political machine in Arizona. He continued to hold political appointee positions, but all of them low-grade. Behan's fatal mistake was that he let his hatred for Wyatt over alienation of Josie's affection interfere with performance of duty. He wanted to get Wyatt so bad that he openly took sides with known outlaws in the county. In short, he just got in too far over his head when he tackled the Earps.

Ike Clanton took his rustling operation to the White Mountains where, in 1887, he was shot and killed on Eagle Creek, near Clifton, by a correspondence school detective named Rawhide Jake Brighton. Brighton was a deputy sheriff of Apache County at the time. Doc Holliday died that same year of consumption at Glenwood Springs, Colorado.

Tombstone itself was dying. The "Comstock of Arizona," which had pulled Arizona out of an economic abyss, came into hard times. The mines started to flood in 1883. A few years later, new pumps were installed, but a fire put them out of action and they were submerged. They are still there under water. The labor movement was gaining momentum, along with the demonetization of silver, which also caused many mines to shut down. The entrepreneurs and hardrock miners went on to greener pastures. Things began to quiet down along notorious Allen Street. The sounds of laughter, spinning of the roulette wheels, shuffling of cards and the rinky-tink piano were heard no more. Only the "hangers-on" and wishful thinkers remained.

Tombstone, the great "Sagebrush Sodom" of Goose Flat Mesa, a city that rivaled the likes of Virginia City, San Francisco and New Orleans, and, like many of the famous personalities who walked her streets, was fading from reality into the realm of myth and romance. Tombstone, for better or worse, was one of a kind. (It still is.)

THE COWBOYS
Legends in Levis

"If they are human, they're a separate species."
Charles M. Russell

The men and women in the West are among the most cherished figures in Americana, the rugged symbols of the making of a country, of hard work, honest determination, elemental existence and self-reliance. Of these, the most romantic are the cowboys.

There has never been, before or since, a figure who has held the interest and imagination of so many people, nor has there ever been a figure so misunderstood and misrepresented. The word "cowboy" epitomized the wide gamut of frontier society. Gunfighters, gamblers, outlaws and cowboys are inseparable to all but the most discerning student of the Old West. Often viewed in an overly romantic light, they are idolized and imitated not only in this country, but throughout the world—their jeans, shirts, boots and hats have become an international costume.

It is not enough to simply compare today's working cowboys with their counterparts, the old time cowhands. First, one must look at the subjects, real and imagined, as the world perceives them.

Out of a frontier history that lasted more than 350 years, Americans have taken the era of the open range cowboy, a brief 20-year span, given it immortality and called it the West. The heroic figures who emerged have come to symbolize all the manifestations of character we ascribe to the winning of the West. Most important, those qualities have come to represent our perception of our own self-image as rugged individuals.

The cowboy image universally epitomized the highest and most honorable qualities of mankind, outdoors, freedom, individualism and defense of the oppressed. The cowboy has been romanticized, lionized, analyzed and psychoanalyzed. We have the singing cowboy, drugstore cowboy, Coca Cola cowboy, rhinestone cowboy, tragic cowboy, urban cowboy and instant cowboy. One answer might be that in a society growing more impersonal, with urbanization and computerization rapidly closing in, people instinctively yearn for a sense of place. Solace is found in a vicarious reliving of those simplistic days of yesteryear.

Today's instant cowboys and their silver-buckled bunnies strut around in embroidered, tight-fitting shirts, designer jeans tucked into $300 lizard-hide boots, boots with pointed toes (good for two things only—squashin' cockroaches in corners and kickin' snakes in the fanny). The cowboy's most distinguishable feature, the hat, has been corrupted with enough feathers to do honor to a Sioux warrior. This creeping faddism has encroached into the sacred sanctuaries of modern real working cowboys. Prices for western apparel have gone sky-high. Working cowpunchers, in town for some social imbibing and dancing, cannot afford the ludicrous prices in the cowboy discos that have sprung up. It's said, with some truth, that if you walk into the old Palace Bar, on Prescott's Whiskey Row, on a Saturday night, expecting to see working cowboys, look around, and if you see a feller wearing tennis shoes (tenny-lamas) and a baseball cap—he's likely to be the only real cowboy in the joint.

Traditionally, cowboys were noted for being long on aspiration and short on cash. Wages usually amounted to a dollar a day and all the beef and beans they could eat. Still, they considered themselves aristocrats of the working class. It was said "all you needed to become one was guts and a horse, and if you had guts, you could steal a horse." Fire-eating young heroes came West from all parts of the world and from all walks of life, aspiring to become cowboys. Some succeeded and fulfilled the dream held by virtually anybody who ever read a Beadle and Adams dime novel.

Their brash, rebellious years were brief; a couple of decades made them immortal. There was an aura of romantic mystique and daring that clings to them still—flamboyant figures bigger than life, they are considered by many to be America's last grand image—the idol of an age turned to legend—a timeless symbol for a frontier panorama. Fancying themselves as daring, errant knights of the open range, they collaborated in bolstering the legend:

> Cowboys is noisy fellers with bow legs and brass stomachs that works from the hurricane deck of a U-necked bronco and hates any kind of work that can't be done from atop one. They rides like Comanches, ropes like Mexicans and shoots like Texas Rangers. They kin spit ten feet into a stiff wind, whip their weight in wildcats, fight grizzlies bareknuckle. They bites on the tails of live cougars, hold off the Apache nation with a six-shooter and rides anything that wears hair. Homeless as poker chips, they live in and loves the outdoors, hates fences, respects rivers and independent, why you throw one of 'em in a river and he jest naturally floats up stream.

Most old-time cowboys were aware of the legends being created about them. Some had seen Buffalo Bill's Wild West Show, many had traveled and performed in the East. Those who could read had in their possession the nickel and dime novels of Beadle and Adams.

The works of such turn-of-the-century photographers as Dane Coolidge, L.A. Huffman, Charles Belden and Erwin Smith reveal an air of unmistakable pride and dignity, whether they were with their contemporaries on the range, or in some studio miles from their natural environs.

For the most part, these classic old studio photographs reveal little of the reality of the rigors of cowboy life. Unseen are the blizzards, drought, sickness, injury, arthritis, isolation, boredom and loneliness. The camera couldn't capture the acrid smell of burning hair at branding time, the choking dust and heat or the icy blast of a "blue norther." In reality, they were hard-working young men who bore little resemblance to the tight-lipped, tight-trousered puppets of Western fiction. Their days were spent toiling in a hot, blazing sun, or in the grips of a blizzard; their nights in exhausted sleep. Still, they left behind a powerful tradition that even

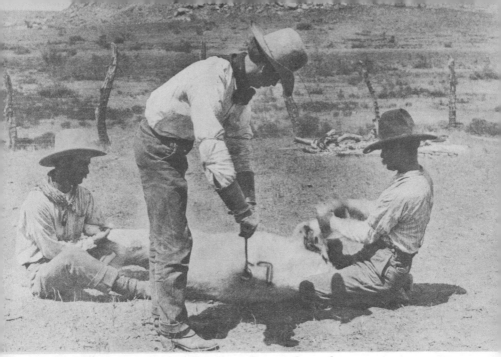
Arizona cowboys branding cattle on the range

when prettied up is a strong and rousing one.

There was little glamour in the endless hours of riding fence, doctoring screwworms, gathering strays, or pulling a cowbrute out of a bog, then having the angry critter run up the rope and try to gore horse or rider. The brutal physical punishment and hard hours working cows took its toll. Bodies got "stoved up" prematurely and parts of fingers turned up missing when they got caught taking up a dally. The elements turned skin to leather and wrinkled faces prematurely. Still, they were a breed all apart and preferred vicissitudes of a cowboy's life to any other. Trail dust has settled and false front saloons are found only on movie sets and at tourist traps, but the legacies of the old-time cowboy live on today. These late-model cowboys still carry on the traditions of this great American legend on working ranches.

The Arizona cowboy was a curious mix of the northern Plains, Rockies, California, Texas and northern Mexico cowboy culture. The influence of all these was strong, yet the Arizona cowboys or vaqueros evolved into a unique breed of their own. In a frontier that was closing rapidly at the turn of the century, Arizona offered one of the last vestiges of the freedom that was associated with being a cowboy.

Perhaps the cowboy's most distinguishable features were their wide-brimmed Stetsons, sometimes called the "John B" in honor of the manufacturer. In the Southwest it was sometimes referred to as a sombrero from the Spanish word *sombra* meaning shade. Like their other trappings, the hat was multi-purpose. It served as a water pitcher for them and their horses, to fan fires, and it kept the dust, sun and rain off their heads. They used to say, "humans dress up, but a cowboy dresses down." The hat was the first thing a cowboy put on when he got up in the morning and the last thing he took off at night. The high crown gave him the opportunity to "personalize it" or style its shape to his own liking. Expensive hats were a status symbol, and a good one would cost the better part of a month's pay. But they were so durable they lasted for years.

Most cowboys donned a pair of chaps when working cows in rough country. The name chaps is derived from the Spanish word *chaparejos* which meant "leather breeches." They saved wear and tear on a man's overalls, kept him warmer in winter and protected him from rocks, cactus and thorny bush. A few wore "hair pants" or angora chaps made from goat skin and worn with hair side out. Many preferred the Mexican "shotgun" chaps. These leggings fitted snugly around the legs and were more like a second pair of pants. They were decorated with a leather fringe on the pockets and sometimes had silver conchos running down the legs. When riding in bush country, however, the chaps with the silver conchos remained in the bunkhouse, as the cowboy didn't want to lose them in the mesquite.

The batwing type was probably the most popular. They were held on with snaps and didn't fit so tightly. Their shape, along with their big flapping leggings, gave them their name.

Trousers worn by the working cowboy were the heavy, blue denim "Levis," when they could get them. Otherwise they wore woolen "California pants." The tighter the fit, the better. Tight pants, especially across the seat, meant less wrinkles to cut into the fanny. Long hours in the saddle caused the crotch to wear out first. One was able to prolong the use by stitching a large leather patch over the worn out part. Shirts were long-sleeved, colorless and made of cotton or flannel. Since there was little pocket space in the trousers, they carried essential items, such as cigarette makings, in a many-pocketed vest which was usually worn unbuttoned.

Knotted around the neck was a brightly-colored neckerchief or bandana. Most preferred the former, saying that bandanas were for farmers. The neckerchief, not only served him as a "range necktie," but it also gave protection from sun and windburn. Worn as a mask, it was a dust filter in a storm or riding drag and could be used as a wash towel, tourniquet or sling.

Boots were of a high-shafted, two-inch heel variety, not for show, but to keep their feet from pushing through the stirrups. Those boots weren't made for walkin', but then they didn't plan to do much walkin' anyhow. Cowboys did not invent the high-heeled boot. They have been in use since the earliest Asiatic horsemen. No expense was spared when purchasing a pair. It was not uncommon for a man earning $30 a month to spend $40 on a pair of custom hand-crafted boots made of leather so fine you could "see the wrinkles in yer socks."

Another distinguishable feature of the working cowhand's rigging were his spurs. Spurs were sometimes worn as ornaments for show, but were more important than reins when it came to maneuvering a cowpony—to signal quick action when working cows or getting over rough terrain. They weren't used to inflict pain, but more as a reminder, usually a simple movement of the leg was all that was required to get the message across.

The working cowboys were mighty particular about their "hoss jewelry," especially their saddle, after all, they spent the greater part of their waking hours seated upon it. The ranch might furnish the horses, but the saddle was nearly always the personal property of the cowhand. A good one cost about a month's wages and was worth more in dollar value than most of the horses he rode. There was a great deal of truth in the saying "a cowboy rode a $10 horse and sat on a $40 saddle." It was so much a part of the trade that "sellin' one's saddle" was a phrase used to describe getting out of the business for good.

The saddle was not only a seat, but a workbench as well. The cantle was high, to keep one's seat firmly in place and rest the back. It weighed 30 to 40 pounds, and it was built rugged to withstand the punishment. The horn was steel forged, wrapped in rawhide then leather, and stout enough to anchor a dallied lariat with a contrary critter on the other end. The pommel might be a swell fork or slick, and the rigging and cinch a "rimfire," "centerfire" or a "three-quarter" rig, depending on one's locale or preference.

The rest of the working cowboys "hoss jewelry" was the headgear— reins, bridle and bit. Most important is the bit. The three standard types of bits are curb, snaffle and bar. Each has its own variations, but the curb is the simplest, most humane and therefore the most widely used. Some were cruel and severe, like the Spanish ring bit, but most cowboys found the most suitable bit was one that had the psychological effect of directing the horse's movement with only the slightest motion of the reins. Regardless of how severe the bit is, the real talent in making a horse perform remains in the lightness of hand on the part of the horseman.

The rope or lariat was the most important tool of the cowboy. At one time or another, each cow had to have a loop tossed around its neck. A rope enabled a 150-pound man to easily throw a 1,000-pound cow. Cowboys then and now considered roping as the feature that separated real cowhands from pretenders. Even today, good cowpunchers won't stay with an outfit long if it doesn't provide them with the opportunity to use their ropes.

The Spanish, and later the Mexicans, preferred to use a braided rawhide *la reata,* which was later corrupted into the English lariat. The reatas were from 60 to 100 feet long. American cowboys used a shorter grass rope like a "maguey" made from the fibers of the century plant, of a "manila," made from manila fiber. Others preferred the "seago" for their roping. The seago was short for seagoing or a maritime rope. Disdaining the longer Mexican rope, one cowboy said, "You only need one that long to catch something down in a well."

It was not the cow that made the cowboy; it was the horse. In the early days it was a range mongrel known as the mustang, those sturdy, unpampered descendants of the Spanish breed that were the greatest contributors to a cowboy's self-image. There was an aura of aristocracy, shared by the fraternity of horsemen, that bridged all cultures. The U.S. Cavalry felt a strong sense of superiority over the foot soldier, as did the horse Indian who considered fighting on foot as degrading. To the Spanish, a *caballero* was a gentleman on horseback and *chevalier* and *cavalier* meant the same to the French and British, respectively. To the cowboy, "sitting on the hurricane deck of a cowpony" made him a member of the same elite fraternity—"Nature's Noblemen," cowboy artist Frederic Remington called them. The horse was the apparatus on whom the cowboy and the range cattle industry depended for survival. Without them it would have been impossible to gather, rope, brand, drive the millions of critters to market, which was what the range cattle industry was all about.

Those old time cowponies were not the well-bred animals seen at rodeos and at most working ranches today. During the 1600's, the Plains Indians captured a few barbs and Arabs from the Spanish, and built an entire culture around them. Not much larger than a pony, they weighed only 700 to 900 pounds and stood 12 to 14 hands high. Called range mongrels, they looked more like a scrub of no particular parentage, but appearances are belying; they had undergone many changes through generations of adapting to the demands of their environment. Those broncos used by late 19th century cowboys did not necessarily descend from the mustangs of the Great Plains as is often believed, but came from northern Mexico instead. Generally, the Hispanos were more particular about breeding good stock than the Indians, and it is likely they were the progenitors of the American cowpony. The sires were well-chosen for their bloodlines and confirmation and were not subjected to the long, hungry winters that stunted the growth of the wild horses on the Great Plains.

Most cowboys regarded horses as a necessary tool of the trade and nothing more. However, extraordinary cowponies were held in high regard and provided the inspiration for much bragging during "lying hour" around the bunkhouse. Tall tales abounded about the prowess of cutting horses that could spin and turn quicker 'n a cowbrute could duck or dodge, and the term "horse sense" subsequently has become a part of the Engligh language. It was said by many that they knew more than their rider when it came to doing the right thing at the right time. Good cow horses in an outfit were sometimes better known and longer remembered than the men who rode them.

Most had been ridden only four or five times by a bronc twister when they were turned over to the cowboy to tone up the rough edges and had to be blindfolded before being mounted. One old-timer described one of these experiences: "The horse changed ends under me and was, before I knew it, going the other way." Another said that "some of the snuffy cayuses in his string galloped a little high. The trick is to keep falling off and climbing back on again until the horse becomes bored." To meet one's shadow on the ground, in a land where you could look further and see less, a man left afoot had about as much chance as a one-legged man at a kickin' contest. It was said that the only thing a cowboy feared more than being left alone in a room with a decent woman was being left afoot in the middle of nowhere. The plight of a cowboy who was long overdue back at the ranch would be discussed in relation to what particular horse he might be riding. If it was a dependable one, nobody showed much concern. However, if the horse was "green," the available hands would ride out to look for the rider.

When a horse was sick or lame enough to call a horse doctor out, the monetary value of the horse was never a topic of discussion, nor did anybody ask how much the treatment would cost. The only thing that might be said was "save him if you can." Most of the talk centered around what a good horse he'd been, how much he'd helped the ranch and his exploits on the range. Good horses are as important to a working ranch today as years ago. Some outfits buy their replacement horses from sale barn auctions or by treaty, while others do their own breeding. There's an old adage among cow-bosses that good horses will go a long way towards holding a man to an outfit.

Texas folk historian J. Frank Dobie called the long-eared, rangy longhorn "the bedrock on which the range cattle industry was founded." No other breed of cattle has ever been as unique and no two longhorns looked

Arizona cowboys throwing cattle. (Az. Historical Society)

exactly alike. Colors ranged from black and brown to red, white and pinto. Anyone who ever witnessed the longhorn running wild and free on the range had to agree there was something special about the critter. They were tall and bony with an enormous horn span that reached seven to eight feet tip to tip, a coarse-haired coat, an ornery looking face, thin flanks and a swayback. They were aptly described as a "critter with four legs hitched to a set of horns." These "hairy greenbacks" were a race apart, and without them there might never have been open range cowboys. A descendant of the racy-looking Mexican corrientes, the harsh environment, geography, and mix combined to produce a unique breed—a formidable beast, unpredictable, mean and fearing nothing. They had the ability to recover much more quickly from prolonged drought and could travel 60 miles without water, endure extreme cold and heat and were adaptable to all kinds of terrain. It was said, perhaps in exaggerated admiration, they could jump a six-foot fence standing flatfooted. During the early part of this century, the longhorn came closer to extinction than the buffalo. Today, in some regions the longhorn is making a comeback. Cattlemen are as lavish in their praise of the beast as their predecessors were, saying they calve easier, with less death loss in the first year heifers, and there is less cholesterol in the meat compared to heavier beef.

During the early 1880's, the public demand for a better grade of meat caused cattlemen to begin looking for a breed that would gain weight faster than the longhorn, but was hardy enough to survive under the harsh conditions of the arid lands known as short grass country. Several breeds were tried, including the placid, blocky, short-legged Hereford. The winter of 1880-81 was a particularly harsh one, and it was feared the severe weather on the Great Plains would be too much for the imports. Much to their surprise and satisfaction, when spring rolled around, the durable white-faced were thriving on the range. The day of the longhorn was over, and a new breed began to dominate the range cattle industry. The sturdy, durable, big-boned cows, with decent forage, weighed a thousand pounds long before reaching two years old, as compared to the longhorn who was four or five before reaching the same weight.

The first Herefords were brought into southern Arizona in 1883 by Colin Cameron. Soon after, they were grazing on the nutritious grasses above the Mogollon Rim. Preferring good purebred Hereford cattle to heterogeneous mixtures, ranchers began importing expensive registered Hereford bulls, gradually breeding over to full-blooded herds, keeping the best of the cross-bred heifers to be their mother cows.

Today, these bald-faced, mahogany-coated critters are by far the dominant breed in Arizona, ranging in the grass-carpeted rolling hills of Santa Cruz County, the high chaparral and desert country, the pinyon, juniper and malpais plains of the Coconino Plateau, and the pine-covered, grassy-meadowed high country of the Mogollon Rim and White Mountains.

OPENING of the SOUTHWEST'S LAST FRONTIER

"Our Plains are stocked with thousands of cattle and sheep, and still there's room for more." —**Holbrook Times** (1884)

With the exception of the Indians who lived there and a few buckskin-clad mountain men who crossed it, northern Arizona was pretty much *terra incognita,* until the Army Corps of Topographical Engineers began surveying routes along the 35th parallel for a transcontinental railroad in the 1850's. Among those mapping the area was Lt. Edward Fitzgerald "Ned" Beale and his famous Camel Corps who plodded a trail across the plateau that eventually became the fabled Highway 66. The Civil War broke out soon after and delayed the actual construction for several years. In the early days of the war, federal troops were withdrawn from the area to the Rio Grande and marauding bands of hostile Apaches and Navajos caused all but the most daring to avoid the entire area entirely. The vast region that held the world's largest stand of Ponderosa pines and some of North America's most nutritious range grasses, the Grand Canyon, and numerous other natural wonders and resources remained a sleeping giant.

During the 1860's, the Federal government devised a clever scheme to finance the building of railroad lines in the western territories at virtually no cost to the taxpayers. Since the nation was too poor to finance the enormous costs, the railroads were given large land grants along the right of way as incentives. The grants awarded the Atlantic & Pacific (Santa Fe) in northern Arizona were in twenty-mile sections along each side of the track. The railroad was given deed to the odd numbered sections in each township. The vast, isolated regions weren't worth much until the railroad stretched its ribbons of steel across, then the land value soared. By selling this land back to ranchers and settlers, the railroad could earn back the cost of building the line. In this manner, the western lands were opened for settlement, and the east was linked up with the Pacific coast by the fast-moving steam-driven locomotives and their steam cars.

Arrival of Mormon colonists in 1876 heralded the first permanent Anglo settlements in northern Arizona. Isolated but self-sufficient communities around the Little Colorado River Valley such as Snowflake, Joseph City, Woodruff, Springerville and Eager trace their beginnings to those families who made the trek southward from Utah along the Hamblin Trail. Arizona has the unique distinction of attracting vast numbers of settlers from the four cardinal points. The backwash of the forty-niners brought Californians from the West. Mexicans migrated from Sonora to the south, Mormons from Utah and eastern emigrants caught up in the westward migration.

Even though stock raising was one of the territory's largest industries, the ranges in northern Arizona remained virtually undiscovered. Most of the cattle were dairy cows brought in from Utah by Mormon settlers.

The railroad brought new life to the sleepy little settlements along the old Beale Camel Road in 1881 when the A & P railroad linked northern Arizona with the rest of the civilized world. Horsehead Crossing, on the Little Colorado River, was now being called Holbrook, and Brigham City became Winslow.

The coming of the railroad in 1881 was the primary reason for the great change that was about to take place. That year, John W. Young, a son of Brigham Young and a pioneer settler in the area, was contracted to deliver 50,000 ties for the new line. He built a camp for his tie-cutters in what is today Fort Valley, nine miles north of Flagstaff. The threat of raids by bands of Apache and Navajo warriors caused Young to turn the camp into a fortress which he called Moroni, after the Mormon angel. A log cabin some 75 feet long acted as one side of the bastion. The other three sides of the square consisted of railroad ties set in the ground on end. A tent city was established inside the stockade to shelter the tie-cutters. The Indian raids never materialized and the fortress walls were torn down and used for firewood. The arrival of iron-bellied locomotives the next year marked the real beginning of the cattle business in northern Arizona. Young and several companions organized the Mormon Cattle Company that same year, stocking the ranges around Flagstaff for the first time on a large scale. By 1883 the price of beef was $50 a head, up from $15 a head just two years earlier.

Holbrook with some 250 inhabitants became an important shipping center for cattle, wool, hides, and merchandise for the Army, Indians, cattlemen and settlers. This bibulous Babylon on the Little Colorado also attracted a full complement of social outcasts who could usually be found bellied up to the bar in one of several saloons along either side of the tracks. Lawlessness and violence were prevalent among this wide gamut of frontier society where voluminous comsumption of snakehead whiskey and the slightest provocation or misdeal of the cards was apt to bring the hammer down on 40 grains of black powder.

Hell-raising, devil-may-care cowboys, in from the open range, took great delight in the challenge of trying to "down a shot of whiskey before it touched the bottom of the glass" before heading over to pay a visit to the "ladies on the line."

In Flagstaff, newspaper accounts of the time tell of citizens' outrage when cowboys periodically drove several hundred range cows down the town's main street or when law-abiding folks were sent scurrying for safety as drunken cowpunchers rode hell-for-leather through town, waving their revolvers in the air, "shootin' holes in the sky."

The local chronicle expressed its displeasure at the behavior of Flagstaff-area cowboys in an article on September 20, 1883, which read:

Hashknife cowboys in Holbrook

"They are bragging, whiskey-drinking bummers who delight in six-shooters, fine horses, saddles and fast women. Their aim in life seems to be to have a good time. They delight in disconcerting the eastern tenderfoot. Nearly all die with their boots on and no one mourns their death."

For all its reputation as a frontier Sodom and Gomorrah, Flagstaff was no worse than most of the other western boomtowns, and better than most. As in any developing community, the more populous genteel side of law-abiding citizens, merchants, churches and schools soon prevailed. The town bragged, with a great deal of civic pride, in the healthy climate and opportunity for, as Bret Harte said, "a fresh deal" to those who would give up their relative security in the east to settle in the new town nestled at the foot of the titanic San Francisco Mountains in what has to be one of the prettiest settings for a community anywhere in North America.

In what could pass for a Department of Tourism commercial, newspaperman George Tinker wrote in 1887, "The climate of northern Arizona is moderately dry, the days warm and the nights cold ... the air is dry, the soil porous, the water pure, scenery cheerful and sunlight brilliant ... the value of the climate as a remedial agent is demonstrated daily ... around Flagstaff the sun shines nearly every day, and but few are cloudy. Even during the rainy season which begins in July and lasts about six weeks, the daily showers are followed by the brightest sunshine."

The name Flagstaff was given to the site by a party of immigrants on

July 4, 1876, who paused to raise the colors in honor of the 100th anniversary of the Declaration of Independence. The first permanent settlement at Flagstaff occurred a few years later in 1880, when work crews building the transcontinental line for the Atlantic & Pacific Railroad established a camp at the springs where old town is today.

By 1886, Flagstaff was the largest city on the main line of the Atlantic & Pacific between Albuquerque and the Pacific Coast. It was also set to be the northern terminus of the Mineral Belt Railroad, an ambitious, but ill-fated line that attempted to bore a hole through the Mogollon Rim and lay tracks to the prosperous mining camp of Globe. The 160-mile line had to be built through some rough terrain, the most notable being a 3,100 foot tunnel through the Rim. This precipitous raw edge of rock and faulted displacement which separates Arizona's high country from the lowlands would require a grade rise of 2,000 feet in just a few miles. The visionary scheme might have worked; however, after they had laid some 40 miles of track and tunneled 70 feet into the Rim, the promoters ran out of funding, and enthusiasm for the project evaporated.

Large cattle ranching had its beginnings in 1883 when John Young teamed up with a group of Eastern capitalists that included Col. Jake Rupert, the man who owned the New York Yankees during the heyday of Babe Ruth, and founded the Arizona Cattle Company, headquartering at Ft. Moroni.

Young, a polygamist, didn't stay in the business long. In 1885, a warrant was issued for his arrest and he was forced to sell his share and make a hasty exit.

After Young left, the outfit built several new buildings at Ft. Moroni and renamed it Ft. Rickerson, in honor of C.L. Rickerson, an officer in the New York based firm. During its heyday, the Arizona Cattle Company, or *A1,* ran some 16,000 head of cattle on some of the finest cattle country in Arizona. They ranged from south of Flagstaff near Lake Mary, north to the Grand Canyon and from Ashfork on the west to the Little Colorado River on the east, on 132,000 acres of land purchased from the railroad for 50¢ an acre.

In late 1885, the absentee owners selected a field manager, a colorful, picturesque, ex-Chicago fire captain named B.B. Bullwinkle who literally talked his way into heading up one of northern Arizona's biggest cattle ranches. In spite of his inexperience, Bullwinkle learned the cow business quickly. His commanding presence more than made up for his lack of knowledge and the ranch flourished with the Captain at the helm. He erected fences, built barns and bridges on the ranch and even strung a telephone line from Ft. Rickerson to Flagstaff. The outfit maintained ranches at Cedar Mesa, north of the San Francisco Peaks, and the Fort, along with winter camps at Squaw Tank and Tappan Springs. Texan Bill Thomas was the outfit's first range boss. He was later replaced by the noted Jack Diamond who ran it until the company folded in 1899.

Bullwinkle was a gentleman who liked pretty women, fast horses, and poker. The epic poker games the flamboyant Captain Bullwinkle engaged in with other cattlemen were a reflection of the man and his time. Vast properties were won and lost on the turn of a card. A story that appeared in the May 9, 1887, edition of the *Arizona Champion,* tells of one such game.

One of the editor's friends dropped in this week and told us a story about a poker game Saturday night between Captain Bullwinkle and Frank Vanderlip, local cattleman.

Vanderlip had no money with him but plenty of cattle and an immense desire to play poker with Captain Bullwinkle. The latter is known for his great natural resources and he swept away the seemingly insurmountable difficulty by proposing a game of one steer ante, two steer to come in, and no limit. They played on this basis. The captain dealt and Vanderlip anteed one steer. Both came in and the game opened with four steers on the table. The Captain drew two tens and caught an unexpected full, while Vanderlip passed out.

The third was a jackpot, and it took three deals to open it. Vanderlip finally drew two jacks and opened the pot with a fine breeding bull, which counted six, The Captain covered this with five steers and a two-year-old heifer, and went him twelve better. Vanderlip, who drew another Jack, saw the twelve cows and went him fifty steers, twenty two-year-old heifers, four bulls, and twenty-five calves better. The Captain looked at his hand and placed upon the table six fine cows, five bulls, one hundred two-year-olds, fifty prime to medium steers, and with a side bet of a horse to cover the bar bill. Vanderlip made his bet good with an even two hundred and fifty straight halfbreeds and twenty-four mustangs and a NE ¼ of the SW ¼ of Section 10, Township 24, Range 2 East and called. The Captain held three aces and put in his hip pocket seven hundred sixty-two steers, heifers, etc., and a big stock ranch.

As previously mentioned. B.B. Bullwinkle lived hard and loved fast, well-bred horses. He imported some of Kentucky's finest running stock for the ranch and took great delight in riding at breakneck speed across the range. It was just a few days after the previously mentioned article appeared that Bullwinkle was killed when his horse took a fall while racing into town. Cowman Frank Livermore took over the outfit and it prospered until a prolonged drought and overstocked ranges drove the company out of business in 1899. That year, range boss Jack Diamond gathered and shipped a record 10,000 head to eastern markets.

When the ranch was sold, the tall stands of Ponderosa pines on the property were sold to the Manistee Lumber Company of Michigan, which later combined with Saginaw Lumber Company, marking the beginning of Flagstaff as a boom-town in lumber as well as cattle.

Mormon pioneer Lot Smith was another of northern Arizona's pioneer cattlemen. Smith, an iron-fisted, temperamental man, owned the large sprawling ranch that ranged between Tuba City on the Painted Desert and Mormon Lake. The rugged Smith, who was one of Brigham Young's captains, led a party of Mormon colonists to the Mormon Lake area where he established a small settlement. His ranch, the Mormon Dairy, with its *Circle S* brand, was one of the bigger outfits of its day. Smith, like many of his contemporaries, had a fondness for fast horses and was noted for his well-bred Kentucky stallion which he bred with range mares. The result was a strain noted for speed and endurance. Old timers used to tell of how the hard-riding cattleman would ride from the Mormon settlement at Tuba City to Fort Moroni in a day, and at the first light of dawn, to Mormon Lake, a distance of 130 miles—on the same horse. The fiery rancher was killed in June, 1892, in a gun battle with Navajo sheepherders, during a feud over grazing rights.

Another Eastern-owned outfit, the Aztec Land and Cattle Company, better known as the *Hashknife,* was the most spectacular of the 19th century ranching enterprise, not just in northern Arizona, but throughout the territory. The company ran as many as 60,000 cows and 2,000 horses on some two million acres of private and government-owned land north of the Mogollon Rim between Holbrook and Flagstaff, with nothing but a brand burned into their hides to prove ownership. Until the company sold out in 1902, the *Hashknife* was considered the second largest cattle ranch in the U.S. Only the legendary XIT in Texas was larger.

The great adventure began in the Spring of 1884, when a stockholder for the A & P Railroad, named Edward Kinsley, went west to inspect the new mainline across northern Arizona. Unusually heavy winter rains had provided an abundance of lush, nutritious grasses on the rangelands and water along the Little Colorado River Valley. Kinsley was sure he had found one of America's great feeding grounds where one could turn a $4 yearling into a $40 steer. He returned to New York and persuaded a group of business associates to invest more than $1.3 million and incorporate a cattle ranch, and thus was born the fabled Aztec Land & Cattle Company. Other investors included Henry Kinsley, Frank Ames, James McCreery and the Seligman brothers. Interestingly, these men were also major stockholders in the A & P. The following year, the railroad offered for sale 20 million acres of grazing land at prices ranging from 50 cents an acre to $1.50, and turned around and sold one million acres to the Aztec Land & Cattle Company for 50 cents an acre. Next, the fledging cattle barons brought a large herd of Texas cattle to stock their new range, and in doing so acquired a brand, the *Hashknife* ⌂ so called because it resembled a cooking tool used by chuckwagon cooks. The company also imported a large number of Texas cowboys who brought along all their vices and virtues. It was said that many of those punchers left Texas to seek greener pastures because they were not wanted in Texas and a good many others left because they were wanted in Texas. The Texas range country had been suffering through a long drought and the cattle were too poor to be driven, so they were loaded on the A & P and shipped to Holbrook. From that day on, Horsehead Crossing would never be the same. The local newspaper reported: "Since the construction of the Atlantic & Pacific Railroad the whole northern portion of the territory seems to be undergoing a great change. Our plains are stocked with thousands of cattle, horses, and sheep, and still there is room for more. We are astonished at the immense number of ranches that have been located during the last 18 months in this county alone."

The ranges of northern Arizona had filled with cattle by the mid 1880's. Estimates ran as high as 1½ million head in the territory by 1891. Cattlemen saw no end to the prosperity and crowded the ranges with more cattle than the native grasses could sustain. In earlier times, cattlemen simply grazed out one range and moved on to the next, but times were changing, and by the 80's cowmen were establishing permanent locations. Unfortunately, Federal land laws were not designed for the arid lands west of the 98th Meridian, where it might take 50 or 60 acres to support one cow-calf unit, and ranchers needed at least a hundred cows to make a living. The Homestead Law of 1862, which provided for the free distribution of 160-acre parcels to anyone who could improve up or remain on the land for five years, clearly demonstrated the lack of understanding on the part of the Federal Government. Cattlemen were able to take advantage of the situation by securing title to lands along natural streams, which also gave them control over adjacent lands. Big outfits were developed, as cowboys staked out claims under the Homestead Act, then signed the parcels over to their bosses. The Timber and Culture Act of 1873 was basically an extension of the Homestead Act, and the Desert Land Act of 1875 modified the Act of 1862 and allowed parcels of 320 acres, something which further compounded the problem of range management by increasing the number of small ranches.

These land acts allowed cattlemen to increase their ranges and subsequently, the size of their herds. The rich, nutritious stands of grama and other native grasses suffered under the onslaught of hungry cattle. Range grasses were eaten down to the rocks and the ground pounded until the surface was hard as concrete, preventing the growth of new grasses. Rainfall on the ranges carried off rich top soil. Cattle trails became small arroyos; channels that had been narrow with firm banks became sprawling washes; scrub brush, such as juniper, sprang up and proliferated where the native grasses had once prevailed.

The eternal enemies of all cowmen—the elements and hard times— combined in the 1890's to cripple the industry. Heavy rainfall in the winter of 1888-89 brought forth high hopes for the new decade, but then came the national depression of 1893 and with it, a severe drought. Wells and natural water tanks went dry. Ranchers, who had been holding on to steers during the depression, in hopes of getting a better price, later found there was not enough feed to fatten them up for market. Creditors called in their notes, and cattlemen had to sell their stock low in order to pay off. A large number of ranchers went broke.

The free-wheeling days of the great open range in northern Arizona drew to a close with the dawning of a new century. Gone were the days when large ranches enjoyed free use of government land to graze their vast herds of cattle. Newcomers moved in carrying a piece of paper that gave legal claim to small plots under the Homestead Law. Joseph Glidden's newfangled contraption "unraveled the devil's hat band," mass producing miles of barbed wire which the settlers used to fence off their ranchitas. Soon there were enough to gain control of county politics. Rustlers and small ranchers bent on "stealing a start" in the cattle business hung around the fringes of the big outfits like a pack of timber wolves. The Eastern-owned ranches like *A1* and the *Hashknife* suffered the most. Public sympathy was usually against them, and a small rancher caught rustling cows could usually get off easily by simply getting a couple of friends on the jury. The community attitude was that the big outfits had been grazing their cows for free on government land, so the citizens had the right to rustle a few beeves now and then. A more serious blow, however, was dealt by Ol' Ma Nature. Cattlemen had overstocked the ranges with cattle for years, leaving the land in poor condition, and a series of prolonged droughts in the 1890's brought forth a day of reckoning.

By the early 1900's, both the *A1* and the *Hashknife* were out of business. The old days of the open range were over. The big outfits were not gone from the ranges of northern Arizona—they had just undergone many changes. The introduction of purebred cattle, better range management techniques, and expert management guaranteed the continuance of ranching on a large scale, despite constant warfare with cattlemen's greatest enemies—the elements and bad markets.

Three of the largest were consolidated into the *CO Bar* owned by the Babbitt brothers of Flagstaff. The Babbitts acquired the sprawling *Hashknife* range in 1901. That, in addition to the *A1* and Lot Smith's *Circle S,* along with the emergence of their vast mercantile business, made the Babbitts one of the Southwest's greatest enterprises.

The Babbitts didn't confine their operations to Arizona alone. By the late 1890's they were running cows on 100,000 acres in Kansas. Later they would add ranches in California and Montana to their far-flung operations.

Sheepmen had discovered the ranges of northern Arizona about the same time as cattlemen and had moved thousands of head in from California,

A scene on the CO Bar range

Henry Ashurst, father of Arizona's first U.S. Senator, and the Daggs brothers began running sheep on the ranges around Flagstaff in the 1880's. Until then, sheep were raised mainly for wool. However, the coming of the railroads provided sheepmen with a suitable means of getting the critters to market.

Competition between cattlemen and sheepmen for the limited grasses increased as the ranges became more crowded. The woolies grazed in clusters moving the grass down "pretty near to bedrock," devastating the range lands, especially during droughts.

By the early 1900's, the large sheepmen had formed an alliance and had gained much political influence in county politics. Something an Arizona cowboy feared most during those times was being hauled into some county court to stand before a jury of sheepmen. Early on, the Babbitts recognized the market advantage of sheep raising and were one of the first cattle outfits to run sheep on their ranges. There is no doubt they provided a powerful, steadying influence and lessened the danger of open warfare between cattlemen and sheepmen. By the turn of the century, most cattlemen in northern Ariona were resigned to sharing the range as a fact of life.

Legislation in the early 1900's went a long way towards regulating the public lands of Arizona by designating areas where sheep could be trailed. Likely as not, it also prevented all-out warfare between cattlemen and sheepmen in some parts of the territory. Also, forest reserves were established to regulate timber cutting and protect the watershed. Teddy Roosevelt's administration pushed it through, calling it the "greatest good for the greatest number of people in the long run."

The lack of control on the public ranges continued well into the 20th century. In 1906, the Arizona Cattle Growers Association became the first of such organizations in the west to support Federal control of the public domain. Still, it was several years before Congress saw fit to pass a natural law providing for regulated control of unappropriated grazing lands. Former range boss of the *Hashknife* and captain of the Arizona Rangers, Burton Mossman, was instrumental in designing much of the legislation and regulations for what was to become known as the Taylor Grazing Act of 1934. Grazing districts were established and permits to graze, based on the carrying capacity, were issued to cattlemen for a fee. Permits at the time were granted to a period of up to ten years. Ranchers could construct reservoirs, fences, wells and other improvements on the permit areas and a percentage of the fees was designated for range improvement.

During the 20th century, the cowman's old nemesis, the elements and hard times, continued to dog him. Cyclic droughts in the early 1920's, in the early 30's, and again in the 50's, along with howling blizzards, most notably in recent memory 1948-49 and 1966-67, temporarily dealt crippling blows to the industry.

The STORIED BARONS
of NORTHERN ARIZONA

On a cold, wet February morning in 1886, David and Billy Babbitt stepped down from a westbound A & P passenger train and took their first look at the raw, boisterous frontier town of Flagstaff. They weren't much impressed with what they saw. Actually there wasn't much left of Flagstaff, since the town had been completely destroyed by fire three weeks previous. The depot house where they stood was a converted box-car. There was little doubt in the mind of either that the visit would be brief.

Flagstaff, at that time, boasted a population of some 600, profession-ally served by "able lawyers, skillful doctors, honest preachers and scien-tific gamblers." Lumbering, cattle and the railroad provided the main source of income for the community. It was also a favorite gathering place for nefarious scalawags along the mainline, whose only visible means of support was rowdyism. It was said that some 250 saloons were scattered along 350 miles of track. Flagstaff boasted having more saloons than all other businesses combined and they provided most of the inspira-tion for the rowdyism. One saloonkeeper was said to keep order in his establishment by sitting in a loft above the crowd, armed with a sawed-off shotgun.

During the building of the transcontinental railroad, an angry mob of railroad employees lynched a contractor when the payroll failed to arrive on time. On another occasion, a section hand stole a $10,000 payroll. In his haste to escape, the outlaw lost a sack containing $6,000. He was later captured but couldn't remember where he lost the money. The posse decided to hang him anyway. The unfortunate fellow made his last request, watched the noose being fitted over his neck and saw the other end of the rope tossed over the limb of a tree. While he was waiting in a melancholy mood for the jerk of the rope, a bolt of lightning struck the tree. Believing it an act of the Almighty, the posse reconsidered hanging and the man was placed in jail. Several years later, the missing sack of money was found accidentally and the man was eventually released from jail.

Hard-headed miscreants were plentiful around Flagstaff. One such character was a notorious train robber named "Doc" Smart. Doc consi-dered himself a pretty tough hombre. But he robbed one train too many and found himself facing a life sentence at the territorial prison. Not being able to cope with confinement, Doc tried to take his own life by shooting himself in the head four times with a .38 revolver. The bullets flattened against Doc's skull and were soon extracted by a local physician who pronounced his patient "not seriously hurt."

It is no wonder that Dave and Billy were a bit skeptical on their first visit to the new town nestled near the foot of the San Francisco mountains. They had come to Flagstaff on the advice of a railroad clerk in Albuquerque. The young men from Cincinnati were looking for a place to start a cattle ranch. They brought with them the accumulated savings of the Babbitt family store in Ohio, an enterprise run by them and brothers Charles and George.

Evidently, the more they looked the more they saw potential in that part of Arizona, a region that boasted some of the best cattle country in the Southwest.

The two brothers quickly recovered from their initial shock and invested nearly all their $20,000 savings in a cow outfit east of town and thus marked the beginning of the most famous mercantile and ranching dynasty in the history of the Southwest.

The history of this remarkable family, as related to the Arizona scene, began in Ohio during the mid 1850's, when David Babbitt bought a 200-acre farm on the outskirts of Cincinnati. Here, he and his wife, Catherine, raised a family of seven children, of whom five boys would survive. These adventuresome lads, David Jr., George, William, Charles, (or C.J., grandfather of the Arizona Governor), and Edward were to form the nucleus of the Babbitt family—the "Storied Barons of Northern Arizona."

David Sr. died in 1869, shortly after the birth of Edward, leaving Catherine with the task of raising the family. As the children grew older, each assumed the responsibility of helping provide.

In the early 1880's, the four oldest brothers opened a grocery store in Cincinnati. It was here that perhaps a little fate intervened. The Babbitts had the good fortune to locate their store on a corner diagonally across the street from a wealthy Dutch merchant named Gerard H. Verkamp. Verkamp was not only a successful businessman, he was the father of four lovely daughters. It wasn't long before romance blossomed between the Verkamp girls and the enterprising young Babbitt brothers. Eventually David, C.J. and Ed all succumbed to the charm and beauty of Verkamp's daughters. A fourth brother, George, came close to marrying a Verkamp girl, but instead married the daughter of another local merchant. Billy remained a bachelor until 1915, when he married an employee in the company.

When C.J. and Billy Babbitt first arrived in Flagstaff, neither had any real knowledge of the cow business. They had heard stories of the vast fortunes accumulated in the fabled West and like many others of their time, were determined to pull up stakes and go west in search of prosperity.

After a careful examination of the Flagstaff area, Dave and Billy Babbitt bought 1,200 head of cattle from a down-on-his luck cowman near Canyon Diablo. The rancher threw his experienced range boss, Sam

French, in on the deal, and the Babbitt brothers were in business. They branded their cows with the *CO Bar*, for Cincinnati, Ohio. In those pristine days when grass grew "belly high" all a rancher had to do was select rangeland with water on it, brand his cows and turn them loose. They gathered in the spring and fall, sorted out their cows and shipped them to market on the A & P Railroad (Santa Fe).

In the years that followed, C.J. and Billy ran the cattle end of the business. They became the predominant "movers and shakers" of the cattle industry in northern Arizona. Always innovating and expanding their enterprise, the Babbitts soon held controlling interest in most of the large ranches in the northern part of the state, including the *Circle S, A1,* and the famous *Hashknife* outfit. In the early 1900's, Babbitt cattle ranged on millions of acres across the heart of northern Arizona, from Ashfork on the west to the New Mexico line on the east. C.J. and Billy spent most of their time in the saddle, as active as any common cowboy. They dressed like hired hands and oftentimes were mistaken for range bums by their own employees.

C.J. and Billy were ideal partners. When the two engaged in negotiations on the sale of a new ranch to the Babbitt empire, C.J. would talk to management while Billy would mosey out to the bunkhouse and talk to the cowboys about the ranch. Later, C.J. and Billy would get together and exchange notes on what the other had learned.

Billy was perhaps the most colorful of the bunch. He never carried a revolver but feared no man. He was always bailing one of his hired hands out of some predicament and was respected by all, not only as a square dealer, but a good cowman as well.

The heyday of the Babbitt cattle empire was from 1907 to 1919. During those years they entered into partnerships, held an interest in, or financed most of the cow outfits in the area. During the 40 years after the founding of the *CO Bar* in 1886, nearly a hundred ranches came under Babbitt control. "What they didn't own, they held mortgages on," one said. The partnerships worked to the benefit of both. Usually the Babbitts put up the money and the ranchers supplied the management. Small ranchers needed a partner with money. By and large, the Babbitts were benevolent landlords, giving their partners almost unlimited credit. At times this worked to their detriment. By giving their partners such a free hand with operations, it was not uncommon for some larceny to take place.

The Babbitts were probably the first in northern Arizona to run sheep and cattle on the same ranges. By World War I they owned more than 100,000 head of the wooly critters. Sheep were easier to keep track of than cattle, since they grazed close together in flocks. The working conditions were better, too. Sheep were taken to the milder climates of the Verde and Salt River Valleys in the winter and spent the summers in the cool high country ranges.

Old timers around northern Arizona used to say that the sheep on the

The Babbitts of Northern Arizona: (from left) George, Charles (C.J., grandfather of Bruce Babbitt), Edward, William, and David, Jr.

ranges were continually reminding folks who their owners were. One said, "The Babbitts have so many sheep that if you listen to any herd you pass after you leave Holbrook, you will hear them saying Baa-ab-bitt, Baa-ab-bitt,"

Back in 1886, when the Babbitts first went into the cattle business, G.H. Verkamp sought to convince his sons-in-law on the wisdom of diversification. The cattle business was much too speculative. It didn't take a whole lot of convincing, for the young entrepreneurs were always looking for some new business venture. The senior Verkamp grubstaked David to the tune of $50,000 to enter into the mercantile business. Just a few months after the big fire, Flagstaff was three times larger than before. The whole region was booming, and the citizens were crying out for supplies. It was well they heeded Verkamp's prophetic advice, for the bottom fell out of the cattle market the following year.

As the Babbitts expanded their operations, C.J. and Billy took charge of the cattle business, David opened a lumber and hardware store. Edward was still in school back East and had not yet made the scene. George, who had remained in Cincinnati to liquidate the Babbitt interest, did not participate in the cattle or retail business at first, but busied himself with other interests. He invested his money wisely in real estate, small businesses and mining properties. He was the best looking of the five brothers, more outgoing and gregarious. Unlike his frugal brothers, he enjoyed spending money on himself and others. He was forever lending or giving money to friends in need. Old timers used to say that Dave, C.J. and Billy worked hard to earn the family fortune and George worked harder trying to give it away. His lifestyle was fitting to that of a happy millionaire. The others accepted George's ostentatious ways philosophically. "George is our rich brother," they conceded. He took an active interest in politics, holding many city and county offices, and was an advisor and confidant to Governor George W.P. Hunt, Arizona's "perennial governor." In 1920, just as his own political star was rising, George suffered a fatal heart attack. It was generally agreed that he would have been elected governor had death not intervened.

Dave Babbitt made a success of the mercantile operation almost overnight. He took advantage of cheaper rates, buying stock by the carload. Soon he was in the wholesale business, expanding to clothing and household goods. Ranchers and traders were coming in to exchange everything from Navajo rugs to town lots for much-needed supplies. By the end of 1889, Dave had built his enterprise into the largest in Flagstaff. It was time to bring the brothers into partnership, and the Babbitt Brothers Trading Company was founded. Two years later, they were the leading retail and wholesalers in the Southwest. In the early 1900's, the Babbitt mercantile operations spread to Ashfork, some 50 miles west of Flagstaff, and Holbrook, 90 miles to the east of the home office. When gold was discovered in Mohave County in 1916, the Babbitts opened stores in Kingman, Oatman and Yucca. A few years later, stores were built at the Grand Canyon and Williams.

If the Babbitts were guilty of anything during these years, it was over optimism. They were willing to invest capital in almost any interesting deal that came along. When the nation went into depression in 1893, the Babbitts found themselves vastly overexpanded, and creditors started hovering vulture-like around the company offices. G.H. Verkamp calmly informed these creditors that he would back his venturesome sons-in-law through the difficult period. When the creditors asked how far he would go, Verkamp replied tersely, "Up to a million dollars if necessary." They backed off, the Babbitts recouped their losses as the economic situation improved. Thus, Verkamp halted a financial panic without spending a nickel.

The Babbitts always enjoyed good employee relations. Company philosophy was to pay higher wages than others, thereby attracting a better class help. Just how loyal these employees could be is illustrated by an incident that took place on a dark depression day in 1893, when the Babbitts were desperately low on ready cash. Employee John Lind walked into the business carrying a black satchel; its contents consisted of his life savings. He handed the cash, some $4,000 to the astonished Babbitts, saying "It's yours as long as you need it. I'm willing to sink or swim with you." As it turned out, that was just enough money to keep the firm afloat.

The Babbitts, of course, were rightly proud of this kind of employee support. On the other hand, there were many occasions when partners and employees took advantage of the firm's benevolent generosity and there would be even greater economic reversals for the company in the future.

Although there have been several critical periods in their rags-to-riches history, there were only two major economic crises in the 90 years since the Babbitt brothers organized, but they were of epic proportion. The banks took over management of the company in the early 1920's. The Great Depression years, 1930-34, also took its toll on Babbitt operations. The visionary brothers, always eager to experiment and diversify, had overexpanded again. Because of their reluctance to let money sit in a bank, Babbitt cash reserves were always low. They were continually buying up ranches and other properties with spare capital. When a financial crunch came, they had no ready cash to fall back upon.

Another of their shortcomings, at least according to their creditors, was their refusal to "tighten up their cinches," so to speak, or let go of certain valuable properties during hard times. Several business ventures were sold off by tight-fisted, carpetbag management during those years. A prize ranch in California, the Laguna, was forcibly sold for $1.5 million. Less than a year later, the ranch was resold by the creditors for more than twice that amount.

It has been suggested that some of the large creditor banks were calling in their notes in an effort to crush the Babbitts and pick up the pieces for themselves. One outsider called it "legal robbery without a gun." Fortunately, not all the bankers were so greedy, but in the end the Babbitts were required to let the banks provide a manager to oversee their interests. The terms were tough. The carpetbag manager was DeWitt Knox, best known for his refusal to grant a loan to a young entrepreneur for the purpose of opening a second mercantile store. The young man's name—James Cash Penney.

An outbreak of the dreaded hoof-and-mouth disease struck their California cattle operation with devastating effect in the 1920's. The following year, "scab" decimated the northern Arizona herd. Hundreds of prize cattle were herded into trenches and shot to prevent spread of the disease. The cattle operation lost nearly a million dollars before it was over.

Through these difficult years and those to follow in the early 1930's, the persistent Babbitts prevailed. Always optimistic, they opened a new retail lumber yard in Flagstaff in 1931, during the height of the depression.

The general public was never aware of just how near collapse the Babbitt empire actually was. They always presented a calm, affluent profile. Their creditors, and for that matter, the U.S. government pre-

A scene on the CO Bar range

ferred to keep quiet about the economic state of the company. Their operations were far-flung and involved many people, not just in northern Arizona, but throughout the Southwest. If the Babbitt empire collapsed, the domino effect would be catastrophic.

One of the most profitable ventures of the Babbitts, year in and year out, has been the trading posts on the reservations. Since they opened a store at Red Lake in 1891, the trading post business has been a good hedge against hard times. Business is always brisk, the overhead low and profit margin good. There have been times when the company wished it had more trading posts and fewer cattle ranches. Today, Babbitt trading posts range in style from traditional, such as can be found at Red Lake, to Cow Springs where the decor is modern. The Babbitt sensitivity to native customs is perhaps reflected best at Tuba City where the design is in the shape of a hogan and provides for a Navajo-style single exit towards the east. A near disaster was averted at this store in 1920, when a Navajo who was dying commenced to take his final breath in the trading post. The quick-thinking manager assisted the dying man outside. The Navajo will not enter a structure in which a person has died. It would have been a taboo for any Navajo to enter the store again. Such an event did occur at another trading post in Navajoland. Today that abandoned building stands in decay, mute testimony of a people's adherence to an ancient tribal custom.

Time was beginning to take its toll on the five original Babbitt brothers. George died suddenly in 1920. David passed away in 1929, Billy a year later. Edward sold his interest in the family business in 1929. He had never spent much time in Arizona and was not as active a participant as the others. C.J. remained as the last active member of the original five brothers, although there was never a shortage of Babbitts in the prolific clan to help run the business. C.J. worked right up to the end. He died at 91 in 1956, just ten weeks after taking his retirement.

By the 1950's there were three generations of Babbitts on the company board of directors. During this time, the firm began to streamline operations by remodeling stores and supermarkets. On the ranch, new wells were drilled, holding tanks for natural rainfall were gouged out on the Babbitt ranges. Breeds were improved and fences constructed. A new era was dawning in northern Arizona, and as usual, the farsighted firm, not as large as in the early days, but more efficient, would take its natural place as the pacesetter for growth in the northern part of the State.

There were many explanations for the phenomenal Babbitt success. Their arrival in the region could not have been better timed. Northern Arizona was a sleeping economic giant when they arrived in 1886. No doubt the Verkamp grubstake played an important part. They fought back tenaciously from economic setbacks when others equally well-financed and more experienced failed and moved on. It took a great deal more than luck and financial backing to survive the vicissitudes of business on the Arizona frontier. The brothers were resourceful, patient, energetic and venturesome gamblers. It is doubtful that they ever seriously considered pulling up stakes and quitting.

Obviously, they wielded a good deal of clout in northern Arizona, yet that power was of a benevolent nature. They never tried to "run the town," although they could have easily, a trait rare in the annals of powerful families. There were no Babbitt mansions for tourists to gape and stare at today, for the families lived unpretentiously in upper middle-class homes.

During their heyday, the Babbitts ran thousands of cattle and sheep on some 100,000 square miles of range in three states; had the largest retail and wholesale mercantile business in the Southwest; owned a vast network of trading posts on Indian reservations; were proprietors of Flagstaff's first automotive garage and dealership, a dealership that is today one of the oldest Ford agencies in the nation; owned Flagstaff's only ice plant, bank, and opera house, a livery stable, beef slaughter house and packing plant, including a mortuary. The undertaking business demonstrates their affinity for entrepreneuring any legitimate enterprise. This was a prime example of defying the old maxim of avoiding entering into a business one knows nothing about. The mortuary opened in 1892 and the operating partner was a local character whose only prior job-related experience was that he was an ex-buffalo hunter. In spite of the man's dubious qualifications, the business prospered for years.

It has been said "God made northern Arizona and then he turned it over to the Babbitts to run." Some might question a statement so presumptuous, but it cannot be denied that for nearly five generations they have, in the words of one writer, "fed and clothed and equipped and transported and entertained and buried Arizonans for four generations, and they did it more efficiently and more profitably than anyone else."

ARIZONA'S LOST MINES
and TREASURES

Some of Arizona's greatest natural resources are the fabled lost mines found "somewhere out there" in the rugged mountains and fearsome deserts. If you had to lose one, Arizona was a good place to do it. Although some of these romantic tales exist only in the minds of believers, they provide a wonderful source of the stuff that dreams are made of. They belong to nobody, yet they belong to all. They are rooted deep in the heritage of this land. Since nobody knows for sure where these secret mines and hidden treasures are located, developers are unable to erect fast food franchises, motels, trails or parks and campgrounds in their midst. Most important, they don't pollute the air or collect garbage. And you say you've tried the lure of beckoning mirages, tramping the hills, and unflagging expectations, all to no avail?

You've missed the whole point—the real adventure is the search. Any prospector who ever swished a pan, rocked out a cradle or cleaned out a sluice will swear the real treasure is—being there—the seeking—for them, a course of life.

The fabled jackass prospectors were the trail blazers, leading the vanguard of society into the brawny western mountains. The rich mining industry could never have been developed without those incurable sourdoughs and their inseparable, but cantankerous burros. The mountains guarded their secrets well. The Indians saw little value in the soft, malleable yellow metal. Mountain men were usually more interested in securing the pelts from the plentiful beavers for a booming fur market in the 1820's and early 1830's. It was the interloping prospector who braved the perils of life in the steep-sided, Apache-infested canyons who led the way and set the stage. Following the footsteps of these harbingers of society, for better or worse, came the developers, merchants, farmers and cattlemen—and to protect this new frontier phenomenon, the U.S. Army.

Few of these prospectors became wealthy. Many lost their scalps or left their bones to bleach in some lonely isolated canyon or desert. The fervid belief that the mocking mirage of *El Dorado* was just over the next hill waiting to be kicked over by the toe of a hob-nailed boot was all the inspiration they needed.

The first grand entrada into this land by white men, in 1540, was in quest for the fabled Seven Cities of Gold. It is one of Southwest history's great ironies that Francisco Vasquez de Coronado rode within a stone's throw of great riches at what would become Bisbee, Tombstone, Clifton and Morenci, not to mention the lands he traversed outside the boundaries of today's Arizona. It was the luck of the deal that he returned home a failure after two years of searching.

Whoever said you can't take it with you forgot to reckon with the moribund old gold seekers who took their secrets to the grave.

In spite of embroidered narrations and alleged deathbed ruminations, the whereabouts of the legendary Lost Adams, the mislaid Peg Leg, and the misplaced Phantom Peralta, to mention only a few, remain "somewhere out there." The rugged terrain, restive Apaches and Navajos, and notorious banditos made it an excellent location for growing and nurturing lost mine and treasure stories. The best advice this writer can offer to aspiring treasure seekers is to take a lesson from history. Lost treasures are usually found by accident, so if you are accident prone, your chances of being the chosen one are enhanced. History also tells us that numerous discoveries, including the fabulous finds at Silver King, the Vulture, and Rich Hill, were located or at least assisted by contrary burros. So, forget the four-wheel-drive gas buggy and elaborate metal detectors and get yourself a desert canary. Thus equipped, you're ready to embark on the magical quest for the elusive *madre del oro*.

Arizona's most notorious lost treasure story for both believers and otherwise takes place in the mysterious Superstition Mountains.

The rugged range of mountains east of the Salt River Valley encompasses some of the most breathtaking, untouched wilderness recesses in America. There is also an aura of mystical beauty that can possess the soul. They are regarded as religious shrines by both the Pimas and Apaches. They provided the setting for much bloody violence between those warring tribes before the coming of the white man. During the latter part of the 19th century, the mountains became a formidable sanctuary and one of the last vestiges of the Apaches who refused to become reservation Indians. They used the twisting canyons and impenetrable maze of rocks, defying sustained efforts by the military, for over twenty years.

Closing of the frontier in the 20th century has not lessened the violence of the mountains. People still get lost and perish in the vast wilderness. Occasionally gunplay between treasure seekers occurs. The Superstitions, it is said, can take a normal, peaceable individual and turn him into a gun-toting crazy, once he comes under its mystical spell.

Now a few well-educated, reasonably sane friends of this writer have attested to the fact they they never ride into those mountains without going well-armed, prepared for close encounters with the worst kind of humanity who are reputed to inhabit the region. They also admit to becoming a little crazy themselves upon entering the Superstitions.

As is usually the case, most people going into the mountains regard everybody else crazy and violent, so they arm themselves for self-protection. Since everybody in the area is armed and considers *himself* the only sane person in the mountains, there is bound to be some suspicion when two people meet along the trail. One innocuous word or gesture could be taken by the other as a prelude to violence and the fun begins.

What brings out this craziness? Most would suggest it is the frenzied quest for fabled Lost Dutchman Mine.

Why has this particular lost mine captured the imagination of so many? The mysterious mountains themselves provide the Dutchman Mine with the ideal location to hide a lost treasure. Its convenient location to a large metropolitan area is one reason. It's one of the few places where the part-time treasure-seeker can escape from the concrete, glass and steel jungle and for a brief period relive those dreams we all share at one time or another—that of locating some fabulous cache of riches. For we are, in the immortal words of Texas folklorist, J. Frank Dobie, "Coronado's children."

The legend itself has all the basic ingredients of the consummate lost treasure tale—deathbed ruminations by an enigmatic prospector, then embellished and improved versions, fruitless searches, a ballad or two, and that important ingredient—violence. All contribute to make the Lost Dutchman one of America's most enduring legends.

Paradoxically, the Old Dutchman, Jacob Waltz would be surprised and bemused by all the notoriety since his death in 1891.

He seems to have lived a very nondescript life, arriving in America from Germany about 1840, to Arizona in the early 1860's and to Phoenix in 1868. He was one of the Valley's first settlers. Earlier, he prospected around Prescott and Crown King, but his name does not appear on any claim after 1865. There was no reference to a claim or mine by Waltz in the Superstitions during his lifetime. Contrary to stories of hoarded gold, he lived out his final years on his homestead at Henshaw Road (Buckeye Road) and 7th Street in poverty. He literally sold himself into peonage by deeding his property to a neighbor in exchange for that neighbor's taking care of him for the rest of his natural life. His only spoken words regarding a treasure are handed down from people who befriended him during his last days, like Julia Thomas, a young lady who owned a confectionery store, and Rhinehart Petrasch, a neighbor.

The disastrous flood in Phoenix during February, 1891, was Waltz's final undoing. His homestead was inundated and the old man suffered from exposure. He contacted pneumonia and died several months later. During those last days he is supposed to have told Mrs. Thomas about his hoard of gold in the Superstitions.

Soon after Waltz died, she and Rinney Petrasch, along with his brother Hermann, ventured into the mountains to search in vain for old Jacob's gold. Had it not been for the brief publicity generated by Mrs. Thomas and the Petrasch brothers, the legend of the Lost Dutchman mine might have died then and there. It would remain for the yarn spinners and tall tale tellers to embellish the legend. Julia Thomas hocked her small business to grubstake the expedition. She would not be the last modern-day argonaut to make that mistake. She did reap some profit from the venture, however. The resourceful Julia sold the first of a long line of treasure maps for seven dollars each, or whatever the market would bear, for several years, thereby distinguishing herself as one of the few who made a few bucks for her trouble. Another was author Oren Arnold, who was also one of the founding members of the Don's Club, a group of hardworking history buffs. Arnold happily laid claim to finding riches beyond his wildest dreams by sitting down at his typewriter for a couple of hours and writing a popular pamphlet on the elusive Lost Dutchman.

There are usually four theories surrounding old Jake's mine or cache of gold. Some say he highgraded ore out of the Vulture near Wickenburg, then circled across to the Superstitions. However, Waltz's name does not appear on any records nor does he seem to have spent any time around the Vulture mine.

Another theory is that he found a hidden cache of processed gold left by Jesuit priests prior to their expulsion in 1767. Most historians agree, however, the Jesuits could not possibly have hidden any gold in the Superstitions.

A likely theory, if Jake Waltz did have a cache of gold, was that he found it west of the Superstitions at Goldfield. It is a fact that a large amount of the yellow metal was taken out of the Mammoth Mine and others in 1893. Another possibility was east of the mountains. The fabulous Silver King near Superior mined some $19 million in its heyday, so the region was certainly not devoid of mineral; but the area where most treasure seekers congregated, Weaver's Needle, does not appear to be mineral-bearing.

Unfortunately old Jake died, lonely, forgotten, obscure, pitiful and broke. In spite of all this, the legend continued to grow.

The fourth theory concerns the fictitious Peralta Mine.

The story took on an Hispanic flavor around the turn of the century, when it was said Mexican gambusinos had worked the area prior to the U.S. acquiring it with the Gadsden Purchase in 1853. The story was told that a Mexican gentleman had befriended Jacob Waltz and his partner Jacob Weiser (there seems to be no evidence of there ever being a Jacob Weiser) in Sonora, and agreed to take them to the mine in the Superstitions called the *Las Minas Sombreras*. After taking some gold, the Mexican returned to Sonora and soon after, Weiser, according to one version, was killed by Apaches, in another, by Waltz. During these tellings, the character of Waltz transforms into that of a sinister, steely-eyed reprobate who ambushed those who tried to follow. In reality, old Jake was incapable of the violent nature attributed to him by mythmakers.

Around 1930, the name of this "mysterious Mexican" materialized into that of Don Miguel Peralta. The Peralta name is rich in the annals of Southwest history and gave credence to the legend. The great Peralta Land Grant swindle was still fresh in the minds of most Arizonans, although the huge grant had been conjured up in the fertile mind of a con man and would-be Baron of Arizona named James Addison Reavis and had been proven a fraud, many people still believed in a Peralta land grant. This seems to have enabled yarn spinners the opportunity to incorporate the name Peralta into the legend.

In reality, there was a Don Miguel Peralta. He traveled from Mexico to California during the gold rush and thence to Arizona where he hoped to hit paydirt. He and his party were not ambushed and massacred in the Superstitions by Apaches. The Peralta Mine was located in Yavapai County's Black Canyon, near Bumble Bee. Apparently it was moved to the Superstitions later for convenience.

Still, the Lost Dutchman would be just another obscure legend had it not been for Dr. Adolph Ruth, a crippled, old, amateur treasure-seeker who ambled into the Superstitions in 1931. Dr. Ruth carried with him a map giving the location of the Peralta's *Las Minas Sombreras*. When Ruth failed to reappear from his sojourn, a search party went looking but could find no trace. Several months later, Ruth's skeleton was located. The skull appeared to have been perforated by a bullet. He was killed for his secret map, the yarnspinners said, and a whole new generation of treasure-seekers joined in the search.

A full-scale feud broke out around Weaver's Needle between a friendly old cuss named Ed Piper and a good-natured lady named Celeste Marie Jones. Both were seeking the mythical Lost Jesuit treasure and that is what created the contention. Celeste, a black woman, reputed to be an ex-opera singer, carried a sawed off .30-06 and a pistol strapped to her hip. Piper went similarly armed. Neither seemed capable of violence; however both hired an assortment of baleful bodyguards and they were catalyst for what followed.

A saloon in Apache Junction joined in the fun, hanging recruiting poster sign-up sheets on the walls for each army. The frivolity ended when real violence broke out among the hirelings and three people died violently.

The feud ended when Piper died of natural causes in 1962 and Ms. Jones abandoned her claim for parts unknown.

These stories and others have continued to perpetuate the legends of the Superstitions and the Dutchman's gold.

While historians and some writers refute the existence of the Lost Dutchman and the stories of buried treasure in the Thunder God's Mountains, the legends live on and the Dutchman hunters still persist.

The entire matter was summed up three centuries ago, when a Spanish chronicler noted wryly, "Granted they did not find the gold, at least they found a place in which to search."

You ask me—does the Lost Dutchman exist? Is there a treasure in those Superstitions Mountains? You bet there is a Lost Dutchman. It lives, if only in the minds of those who choose to believe. And that is their privilege and right. A treasure in that magnificent theatre of nature? Yessir—it's called "being there."

To the last man:
JIM ROBERTS
and the Pleasant Valley war

Author's Note: In the early 1970's I had the opportunity to spend many hours with the legendary lawman's son, Bill. Bill Roberts was dying of cancer at the time and was in a great deal of pain, but never tired talking about his famous father. Much of the information contained in this story is the result of those interviews.

Arizona's central mountains, in the closing years of the 19th century, were the last refuge of the old West-style badmen. The terrain was rugged and remote, strewn with countless side canyons and hidden valleys. Few roads led into the brawny mountains and only the bravest of lawmen dared venture into the outlaw sanctuaries. Honest citizens in the area had no choice but to tolerate the outlawry, especially the livestock thieves. To have resisted the organized packs of pariahs would have been fruitless. Citizens could not cooperate with peace officers, for the lawmen were only passing through, so to speak, and the resident cow-horse thieves could take their vengeance out on any honest rancher who cooperated with the law.

Pleasant Valley, in the Tonto Basin, became a classic place-name of contradiction in the early 1880's when the cattle and horse rustlers moved in. The valley was an isolated piece of geography bordered on the south by the Sierra Ancha Mountains; to the west were the towering Mazatzals; on the east was Apache land, and on the north was the precipitous Mogollon Rim. The rugged wilderness of forest was interspersed with grassy meadows and sparkling mountain streams. The climate was generally mild. In short, it was a cattleman's paradise.

The county seat in those days was Prescott, some 150 miles to the west. Globe was 75 miles in the other direction. Flagstaff was just a small burg on the A & P railroad line and Payson was not much more than a cross-road.

Over the next few years, this valley with the tranquil name would be the setting of the most notorious vendetta in Arizona's history. Before the feuding factions and the local vigilance committee ended their work, some 30 people would die a violent death from faceoff gunfighting, back-shooting, ambush or the lynchman's noose.

The two prominent families in the feud were the Tewksburys, led by eldest brother Ed, and the Grahams, ramrodded by their eldest, Tom.

It's commonly believed that the so-called Pleasant Valley War or Graham-Tewksbury feud broke out in 1887 when the Daggs brothers, a sheep outfit headquartered at Flagstaff, drove a large herd of woollies into Pleasant Valley, under the protective guns of the Tewksburys. Novelists have created the myth that it was strictly a sheepman-cattleman war. In reality, it began several years earlier.

The Tewksbury boys were among the earliest settlers in that remote region of the Tonto Basin. Years before, their father, John D. Tewksbury, Sr., had settled in the Humboldt wilderness of California and married an Indian woman, who bore him four sons. Following her death in 1878, John Sr. packed up his sons, Ed, John Jr., Jim and Frank and headed for the boomtown of Globe. The following year, the Tewksbury boys started a ranch on Canyon Creek in Pleasant Valley. Evidently they were good, hard-working cowmen. Two years later, Jim Stinson, someone who would figure prominently in the outbreak of the feud, moved into the area with some 600 head of beeves. Stinson planned to live in the Salt River Valley and check on his Pleasant Valley holdings only periodically, so he hired a rather notorious Texan of limited intelligence named John Gilliland to run the outfit.

During the summer of 1882, the Graham brothers, Tom and John, came to Globe from California, liked the area, and decided to start a ranch. Ironically, one of the first men they met was Ed Tewksbury, who told them of the wonderful range country in the Tonto Basin.

Tom Graham, handsome and dignified looking, seems to have been an impatient man. Not content to let his small herd multiply by the natural laws of biology, he and his hirelings were soon putting their stamp on every calf they found, regardless of its mother's brand. Before long, he had to hire more punchers to keep up with his growing herd, and among those hired was young Jim Tewksbury. When Tewksbury told his older brothers about the Graham's rustling activities, they persuaded him to quit the outfit. From that time on, hard feelings developed between the two families. Soon after, Jim Stinson, the absentee owner of a neighboring ranch, accused the Grahams of stealing his cows, but when the district court met at St. Johns, witnesses failed to appear and the charges were dropped. Stinson's foreman, John Gilliland, was a good friend of the Grahams, and tried to divert attention from his cronies by shifting the blame on the Tewksburys. He got his chance later when two heifers that belonged to Stinson were found wearing Tewksbury brands. Ed openly admitted the mistake and offered to return the cows, but Gilliland insisted on pressing charges. Ed decided to go around the ill-tempered foreman and wrote to Mr. Stinson explaining the situation. Stinson accepted Tewksbury's story and ordered his foreman to drop the issue. Needless to say, Gilliland was upset but did as he was ordered.

However, on January 11, 1883, he braced himself with a few shots of whiskey and rode over to the Tewksbury ranch looking for stolen cattle. With him was a 15-year-old nephew, Elisha, and a ranch hand. Following a brief argument between him and Ed Tewksbury, Gilliland, who was still mounted, jerked his revolver and fired off a round but missed. His nephew pulled his pistol and fired, but in his haste the shot went wild also.

Edwin Tewksbury

Thomas H. Graham

Tewksbury grabbed a .22 caliber rifle stashed nearby and fired off two rounds, one hitting Gilliland in the leg and the other the calf of young Elisha. The lad fell from his horse and was left to look out for himself as the frightened Gilliland rode off in a cloud of dust. He stopped at the Graham ranch where he reported the unprovoked attack by Ed Tewksbury and added that Elisha was mortally wounded in the ambush. Rumors were quickly spread by the Grahams and Gilliland that young Elisha had been murdered. Elisha quickly recovered from his wound, but the Grahams wouldn't let matters rest. Avoiding the obvious facts of the case, they insisted on pressing charges against all the Tewksburys. In January of 1884, a trial was held in Prescott and the charges were quickly dismissed. The judge chastised the Grahams for trying to create such a ruckus over nothing, and as far as the law was concerned, the matter was ended.

However, as a result of the long, chilly horseback ride to and from Prescott to stand trial on the trumped-up charges, young Frank Tewksbury caught pneumonia and died. The Tewksburys bitterly blamed his death on the Grahams.

For the next 18 months, the men of Pleasant Valley lived under an armed truce, each keeping a wary eye on the other. The volatile atmosphere took a turn for the worse in early 1884 when "old man" Mart Blevins and his sons, John, Charlie, Hamp, and Sam Houston pulled up stakes in Texas and moved their operations to Pleasant Valley. Another son, Andy, alias "Andy Cooper," would arrive later. The Blevins closest neighbors were the Grahams, and since the residents were dividing into factions, the two families joined forces. One of the main characteristics of a frontier feud was that it was not possible to remain neutral. To attempt to do so would likely incur the wrath of both warring factions. So the Blevins family were left with little choice but to join their neighbors.

Andy Blevins or Cooper, as he preferred to be known, was a desperado from Texas. His arrival in Pleasant Valley, along with a number of others of dubious reputations who drifted in, swelled the ranks of the Graham partisans. Most of these newcomers were refugees from some other troubled region, such as Lincoln County, New Mexico. Unhappily for the honest settlers and ranchers in Pleasant Valley, they brought their vices along. Soon, a well-organized band of rustlers was headquartering in the Valley, using the region as a staging area for stolen livestock.

Into this valley of turmoil rode a peaceful man from Macon County, Missouri, named Jim Roberts. He was a handsome, mild-mannered young man of medium height, close-cropped blond hair parted on the side and a mustache. He had an aquiline nose, square, determined jaw and penetrating eyes. Unlike many others who came looking for action, Roberts quietly went about his business, which was raising well-bred horses. He had spent his entire stake on a broad, deep-chested stallion. Roberts preferred not to join either side, but when his prize stallion was stolen and the tracks led to Graham partisans, and when they burned his place, he joined the Tewksburys. The Grahams, in driving the quiet Missourian into the Tewksbury camp, made a serious, tactical blunder. Behind that disarming, easygoing personality was a resolute man as tough and determined as the outlaws. Contemporaries on both sides agreed on one thing, Roberts was the best gunfighter in the war. A crack shot and expert tracker, one of the participants later called him the "coolest, deadliest fighter of them all."

In February, 1887, Bill Jacobs, a friend of the Tewksburys, in the employ of sheepmen from Flagstaff, drove a herd of sheep into what had been cattle grazing land. Immediately, a Basque sheepherder was shot to death and beheaded. The sheepmen wisely removed their herd from the valley and that abruptly ended the sheep business in the area.

Events began to unravel quickly. The following July, Mart Blevins, father and leader of the Blevins clan, disappeared and was presumed murdered. It was naturally assumed he was killed by Tewksbury partisans. A couple of weeks later, John Paine, Bob Gillespie, Tom Tucker and Blevins' son Hamp, rode brazenly up to the Newton Ranch where the Tewksburys and Jim Roberts were staying and tried to invite themselves in for dinner. When refused, a fight broke out. After the smoke cleared, Blevins and Paine lay dead and the others were all wounded. There were no casualties on the other side. After the shootout, Yavapai County Sheriff William Mulvenon and a posse came over from Prescott, remained only briefly and returned to the county seat. Apparently, after gauging the scope and size of the feud, they decided at least for the time being, that discretion was the better part of valor.

A few days later 18-year-old Billy Graham was shot and killed by Jim Houck, a brother-in-law of the slain Basque sheepherder. Houck, also a friend of the Tewksburys, was acting as a deputy for newly-appointed Apache County Sheriff Commodore Perry Owens. The shooting occur-

Jim Roberts, last of the gunfighters (Photo: courtest Bill Roberts)

Commodore Perry Owens, Apache County sheriff (Arizona State Lib.)

red when the two met on a lonely trail. Both went for their guns, but Houck was the better man that day.

Thirsting for revenge, the Grahams, along with Andy Cooper and some of his friends, decided to try to even things up with a sneak attack on the Tewksbury's ranch. On the morning of September 2, 1887, the men concealed their horses and quietly surrounded the ranch house. Inside were Ed and Jim Tewksbury, along with his father, Ed Sr., and Jim Roberts. Although it has been disputed, many also believe that Eva Tewksbury and her infant were also present. Two others, Bill Jacobs and John Tewksbury, husband of Eva, were outside the house, unaware that several rifles were trained on them.

The stillness of the crisp late summer morning was broken by the sound of rifle fire. Jacobs and Tewksbury fell dead, their bodies riddled by the stream of gunfire. The Graham-Cooper gang then turned their attention to the ranch house, pouring round after round into the stout structure. Inside, Roberts and the others fought desperately against overwhelming odds. During the fight, a herd of semi-wild hogs moved in and began to devour the bodies of the slain pair, in full view of their allies and families. A plea, made from inside the house for a cease fire to remove the bodies, was refused. It is said that at this point Eva Tewksbury stepped outside, grabbed a shovel, drove off the hogs and buried the two men in shallow graves. During this time, all gunfire ceased. After Mrs. Tewksbury finished her grisly chore and returned to the cabin, the fighting resumed. The siege ended when a posse from Prescott arrived and scattered the intruders.

A dramatic spinoff of the war occurred just two days later when Andy Cooper was gunned down along with two others in Holbrook by the long-haired Sheriff of Apache County, Commodore Perry Owens.

Cooper had left Pleasant Valley and was visiting at the Blevins family home on Center Street, next to the railroad tracks. Witnesses later said he had been boasting in the saloons about killing two men in Pleasant Valley two days earlier. He was at the Blevins house later that day when Sheriff Owens stepped up on the front porch and attempted to serve a warrant on him for horse stealing. Andy cracked open the door and raised his revolver, but before he could fire, Owens, armed with a Winchester, put a round through the door and into Andy's midsection, mortally wounding the outlaw. From the opposite side of the room, John Blevins pushed open a door and fired at Owens, who cranked another shell into his rifle, turned and fired from the hip, wounding Blevins. A relative, Mose Roberts (no relation to Jim) leaped out a side window at the same time the sheriff moved out into the street. Before Roberts could get a shot off, the Winchester cracked once more, killing him. Meanwhile, 14-year-old Sam Houston Blevins wrestled Andy Cooper's pistol away from his mother and ran out the front door to join the fight. Before he could take aim and fire, Owens shot the youth through the heart.

The battle was brief but furious and goes down as one of the most exciting gunfights in the history of outlawry. Unfortunately, for the descendants of the Blevins family, the legacy of that event haunts them to this day.

Controversy over the gunfight continues. To most, C.P. Owens is a celebrated, legendary hero. Others considered him a hired assassin brought in by county officials to rid the area of desperadoes, but instead, gunned down the Blevins boys and Mose Roberts without giving them a fighting chance. Whichever side one chooses to believe, none can doubt the courage of Owens that day and few, if any, outside the family were sad to see Andy Cooper die with his boots on.

Two weeks after the siege at the Tewksbury ranch, Graham supporters tried another early morning sneak attack, this time at Rock Springs where Jim and Ed Tewksbury, along with Jim Roberts, were camped. Roberts had arisen early and observed the men setting up their ambush and gave the alarm. In an instant, the Tewksbury brothers were up, grabbed their rifles and opened fire. All three were expert marksmen, and when the shooting ended, one Graham partisan was dead and several were down.

At this same time, a large posse had converged upon the valley to arrest prominent gunmen on both sides. The plan was to take the Grahams first, then the Tewksburys and Roberts. The posse gathered at Perkin's Store during the night, hid their horses, and made plans to lure the Grahams into a trap. Deputies were hidden behind a five-foot stone wall near the store. They sent a couple of riders by the nearby Graham ranch, and sure enough, John Graham and Charlie Blevins rode over to check out the two strangers. When the two feudists saw the trap, they spurred their mounts and tried to make a break. A blast from a twin-barreled shotgun knocked Blevins out of the saddle, killing him instantly. John Graham was hit by rifle fire and died a few minutes later. Tom Graham, the last of the Graham clan, escaped capture.

After the shooting of John Graham and Charlie Blevins, the posse rode over to the Tewksbury ranch to make their arrests. None of the Tewksbury partisans offered any resistance. For all practical purposes, the "war proper" had ended.

Leaders of both partisan groups were charged in Prescott and later St. Johns. However, when witnesses for the prosecution failed to appear, charges against both sides were dropped.

Tom Graham left the valley, married and settled down in Tempe—the feud, and the loss of his brothers a bitter memory. He would be shot down nearly five years later outside Tempe by Ed, the last of the Tewksburys. Tewksbury was released on a legal technicality after a lengthy trial. He served as a lawman at Globe until his death a few years later of consumption. Ed Tewksbury was one of the few on either side of die peacefully in bed, "with his boots off."

The worst terrorism was yet to come. A small group of prominent farmers and ranchers formed a viligance committee and sought to rid the valley of all unsavory characters. Any outsider was suspect. Several culprits and some innocent drifters wound up "dancin' a jig 'neath the limb of a cottonwood tree."

Jim Roberts did not remain in the valley after his arraignment in 1887. Like many others, he had lost his investment during the donnybrook and was forced to start over.

The reputation earned as a gunman in the war made Roberts a much sought-after character by law enforcement agencies. In 1889, the noted sheriff of Yavapai County, William O. "Buckey" O'Neill, hired him as a deputy to help tame the new gold-mining town of Congress in the Bradshaw Mountains. Roberts would remain a lawman in Arizona for some 45 years. It was at Congress that he met the lovely Permelia Kirkland. "Melia" was the daughter of pioneer rancher William Kirkland, who had raised the first American flag over Tucson. Kirkland and his bride were the first Anglo couple to be married in Arizona.

Melia, a blond, 20-year old beauty and "belle of the town," was engaged to another man at the time. However, it took little time for the handsome gunman-turned-lawman to win her heart. In late 1891, Sheriff O'Neill gave Roberts another town to tame—raucous Jerome. He and Melia were married in Prescott and headed for Jerome the next morning. The boomtown perched on the slopes of mineral-laden Cleopatra Hill, was a typical western mining town. Jerome, with an abundance of boisterous, devil-may-care reprobates, and dozens of saloons that remained open 24 hours a day, seven days a week, required the services of a fearless peace officer. Jim filled the role perfectly. One night, three men escaped to the outskirts of town after killing a man over a card game. They sent a challenge to Roberts and his young deputy to come and get them.

As Roberts and the deputy approached the desperadoes, the grim-jawed lawman told his protege, "You take the one in the middle and I'll get the other two." When the youngster began to tremble, Roberts told him in a kind but firm tone, "Get out of the way, Sonny, and I'll take 'em all."

Moments later, all three killers were down. On another occasion, two men broke jail, murdered his deputy, and headed off into the night. Roberts tracked the men to a wooded area near Camp Verde and in a running gun battle killed both outlaws.

Over the next several years, Jim Roberts worked as marshal or sheriff at Douglas, Florence and Humbolt. In 1927, at the age of 69, he returned to the Verde Valley as constable at Clarkdale. Arizona's wild and woolly days were over. Law and order had been established and the gunfighter era had passed into the realm of romance . . . and into the hands of novelists and mythmakers. Old Jim by this time was one of only two or three survivors of the Pleasant Valley War, a genuine western idol of an age turned to legend. Unlike many others of his period, Jim didn't have much to say about the old times. He didn't swagger or brag, drink, swear or play cards. He clammed up tight as a drum when anyone questioned him about the Graham-Tewksbury feud. Instead of a fancy fast-draw holster, he carried his nickel-plated revolver in his hip pocket. When the youngsters around Clarkdale tried to persuade "Uncle Jim" to demonstrate his quick draw and uncanny marksmanship, the old man just smiled. The youths raised on the likes of such two-gun galahads as Wm. S. Hart and Tom Mix were quick to notice other incongruities—Roberts rode a mule instead of a white horse—his six shooter looked like it hadn't been fired in 20 years and worse—there were no notches on the handle. "Uncle Jim" neither looked nor acted the part of a legendary gunfighter. Some even began to question his authenticity.

All those doubts about whether or not Uncle Jim was a reality or merely a myth were laid to rest one day in 1928 when two desperadoes robbed the Clarkdale branch of the Bank of Arizona of $40,000. It was the largest heist in Arizona history. The two men jumped in the getaway car and drove off just as the old lawman rounded the corner. As the car sped by, one of the bank robbers leaned out the window and fired at Roberts. Old Jim reached into his hip pocket, drew his Colt revolver and slowly took aim, holding the piece with both hands. The pistol bucked twice in the old man's wrinkled but steady hands. The car skidded sideways striking a telephone pole guy wire. The driver slumped over the wheel with a bullet in his head. The second robber surrendered meekly to the old gunman.

That was Jim Roberts' last gunfight. The last of the old time shootin' sheriffs died of a heart attack on the evening of January 8, 1934, while making his rounds. It seemed fitting somehow that the old lawman should die on the job. The "last man" in the Pleasant Valley War, a notorious gunfighter who pinned on a star and became one of Arizona's greatest peace officers died with his shoes on. Jim Roberts didn't wear boots.

BUCKEY O'NEILL
Arizona's Happy Warrior

Has this country grown too rich, too confused, too disillusioned or too worldly for heroes?

True heroes have become so elusive in our time that, if we seem not to have any, it might be because we aren't able to recognize them and perhaps we don't deserve them. In these times of "kiss and tell" journalism where today's heroes are tomorrow's trivia questions, few can withstand the barrages of intense public scrutiny. Today's heroes are as dispensible as baby diapers and some aren't treated much better. Today, we live in a troubled land of thought-deadening disco bars and cookie-cutter shopping malls. The embodiment of today's hero-types range from sports stars to rock idols. We live under a deluge of continuous blasts of human potential, self-improvement and sensuality which this society has been touting of late. In a society which accepts the tarnished coin of celebrity in place of heroic virtue, our interests seem as broad as they are shallow.

In times like these, we need to look back to the past. As Will Rogers used to say, "The Indians never got lost because they were always looking back to see where they'd been." There are too few statues around these days to honor those hallowed heroes of yesteryear and that is unfortunate, for these shrines provide the necessary inspiration to make us pause for a moment and reflect upon our past.

Prescott is one of Arizona's most historically-conscious communities. Public-spirited citizens have worked long and hard to keep the rich cultural heritage alive. Standing in front of the old Yavapai County Courthouse is a bronze statue of a soldier on a spirited horse. This monument honors a group of young Arizonans who gallantly served their country during the Spanish-American War in 1898. It is also a shrine to one man, Captain William O. "Buckey" O'Neill.

Frontier sheriff, newspaperman, adventurer, politician, and soldier, Buckey O'Neill, was all these and more. There was an aura of romantic daring about him that attracted legions of followers, both men and women. He was a born leader whose hectic career and many-sided personality embraced a life-long idealistic quest for glory. In short, Buckey O'Neill was a reflection and reincarnation of the gallant knights of old. When war with Spain broke out in 1898, it was only natural that he be chosen to lead northern Arizona's Company A of the First United States Volunteer Cavalry, better known as the "Rough Riders." Perhaps, in some poignant way, it was also a fitting climax that he died while participating in one of the most glorious charges in United States military history.

Buckey O'Neill came to Arizona during the wild heydays of the silver boomtowns. He worked as a newspaperman for John Clum's *Epitaph* in the early 1880's during the time of the Earp-Cowboy feud around Tombstone. He was a member of the Prescott Volunteer Fire Department when famed Whiskey Row burned. As newly-elected captain of the Prescott Grays honor guard, he took much good-natured ribbing from his contemporaries when he fainted dead away at the hanging of notorious murderer Dennis Dilda. When Walnut Dam collapsed in 1890, killing more than 100 people in what was Arizona's greatest natural disaster, he directed search and rescue operations. He was court reporter when defendant Patrick McAteer went berserk with a double-bladed Bowie knife and tried to exterminate half the courtroom, including the court reporter. He had just become Sheriff of Yavapai County when outlaws held up the train at Canyon Diablo. Following the pursuit and capture of the train robbers, a contemporary judge wrote these prophetic words nearly nine years before O'Neill's heroic death near San Juan Hill: "Yavapai County's young sheriff with his rough riders . . . has scarcely a parallel for daring and pertinacity in this or any other country."

The darkly-handsome Irishman epitomized those halcyon days known as the "gay nineties." His ego was fairly full-bloomed, his nature gregarious, witty, self-confident, and he was a daring, devil-may-care gambler. He earned his illustrious nickname in the gambling casinos along Whiskey Row by constantly "bucking the tiger," a term used for a faro player betting against the house.

Until he reached Prescott, Buckey was a kind of romantic vagabond who drifted from town to town in search of adventure and excitement. He never really settled for long anywhere until his arrival in the "Mile High City." The beautiful mountain backdrop, mild climate, scented pines, culture and elegant ladies got hold of him and for the last 16 years of his life, he called Prescott home.

The future Rough Rider captain received his first baptism of fire while serving as a special deputy for noted Phoenix city marshal Henry Garfias a few years prior to his moving to Prescott. One June night in 1882, three drunken cowboys decided to whoop it up and went on a shooting spree along Washington street. When O'Neill, Garfias and two other officers tried to arrest the trio, they set up their horses and made a mad dash towards the policemen, firing their revolvers as they came. Garfias dismounted and calmly fired two shots at the leader. The first one knocked the pistol out of his hand, the second blew the surprised cowboy right out of the saddle. The other two, reasonably sobered by the death of their comrade, surrendered meekly.

Prescott Mayor William O. "Buckey" O'Neill was reputed to have been one of the most popular party throwers at the 1885 session of the territorial legislature, that infamous body of lawmakers known as the "Thieving Thirteenth" because of their ultra liberal spending habits.

Prescott was the territorial capital in those days and when the legislators were in session the town was not wanting for excitement. Days were spent engaging in such nefarious activities as fistfighting, wrench swing-

Buckey O'Neill, Populist
Congressional candidate (1894)

Rough Rider monument at
Prescott, dedicated 1907

ing and dueling. This all occurred, incidentally, in the hallowed halls of the legislature, and by the delegates, not the ruffians they represented. Nights were spent in carousing among Prescott's many pleasure palaces around Whiskey Row. Most of the important legislation was decided at the expensive parties thrown for the purpose of promoting various schemes.

Buckey is generally credited as being responsible for Prescott retaining the territorial capital, in spite of the tireless campaign by citizens of Tucson to "steal" the capital and return it to the "Old Pueblo." (Prescott had been the territorial capital 1864-67. Tucson was capital 1867-77, before losing it back to Prescott. Phoenix became territorial capital in 1889.)

As far as can be determined, money did not change hands in these dealings. Lavish parties were thrown by the various delegates seeking political plums for their constituents. At these social gatherings, deals were made and trades were given. Phoenix sought and received an "insane asylum." Tempe was given a normal school. Prescott wanted to keep the capital. Tucson wanted the capital but was awarded the University of Arizona, as a consolation prize. Tucson's delegates had taken the long way around to Prescott by railroad, via Los Angeles, and had not arrived in time to "out party" Buckey's gala affair, so the capital remained in Yavapai County. In the unhappy aftermath, Tucson's delegates were pelted with rotten vegetables upon their homecoming by an ungrateful constituency. The "you can't fool mother nature" award went to the delegates from Florence. They asked for and received monies to build a bridge over the Gila river. Soon after completion of the project, the fickle Gila changed her course and left the bridge standing forlornly in the desert.

O'Neill pulled a mild political upset in 1888 when he sought and won the election for sheriff of Yavapai County. Newspapers began calling him the "Conquistador of Yavapai County," and the public loved it.

He had been in office only three months when four men robbed the Atlantic and Pacific Eastbound Number Two, a few miles east of Flagstaff (then a part of Yavapai County). The passenger train had halted to take on firewood at about 11 o'clock in the evening. The bandits, all cowboys in the employ of the famous Hashknife outfit near Holbrook, took more than $7,000 from the express box at gunpoint, then fled north across the vast Colorado Plateau and into Utah.

Sheriff O'Neill organized a small posse, rushed to the scene of the holdup, picked up the outlaws' trail and followed it into the heart of the Painted Desert. When he was sure of their direction, he sent a young Navajo down to the railhead at Winslow, informing the agents of his whereabouts and requesting that they wire the communities in southern Utah to be on the lookout for the bandits.

Meanwhile, the outlaw band had doubled back towards Arizona in hopes of throwing the posse off their trail. After nearly three weeks, O'Neill and his men caught up with the cowboys-turned-train-robbers near Wahweap Canyon on the border.

When one of the bandits tried to make a run for it, Buckey opened fire, shooting the horse out from under the rider. In the exchange of shots that followed, a bullet struck Buckey's horse, pinning him underneath temporarily. The gunfire had taken the rest of the band by surprise. Their other horses ran off, leaving them afoot, and in short order the posse had them in irons.

The outlaws were returned to Arizona in a roundabout manner. First they were taken north to Salt Lake City, then east to Denver, then south on the Santa Fe line. Near Raton, New Mexico, one of the prisoners slipped out of his irons and escaped. He was later recaptured and reunited with his cronies at the Yuma Territorial Prison. One of the train robbers, Bill Sterin, served his term, and in 1898 enlisted in the First U.S. Volunteer Cavalry Regiment under an assumed name. He is believed to have died at the Battle of the San Juan Heights in Cuba.

Had he never ridden among the exalted ranks of Roosevelt's Rough Riders, Buckey O'Neill would still have been assured a place in the Valhalla of Arizona heroes for his relentless pursuit and capture of the Canyon Diablo train robbers.

O'Neill chose not to run again for sheriff and over the next few years engaged in various mining ventures. He didn't vacate the political scene, taking time twice to run unsuccessfully as delegate to Congress. In 1897 he ran for mayor of Prescott and won handily. It was just a short time later that the battleship Maine made that fateful voyage to Cuba to pay a courtesy call. While anchored in Havana Harbor, she mysteriously blew up.

Almost before the smoke had cleared from the wreckage of the Maine, America was at war. Buckey was sure his services would be needed and he immediately began recruiting a regiment of cowboys and frontiersmen. His personal army of volunteers was ready to go when the official call to arms came in late April, 1898.

In the meantime, the irrepressible Assistant Secretary of the Navy, Teddy Roosevelt, had received permission to raise a force of volunteer cavalry. Roosevelt, a self-styled cowboy of sorts (what he lacked in ability he more than made up in enthusiasm), was in the market for just the kind of cowboy cavalry that O'Neill had organized. Thus, the First Volunteer Cavalry Regiment was born. The outfit was made up of Southwesterners from Oklahoma, Indian Territory, New Mexico and Arizona, along with a sprinkling of adventuresome eastern college "dudes."

The regiment was a mixed bag of rogues, short on discipline and long on energy. Under the leadership of Teddy Roosevelt and Alexander Brodie (the Arizona regiment commander and future governor), the volunteers, or Rough Riders as an adoring press preferred to call them, became a crack fighting outfit. Captain O'Neill, commanding Company A, was the regiment's most popular officer. The men idolized the dashing former frontier lawman, and each man in Company A tried to model himself as a veritable reflection of their leader's colorful personality. His noble sense of justice made him a favorite among the enlisted ranks. During the brief training period at San Antonio, Texas, Buckey not only won the unqualified respect and admiration of his charges, but that of his brother officers as well, especially Roosevelt. To "TR," the handsome Irishman was the personification of the beau ideal Rough Rider.

In a few short weeks the regiment left for Tampa, Florida, the final staging area prior to shipping out to Cuba.

Much to their disappointment, part of the regiment was ordered to remain in Tampa. There were more soldiers wanting to join the fight to free Cuba than there were transports to take them. Not wanting to miss this "splendid little war," many of the volunteers left behind did their best to bribe those shipping out to exchange places.

There was no room for the horses, either, and Roosevelt's "Rough Riders" became "weary walkers." The entire regiment for that matter might not have arrived in Cuba in time for the war had not the forceful Roosevelt commandeered a transport just in the nick of time.

Captain O'Neill had a chance to display his bravery before the troops hit the beaches at Daiquiri when a landing craft carrying members of the famed black "Buffalo Soldiers" capsized. Buckey leaped into the water in a vain attempt to save two men who had been pulled under by the weight of their equipment.

The Rough Riders had their baptism of fire at Las Guasimas on June

24, and when the smoke had cleared, 16 were dead and 52 had been wounded. Included among the casualties were Arizona Commander Major Alexander Brodie and Captain Jim McClintock of Company B. It was a few days later, however, at San Juan Heights, in what Roosevelt later called "my crowded hour," the Rough Riders had their rendezvous with destiny.

"An officer should never take cover," Buckey had often said. Time and time again he had defied the Spanish sharpshooters, walked up and down the lines shouting encouragement to his troopers. At Las Guasimas, the flat, brittle crack of the Spanish Mauser rifles had kept the troops pinned down for hours, yet O'Neill walked through the gunfire untouched, increasing the awe of the men in his command. "The Spanish bullet has never been molded that will kill Buckey O'Neill," he had said jokingly on several occasions. Several years earlier Buckey had written an article called *A Horse of the Hash Knife Brand,* in which he expressed what must have been his own philosophical feelings toward death. It read in part, ". . . the Indians were right. Death was the black horse that came some day into every man's camp, and no matter when that day came, a brave man should be booted and spurred and ready to ride him out."

As the battle raged, he paused now and then to chat or joke with his men, trying to soothe their nerves as the Spanish sniper fire was beginning to take its toll. There was no doubt his calm demeanor had a calming effect on the soldiers. The captain continued to defy death. He turned towards the Spanish lines and began to roll another cigarette. An officer suggested he take cover, but he stubbornly refused. Ignoring the gunfire, he continued to pause and chat with his men. He had just rolled another cigarette and turned to speak to an officer when a Mauser slug, fired from somewhere in the dense jungle, struck him in the mouth. Ironically, Buckey, with his strong sense of destiny, would not make what would have been the crowning achievement of an eventful life—he didn't get to make that dramatic charge up San Juan Hill.

The men of Company A stared in shock and disbelief at the body of their gallant captain lying dead on the battlefield. It was said Company A ceased to function as a unit, as the stunned troopers "went off on their own." Some attached themselves to other units, while others rallied around Roosevelt.

In time, the shock of Buckey O'Neill's death wore off. The war was brief and soon the troops came home to the cheers of hero-worshiping Americans. In 1907, a magnificent bronze statue was unveiled on the courthouse lawn at Prescott. The monument, a creation of noted artist Solon Borglum, was dedicated to the memory of Captain O'Neill and in honor of the Rough Riders and should, rightfully, be called the Rough Rider statue, but to Arizonans who know his story, it will always be a lasting tribute to their happy warrior, Buckey O'Neill.

TOM HORN:
legends die hard

It was a brisk, dreary November morning in Cheyenne, Wyoming, in the year 1903. A few people were stirring about, dogs were barking here and there, but otherwise there was a quietness in the air, casting an ominous pall over the town. Off in the distance was heard the shrill, lonesome whistle of a freight train locomotive as it gathered steam to make its run up Sherman Hill. A chilly wind was blowing the grey smoke from the city out into the plains.

At the Laramie County Courthouse, Tom Horn, legendary government scout, Pinkerton detective, champion rodeo cowboy, and range regulator was taken from his cell and led into the courtyard and up the scaffolding steps to the gallows platform where a hangman's noose was waiting. He paused momentarily to speak briefly with friends and looked placidly at the crowd of witnesses. The group, composed mostly of lawmen, journalists and friends, waited nervously. Horn looked at Sheriff Ed Smalley and commented dryly, "Ed, that's the sickest looking lot of damned sheriffs I ever seen."

While Horn stood patiently, the straps that bound his arms and legs were fastened. He gazed off towards the distant mountains while two close friends, Charlie and Frank Irwin, sang a doleful, but popular tune of the day, "Life is Like a Mountain Railroad," then listened quietly while an elderly Episcopal clergyman prayed for his soul. Finally, the condemned man was asked if he would care to make any final remarks. "No," was the crisp reply. The conventional noose with its 13 wraps was placed over Horn's head. The knot was adjusted in such a way as to break his neck when his body dropped through the trapdoor. When the black hood was placed over his head, Horn concealed whatever emotion he might have felt. No one in the crowd was more composed than he on that fateful morning. Tom Horn was facing death in the same manner he faced life— without a trace of fear.

A few seconds later, the trap door fell open with a crash and the body of Tom Horn plunged through the opening. The massive hangman's knot slammed against the side of Horn's head knocking him unconscious. Horn remained suspended for 17 minutes before attending physicians pronounced him dead.

Tom Horn had gone to the grave unconfessed—accused and convicted of a crime he didn't commit.

Tom Horn's remarkable life began in Scotland, Missouri, in 1861. Almost from the beginning, the restless youth was filled with wanderlust. At 14 he ran away from home and headed for the "great and glowing West." From that time on, his life reads like something out of a Louis L'Amour or Zane Grey novel. No Hollywood script writer could conjure a more suitable, hard-riding hero. Horn was a strapping, broad-shouldered man who stood well over six feet tall. Lean and muscular, he was quite handsome with a couple of exceptions: a prominent nose, and, contrasting with his quiet, mild manner, his small and penetrating eyes. It was said Horn could "stare a hole straight through you."

He arrived in Arizona in 1875, working as a teamster, driving a stage between Santa Fe and Prescott. For the next 15 years Tom Horn would call Arizona home.

The legend of Tom Horn began at 16 years of age, when he went to work as an apprentice for the famed army scout Al Sieber. From Sieber and the Apaches whom he befriended and campaigned with, the youth learned the ways of survival on the harsh frontier where men and the environment asked no quarter and gave none. Horn learned another skill that would benefit him in another trade long after the Apache Wars had ended. The crafty scout and his Apaches taught the youth how to stalk an adversary. It was later said, Horn could "track bees in a blizzard."

Many years later Sieber wrote of his former protege, "a more faithful or better worker or a more honorable man, I never met in my life."

For the next several years, Horn served as packer, government scout, interpreter and chief of scouts for Generals George Crook and Nelson Miles. During periodic lulls in the Apache campaigns, Horn scoured Arizona's rich mountainous country for a glory hole. When silver was discovered at Tombstone in 1877, he was among the first to arrive at the new mining camp.

Horn was in on the action at the Battle of Big Dry Wash on the Mogollon Rim in the summer of 1882, the last major clash between the army and the Apaches inside the borders of Arizona. A year later, he went into Mexco as a packer during General Crook's famous Sierra Madre Campaign. Much of the success of this arduous trek into the Apaches' mountainous sanctuary was due to the ability of the pack trains to sustain the soldiers and scouts for prolonged periods of time.

During the Apache campaign of 1885-86 Horn was promoted to chief of scouts. He was in Mexico again in pursuit of Apache renegades in January, 1886, with Captain Emmett Crawford and a company of Apache scouts, when the officer was treacherously shot and killed by a force of Mexican militia. Horn's scouts had attacked Geronimo's camp and defeated the wily renegade when a large body of *soldados* suddenly appeared and opened fire. Horn and Crawford ran into the open and called upon the Mexicans to cease firing. Moments later, several shots rang out. Horn was hit in the arm and Crawford in the head. The gallant captain died a few days later without regaining consciousness.

The murder of one of Crook's most prominent field commanders caused an international incident, but except for a few angry exchanges between embassies, nothing ever came of it. An interesting sidelight to the faceoff occurred when Geronimo offered to side with the government scouts and "rub out" the Mexican force. Later, Horn played a prominent role in bringing Geronimos's band to the famous parley with General Crook at Canon de los Embudos. Unfortunately, some American whiskey peddlers sneaked into the chieftain's camp and convinced the Apaches they should continue their restive ways. (Certain business interests were reaping a harvest of profits from the war and didn't want to see it end.)

The renegade Apaches slipped off during the night, leaving General Crook in an embarrassing position. He was relieved of his command for putting what some Washington officials called "too much trust in the Apaches," and replaced by General Nelson Miles. One of Miles first acts was to disband the Apache scouts. This put Horn out of a job temporarily. His talents as an interpreter, scout, and packer made him too valuable to keep on the sidelines for long. Soon, Miles put him back on the government payroll and the scout played an integral part in the final subjugation of Geronimo in September, 1886. Officers who had served with the scout considered him to be both honorable and brave. Years later, during his trial, his opponents would portray him as a conspirator among the renegades.

Following the conclusion of the Apache Wars, Tom Horn prospected and ranched in the Globe area. During this time he established a reputation as a champion-class calf roper. When the Pleasant Valley War or Graham-Tewksbury feud broke out in 1887, Horn found himself caught in the middle of the conflict. In his memoirs, Horn denies taking sides despite pressure from both factions. Others have said Horn was a participant. Certainly a man of his reputation would be much sought after.

During these years Horn was a deputy in Yavapai County under Buckey O'Neill and in Gila County with Glen Reynolds. During his tenure with the latter, one of Arizona's most famous murders occurred. One of Sieber's scouts called "Kid" (later Apache Kid) was arrested for murder after he took vengeance upon another Apache who killed his father. The Kid was following Apache custom whereby the oldest son vindicates the transgression. He and some friends made a run for it and in making their escape shot and wounded Al Sieber. A bullet shattered the old scout's leg, crippling him for life. The Kid and his gang were captured after a brief spree and sentenced to long terms at the Yuma Territorial Prison. Tom Horn was to be one of the escort guards for the long ride from Globe to the train station at Casa Grande before fate intervened.

Earlier, Horn had won a rodeo contest at Globe qualifying him for the Territorial Fair at Phoenix. The rodeo was held the same time the prisoners were to be taken to the train. Horn went to Phoenix and Sheriff Reynolds and deputy "Hunky Dory" Holmes left Globe with the prisoners. On the way to Casa Grande, the Kid and his gang plotted their escape. Neither Reynolds nor Holmes could savvy Apache lingo and were unaware of the scheme. Had Horn been present, it was likely he would have understood what the Apaches were saying and thwarted the escape. Reynolds and Holmes were both brutally murdered, something

Tom Horn portrait (left) and
prison photo (above)

Horn never forgot. The championship steer roping prize was of little consolation.

Tom Horn left Arizona in 1890 for Wyoming where he went to work as a range inspector with a commission as deputy U.S. Marshal. His talents as a tracker and gunman were much in demand during those turbulent times of range country feuds. The Pinkerton Detective Agency hired him to help solve a train robbery near Denver. Horn tracked the bandits several hundred miles, taking a notorious outlaw named "Peg Leg" McCoy singlehandedly.

He quit the agency soon after because he found the job too dull. The West was changing. More and more Horn became a man out of place and time.

When the war came with Spain in 1898, Tom Horn sought out his old friends in the military, Marion Maus, Henry Lawton, Leonard Wood and Nelson Miles and offered his services. He was commissioned Chief Packmaster for General William Shafter. In his new position, Horn skillfully managed to transport more than 500 pack mules to Cuba just prior to the battle of San Juan Hill. Horn's pack trains delivered much-needed supplies and ammunition for the military, especially the Rough Riders. Had Horn not accomplished this near-impossible task, there might not have been a Teddy Roosevelt-Rough Rider charge up that now-famous hill. Before the war's end, Tom Horn caught the fever and was sent back to a friend's ranch in Iron Mountain, Wyoming, to recuperate.

The range wars were going strong in Wyoming and Horn quickly found employment as a "regulator" for the large cattle interests. Again his unique talents as a tracker and gunman were much in demand. These were many-sided feuds—large cattlemen against small—sheepmen against cattlemen—politicians vs. politicians. Local politics played such a role in the courts that a cow thief caught red-handed usually got off lightly. Also, public sympathy was decidedly against big business and large cattle ranchers were considered big business. The big cattle ranches retaliated by hiring range detectives or regulators. These range detectives generally acted as judge, jury and executioner to cow thieves. The mere presence of a man like Horn was enough to strike fear in the heart of the toughest of men. It was said the ruthless Horn stalked his victim Apache-style for several days, sometimes waiting in the rain for hours for just the right shot. Horn's reputation was such that the suggestion to a suspected rustler that Horn was stalking him was enough to send the frightened man scurrying from the territory. In effect, the cunning regulator became the "rustler's bogyman." Through it all, Horn did nothing to discourage this kind of legend-making. On the contrary, he encouraged it. Killing is my "stock and trade" he would say mild-mannerly.

A brief feud broke out between two small ranch families, the Millers and the Nickells, when the latter began running sheep in the area. Since the Nickell's sheep were running on the Miller's range and Horn wasn't employed by either, he took no interest in the matter, When 13-year old Willie Nickell's body was found, circumstantial evidence indicated a Miller did the killing. However, the matter was dropped when not enough evidence could be gathered, and the case was added to the growing list of unsolved murders in the region.

U.S. Marshal Joe Lafors, himself a former range detective who would later gain fame for his relentless pursuit of Butch Cassidy and the Sundance Kid, became convinced that the killer of 13-year old Willie Nickell was Tom Horn. Horn was a temperate man when on a job but went on tremendous drinking bouts in between. Lafors caught Horn on a binge and tricked him into "confessing" to the crime. Lafors had concealed a deputy and a stenographer to eavesdrop in the next room while he swapped yarns with Horn. Lafors skillfully led Horn into a conversation about the Nickell's murder where implications and innuendos were made concerning Horn's role in which Horn seemingly confessed. The next day Tom Horn was placed under arrest for the murder of Willie Nickell.

The trial in Cheyenne was inundated with politics. Several members of the jury were men who had reason to hate Horn. He had recovered stolen cattle from their ranches. Newspapers in Denver and Cheyenne pictured Horn as a heinous murderer of children. Large ranchers feared Horn might reveal his employers. The most damaging testimony was the "confession" to Lafors. Throughout the trial and later Horn insisted the conversation with Lafors was a set up and the stenographer twisted facts and filled in the missing parts.

Still the odds were better than even that Horn would be found innocent. (The "confession" would be thrown out in today's courts, but was ruled admissible in the carnival atmosphere of Cheyenne in 1903.)

On October 25, 1902, the jury returned a verdict of guilty and Tom Horn was sentenced to hang. Thus began the long process of appeals.

Horn's attorneys searched vigorously for some kind of legal loophole to gain a new trial for their client. Horn grew restless in his cell and became determined to gain his freedom—one way or another. One plot to escape failed. On another attempt, Horn and a cellmate made a successful break, but were recaptured a few minutes later. These incidents did little to improve Horn's public image.

Glendolene Kimmell, a school teacher who had taught at the Miller-Nickell school and lived at times with both feuding families, made a courageous plea on Horn's behalf. Miss Kimmell testified that young Victor Miller confessed to her the Willie Nickell murder. Her testimony was discounted, however, because it was believed the pretty, young teacher was deeply infatuated with Horn.

On October 1, 1903, the State Supreme Court issued an opinion affirming the lower court's decision. Tom was scheduled to be executed on November 20, 1903.

During the final hectic days, Cheyenne took on a fervid atmosphere. The amount of alcohol consumed was awesome. Rumors of another escape ran rampant. Horn's friends added fuel to the fire by vowing to spring him. A machine gun was placed atop the county courthouse in case they decided to carry out their bold threat.

His last months had been occupied writing, in pencil, his memoirs which were released in book form the following year. The work was subtitled "A Vindication." It was really no vindication, but was instead, a history of his years spent in Arizona. Horn's experiences in Arizona were written from memory. Some of the details are inaccurate and misleading. There is also a bit of yarn spinning in the story. Still, Horn's history of the Apache Wars is one of the most important primary historical documents to come out of that period. He didn't "tell all" in the story, preferring to follow a strict code of loyalty to his employers. Horn went to the grave with lips sealed, a detail which, no doubt, adds to the enigma and romance of this western legend.

The hanging of Tom Horn ushered in a new period in American history—the closing of the frontier and the dawning of the 20th century—the old ways superseded by the new. Tom Horn was a product of the old—a misfit in the new.

The curtain rang down on the gunfighter era, passing into the realm of romance—and into the hands of novelists and mythmakers.

Tom Horn saw himself as the embodiment of a knight in dusty leather maintaining law and order as he defined it—by a means known as "Winchester litigation."

And, there were those who believed Tom Horn did not hang that November day in 1903, but instead, rode off into the "great and glowing west" from whence he came, in search of some new adventure.

ARIZONA RANGERS:
last of the Old West's hard-riding heroes

Arizona greeted the 20th century, a frontier Jekyll and Hyde. Towns like Phoenix and Tucson were growing up, becoming cosmopolitan, populated primarily by a citizenry that demanded respect for law and order. Meanwhile, in many outlying areas, the territory remained tied to the wild and woolly past. Lack of effective law enforcement, bad roads, rough terrain and proximity to the hundreds of almost unguarded miles along the Mexican border, made the place an ideal last refuge for rustlers and outlaws. The Cochise County war and the Pleasant Valley feud were recent memories, and with the building of the transcontinental railroad lines in the 1880's, train robbers were having a heyday. Between 1897 and 1900 there were six robberies on the Southern Pacific alone. Large, well-organized bands of bold rustlers openly defied the law, stealing cattle in broad daylight. Large ranchers had to hire extra riders to ride herd on the cattle and small outfits were going out of business. Payrolls for the mines were also being robbed on a regular basis.

Sometimes there was a mighty thin line between those sworn to uphold the law and those who broke the law. A good example was in September, 1899, when Wilcox constable Burt Alvord, with his deputy Billy Stiles, along with a couple of friends, robbed the Southern Pacific Railroad at Cochise Station, taking several thousand dollars in gold, silver, and jewelry in the heist. They were captured soon after and locked up at Tombstone but escaped and slipped across the border into Sonora.

The most serious problem affecting lawmen was they had no jurisdiction outside their respective counties. A large outcry, especially from mining and cattle interests, for a territorial police modeled after the noted Texas Rangers, began in the 1880's. Nothing much came of it until 1901, when the Arizonans finally decided they'd better clean up their act if statehood was to be achieved. The territory's colorful and sometimes exaggerated reputation as a sanctuary for con men, swindlers, rustlers, Apache renegades and other nefarious skallawags had caused a wave of

Arizona Rangers during the 1903 Morenci strike

negativism on the part of proper eastern politicians every time the question of statehood arose.

The territorial legislature succumbed to political pressure from mining and cattle interests in March, 1901, and passed a bill to raise a quasi-military company of rangers, consisting of 14 men, a captain, sergeant and 12 privates, all serving one year enlistments. Monthly pay ranged from $125 for the Captain, $75 for the sergeant and $55 for the privates. In addition, each man had to furnish his own rifle, six-shooter and horse. In a flamboyant display of generosity, the legislature awarded each ranger $1.50 per day to feed man and horse.

The territorial governor was given direct command over the rangers. This created political animosity from the start, since governors were appointed in Washington and were usually Republicans, while the legislatures were elected locally and the assembly was usually dominated by Democrats. Naturally, the legislators saw the force as Republican patronage, as well as the governor's private army.

During the next few years, the Arizona Rangers would be, at times, the darlings of the territorial press, while other times, editors cried out indignantly for their removal. Even though western writers, traditionally, have romanticized and idolized this band of hard-riding lawmen, the organization was destined to be controversial from the start.

Funding for the Rangers would be generated by a tax territory-wide. This created bad feelings, as not all the territory, especially the populous Maricopa County, had much need for a force of free-ranging, cowboy-lawmen and they resented sharing the tax burden.

In spite of this opposition, territorial governor Nathan Oakes Murphy was authorized to raise a territorial police force whose duties were to assist local law enforcement agencies, prevent train robberies and stop cattle rustling.

Murphy didn't have to look far for a suitable choice to ramrod the Rangers. The leading candidate was Burt Mossman, erstwhile superintendent of the famous Hashknife outfit.

Mossman's life story reads like something out of a Louis L'Amour western. He had a stocky build on a 5'8" frame and weighed 180 pounds. He was born in Illinois in 1867, the son of a Civil War hero, and was of Scotch-Irish stock. By 1882 he was working as a cowboy in New Mexico.

As a young cowboy, Mossman earned a reputation in New Mexico as a wild and restless youth with a hot temper who'd fight at the drop of a hat. In spite of these dubious virtues, the youngster was known as dependable and honest. He once walked 110 miles in 47 hours across a desert too dry for a horse, to deliver an important letter for his employer.

When he was 21, Mossman was made foreman of a ranch in New Mexico that ran 8,000 head of cattle. At 27, he was manager of a big outfit in Arizona's Bloody Basin. By the time he was 30, Mossman was superintendent of one of the biggest outfits in the west, the fabled Hashknife of northern Arizona.

It was at the Hashknife where Mossman gained his greatest notoriety up to that time. The eastern-armed outfit had been running as many as 60,000 head of cattle over two million acres. Gangs of rustlers, both in the employ of the company and those who had set up maverick factories on the fringe of the ranch, had been shipping out by the trainload cattle stolen from the ranch. The rustlers were so accomplished at their trade that in the 14 years before Mossman had arrived, there had not been one conviction. Up to that time, the rustlers had always been able to get a friend on the jury to disrupt things, resulting in a hung jury.

Mossman didn't waste time settling into his new role. His first day on the job, he captured three cattle thieves and tweaked the nose of Winslow's town bully. Next he fired 52 out of 84 Hashknife cowboys and installed trusted cowmen as wagon bosses. In a brief time, he had the Hashknife turning a profit. A prolonged drought followed by a great blizzard finished off the outfit in 1901, and the absentee owners decided to sell out. Despite the failure of the Hashknife, Mossman earned a reputation as a formidable foe of outlaws as well as being a smart, savvy businessman. When Governor Murphy got ready to choose the first Arizona Ranger captain, one name stood out above the rest—Burt Mossman, the man who tamed the Hashknife.

Mossman headed the Rangers from 1901 to 1902 and though the reign was brief, the force achieved its greatest successes. He selected his men carefully, dressed them as working cowboys, and had them operate in secrecy as undercover agents, hiring out for cattle outfits. The Rangers pinned on their badges only when an arrest was imminent.

The first big challenge occurred when the Rangers took the notorious Bill Smith gang after the rustlers moved their operation from New Mexico to the rugged White Mountains of eastern Arizona. After Ranger

Burt Mossman, superintendent of the Hashknife and first captain of the Arizona Rangers.

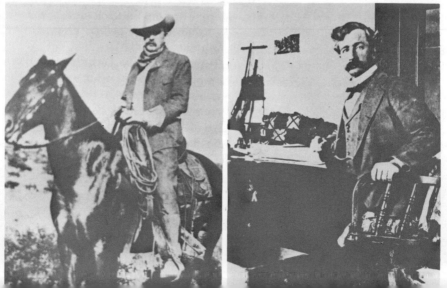

Carlos Tafoya was treacherously murdered by the gang leader, Mossman and his Rangers tracked and battled the gang, decimating their ranks until Smith pulled out for less dangerous environs. Soon after, they invaded the sanctuary of another den of thieves, the George Musgrove gang, capturing one of their leaders and a couple of gang members. Their leadership shattered and scattered, the gang left for other parts. Neither the Bill Smith gang nor the Musgrove bunch ever returned to Arizona. During their first year, the rangers put 125 major criminals behind bars, killing only one man in the line of duty.

Mossman's greatest personal achievement was his daring capture of one of the most notorious outlaws in the southwest, Augustin Chacon. Chacon, a Mexican citizen, once bragged to an officer he had killed no less than 15 gringos and 37 Mexicans. He had unwittingly escaped the gallows, just before he was to hang, by having a ladyfriend use her feminine charm to lure the guard away from his post. During the amorous encounter, Chacon freed himself with a file smuggled in by his resourceful paramour, and headed for the Mexican border. Chacon eluded capture by both Mexico and the U.S. for five years, and his capture became an obsession to Mossman. The ranger captain angled a deal with Burt Alvord and Billy Stiles, two notorious outlaws, wanted for the previously mentioned Cochise train robbery, to recapture Chacon. Mossman knew that Alvord and Stiles were acquainted with the fugitive and was able to persuade them to lead him to Chacon in exchange for testimony on their behalf when the two turned themselves in to authorities.

Captain Mossman's guise was to pose as an outlaw on the run. He hoped to get close enough to the wily Chacon to get the drop on him. True to their promise, Alvord and Stiles led Mossman to Chacon's hideout in Mexico, where the Ranger made a daring, if illegal, capture and returned the fugitive to Arizona where he was subsequently hung for his crimes.

The capture of Chacon was Mossman's "last hurrah" as ranger captain. Despite the expiration of his one-year enlistment, he might have remained on the force, except that politics intervened. Teddy Roosevelt, as president, created a Rough Rider dynasty when he appointed fellow Rough Rider Colonel Alexander Brodie, as territorial governor of Arizona, and Brodie, in turn, appointed a Rough Rider buddy, Tom Rynning, as new captain of the Rangers. Mossman retired from law enforcement and began a long and illustrious career as a cattleman.

Tom Rynning served as captain from 1902 until 1907. During those years, the size of the force grew to 26 men and moved its headquarters from Bisbee to the new border town of Douglas, which quickly established a reputation as one of the toughest towns along the Mexican border.

Under Rynning's regime, the Rangers took on a new look. No longer cloaked in anonymity, they pinned silver stars on their vests. Also, the Rangers spent less time battling rustler gangs and more time responding to corporate interests as strikebreakers.

The first such event occurred in 1903, when the entire Ranger force was called out to put down a strike in Morenci. Threats of violence came when the eight-hour work law went into effect in Arizona, and the mining companies tried to cut wages from $2.50 a day to $2.00. Some 1,500 miners walked off the job to protest the company's action. The company insisted they would be wrecked financially if they continued to pay on a 10-hour scale for eight hours work. Workers found this difficult to believe when reports showed that the company had mined seven million pounds of copper in 1897, and had increased production to more than eighteen million pounds of the red metal just five years later. Company ledgers also showed huge profits during the period.

Before the strife was over and the strike broken, the National Guard and units from the U.S. Army had joined the fracas. Tension was high and violence was likely following an incident where Rangers arrested, but didn't charge, the strike leader. Fate and Mother Nature intervened at this point when a tremendous cloudburst inundated Clifton and Morenci, killing more than a score and wiping out the residential area where most of the miners lived. In reality, the downpour, not the Rangers, Guard or Army, quelled the Morenci strike.

The use of Rangers by Rynning as strikebreakers three years later, was a more serious matter. This time the strike was at the Greene Copper Mines in Cananea, Mexico. In this case, Mexican miners were striking because their American counterparts were given a raise in pay. Norte Americanos were already being paid substantially more for doing the same work, so the Mexicans walked off the job. When rumors of violence against Americans in Cananea reached Bisbee, several hundred locals armed themselves and prepared to march on Mexico. Captain Rynning arrived in time to organize the mob into a loose military organization with his Rangers acting as company commanders. Rynning persuaded the Mexican governor of Sonora to allow him and his army of citizens to cross into Mexico as an unorganized mob. Once across the line, they were sworn in by the governor as "Mexican volunteers" enlisted to aid the beleaguered town of Cananea. Rynning was appointed Colonel and seven Rangers present were made officers. They boarded the Cananea, Yaqui River Railroad and steamed into the strife-torn Mexican mining community. Rynning deployed his volunteers, taking up strategic positions on the hills above the town. The situation almost got out of control when Mexican Rurales arrived and squared off against Rynning's force. At this point, seeing the riot under control, Rynning wisely returned his "army" to Arizona.

Under normal circumstances, Rynning would have been fired and there would have been serious diplomatic developments between the U.S. and Mexico. However, the jingoistic press had a heyday with the affair and Rynning was too big a hero to dismiss. Even President Roosevelt got into the act, praising his former Rough Rider officer. "Tom's all right, isn't he?" Teddy beamed. Rynning left the Rangers soon after to become superintendent of the Yuma Territorial Prison, a promotion, in part, for his Mexican adventure.

Rynning's escapade into Mexico put a strain on what had been cordial relations established between Mossman and Colonel Emilio Kosterlitzky of the Rurales. Up to that time there had been an informal cooperative agreement between the two law enforcement agencies, whereby outlaws could be pursued across the line, or a man wanted by the Rangers who was hiding out in Mexico, would be picked up by Kosterlitzky and handed over to the Rangers without any diplomatic red tape. The agreement had worked to the advantage of both sides many times in apprehending wanted men. During the first ten years of the 20th century, the ruthless Rurales and the Rangers, who were sometimes accused of the same proclivities, maintained order along the border.

Kosterlitzky was a formidable officer whose name struck terror in the hearts of border bandits. He was also one of the most unusual and remarkable men to appear on the southwest borderlands. He was a former Russian Naval Cadet who jumped ship and joined the Mexican Cavalry, working his way up through the ranks until he was top man in the Rurales. He was a brilliant man, fluent in nine languages, including German, who would later move to Los Angeles where he served in the U.S. Intelligence against the German espionage agents in this country during WW1.

The last Ranger captain was Harry Wheeler, the only leader to work his way through the ranks. Wheeler, a former Rough Rider, who stood only 5'4", joined the force in 1904 as a private, becoming a sergeant, lieutenant and finally replacing Rynning in 1907. The colorful Wheeler was by far the shootin'est of the Ranger captains. In his first four years with the Rangers, he killed four men. This is noteworthy in view of the fact that the Rangers overall killed few men in their eight-year career. One of Wheeler's victims died during a holdup at the Palace Saloon in Tucson in a scene that served as fodder for countless Hollywood thrillers. The Ranger walked through the swinging doors just as the outlaw was lining the patrons up against the wall. The outlaw turned and fired as Wheeler reached for his revolver. When the smoke had cleared, the outlaw lay dead with two bullets in him. Wheeler wasn't hit in the exchange.

Harry Wheeler was a bold, fearless type who epitomized some of the better-known lawmen of an earlier time, many of whom were more myth than reality. Famed lawman Jeff Milton called him the best man with a gun he'd ever seen, and he'd seen the best, including the legendary John Wesley Hardin.

Among all Wheeler's many altercations with desperadoes there was one he would likely have chosen to forget, but history writers won't because it has to be one of the most unusual shootouts in Southwest History. It all happened early one morning in Benson in 1906, when the Ranger attempted to arrest a man named J.A. Tracy. Tracy drew his gun,

*Harry Wheeler: Rough Rider,
Arizona Ranger captain, and
sheriff of Cochise County. (Arizona
Historical Foundation: Barry
Goldwater Photo Collection)*

quickly fired four shots, each one missing its target. Wheeler, meanwhile, pulled his revolver and shot Tracy four times. Tracy dropped his arm to his side, saying "I'm all in, my gun is empty." Wheeler unwittingly dropped his pistol on the ground and walked towards the stricken man; whereupon Tracy raised his gun and fired twice more, hitting the Ranger in the thigh and foot. In desperation, Wheeler reached down and grabbed a handful of rocks and started hurling them at his adversary. Tracy, mortally wounded, fell to the ground, literally stoned. In the aftermath, both men lying side by side on the ground, shook hands as each wished the other well. Such gunfights are found only in the real West, not being believable enough for the sagebrush saviors of the silver screen.

During much of their controversial existence, the Rangers were accused of vindictiveness against anyone who crossed them. This was carried to the extreme during Rynning's regime. A good example was the arrest of Graham County deputy sheriff Lee Hobbs on a murder charge. Bad feelings had existed between a couple of Rangers and Hobbs, when the former arrested 69 Hispanics accused of looting whiskey from a store, following a flood. Hobbs, claiming he had no room in his flooded jail, released them on their own recognizance (nearly all were local family men), something that angered the two Rangers. Later, all 69 appeared for their hearing and charges were dismissed against all but one. The Rangers, in what appears to be an act of vengeance, arrested Hobbs for an alleged murder that was supposed to have taken place three years previously on a ship in the South Pacific.

Hobbs had not even been out of Arizona during that time and easily proved his innocence. The press coverage of the event stirred a great deal of anger throughout Arizona and led to a rousing call for disbanding the force.

The well-known Jeff Kidder's murder is another case in point. Kidder had received much bad press for some unnecessary pistol-whipping and other arrogant acts, especially against Hispanics. One night, Kidder crossed the border at Naco, against orders, had a few drinks, got into a brawl with local police and was shot to death. This matter still generates an emotional response to this day among afficionados of borderland history.

Ranger applicants were expected to be fearless, possessing flair for bravado. Facing down a desperate outlaw in some lurid bordertown or taking the fight to a superior force of rustlers was all in a day's work. It was not a job for the meek or fainthearted. Still, some Rangers had a proclivity towards being blustery and swashbuckling and these acts received wide press coverage and undid much of the good accomplished by the force.

In 1908, the Rangers invaded the lair of the Arnett gang, the last of the large bands of rustlers to invade Arizona. The fight ended when Captain Wheeler killed chieftain George Arnett in a gunfight. The rest of the gang scattered for parts unknown.

Partisan politics, not ruthless outlaw gangs, brought about the demise of the Rangers in March, 1909. The previous year, an overwhelming number of Democrats had been elected to the legislature and they sought to reduce the governor's power. The Rangers were accused of having been too actively supporting Republican candidates during the campaign of 1908. Opponents also charged that the Rangers were an unnecessary arm of the governor. Other charges included making too many petty arrests that could have been easily handled, and at less expense, by local agencies.

There was, no doubt, much resentment by local lawmen who felt usurped by the prestigious force of independent, mobile Rangers, and they pressured legislators to disband the group. Professional jealousy on the part of both competent and inept local peace officers wasn't the only reason for animosity. The truth was, many of these county and city lawmen were in cahoots with the outlaw gangs. A disappointed Harry Wheeler later wrote: "I believe the greatest factor ... was the active opposition and bitter hatred of the sheriffs ... especially Cochise, Pima, Santa Cruz, Gila, Pinal and Graham Counties. These men all had friends in the legislature."

The Rangers were a tough, hard-riding outfit. They had to be to survive as some of the most hardbitten, riff-raff in the West hung out along the Mexican border. Their achievements, especially the relentless pursuit of the felonious criminal elements, far outshines the unfortunate incidents when a few of their numbers placed themselves above the law. The old west was passing. The buffalo had vanished, trail dust had settled and the false-front saloons were rapidly disappearing. Like the others, the Rangers were passing, from reality on into the realm of romance. They, too, had outlived their usefulness to a society that was looking ahead to statehood and the 20th century, a society that wanted no vexing reminders of the recent raucous past.

The POWER BROTHERS:
The Old West's last gunfight

Thomas Jefferson Power felt the cold chill in his bones on that February morning in 1918 as he rolled out of his blankets and walked barefoot across the wooden plank floor to the fireplace. A brief winter storm had left a light layer of snow outside the log cabin nestled in the rugged, remote Galiuro Mountains. "Old Jeff" as everybody around that part of Arizona called him, rustled up a few sticks of wood and started a fire. On the far side of the small cabin one of his sons, John, was lazily pulling himself out of bed. Another, Tom Jr., waited under his blankets for the small cabin to warm. Back in one corner, a family friend and ex-army scout, Tom Sisson snored peacefully. John yawned and stretched his stocky frame, lit a coal oil lamp and threw a few sticks of wood in a cast iron cook stove and started another fire.

It started out as just another typical early morning get up, when an unusual noise outside startled the occupants. One of the belled mares thundered across the opening in front of the cabin. The bell hanging around its neck clattered loudly as the horse ran by. Old Jeff, who had reached for his trousers, grabbed his rifle instead. Thinking a cougar might have been lurking about, he opened the cabin door and looked out. A heavy fog shrouded the long canyon, making it impossible to see more than just a few feet.

Suddenly, a voice cried out from the darkness, "Throw up your hands, throw up your hands!" Jeff dropped the rifle and started to raise his arms when three shots rang out. The old man, framed against the lighted doorway, clutched his chest and collapsed in front of the cabin.

John Power, still in his long underwear, rushed to the doorway and reached for his father. Four more shots tore through the cabin. One of the bullets hit an old saddle hanging on the wall, peppering his face with fragments of wood and leather. Another tore a piece of flesh off the bridge of his nose. Tom Jr. sprang from his bed at the first sound of gunfire and grabbed his rifle. He moved in front of a window just as a third bullet shattered the glass throwing slivers into his left eye. The fourth bullet whined by his head and buried itself in the cabin wall. John ran back to his bunk, grabbed his rifle and returned to the door. He pumped two quick shots into the darkness on the left then turned and fired two more to the right. Tom was stunned momentarily, the pain in his left eye caused the right one to fill with water. He wiped the eye on the sleeve of his long underwear and moved towards the window on the south end. A shadowy figure appeared outside. He raised his rifle and fired. The figure slumped to the ground. There were no more shots from outside the cabin—only a deathly silence in the pre-dawn darkness.

Thus ended one of the most furious gunfights in Arizona history. In the span of a few seconds, four men lay dead on the ground, including the sheriff of Graham County and two of his deputies. For weeks, the shootings and the great pursuit that followed dominated the front page of tabloids, usurping even the war news from the Western Front. Other effects were more far-reaching. As a result of the shootout, Arizona would reinstate capital punishment.

The whole story of what really happened that morning of February 10, 1918, will never be known. There are many versions and opinions. Supposedly, the posse went up there to arrest John and Tom Power for draft evasion. Some say there was bad blood between one of the deputies, Kane Wootan, and the Power family long before the fight. The Power boys always insisted that the Wootan family wanted to take over their gold mine in Rattlesnake Canyon. Lee Soloman, who knew both Kane Wootan and the Power family well, testified that Wootan had boasted that he was going into the Power's place and "shoot the hell out of them! And from there, I'll be elected sheriff of Graham County." Others said that the Power family's presence was resented by the tightly-knit Mormon community and the locals took pleasure in harassing the scragly appearing hillbillies ever since their arrival from New Mexico sometime earlier. The posse that surrounded the Power cabin that Sunday morning allegedly had warrants for the arrest of John and Tom Jr. for failing to report for the draft. Why they opened fire on Old Jeff Power as he stood in the doorway of his cabin is a key point in the controversy. The Power brothers always maintained that the posse never identified themselves as such, and when their father was shot, they reacted by gunning down his assailants. They also insisted they were never told to report for the draft. It is worth noting that their version of the incident never varied throughout the trial and the long years of incarceration. The lone survivor from the posse, U.S. Deputy Marshal Frank Haynes, was approaching the cabin from behind and did not fire any shots nor did he see what happened. Haynes high-tailed it back to Klondyke to report that the Powers ambushed his posse.

Haynes' inflammatory remarks inspired Governor George W.P. Hunt to issue an official proclamation offering $1,000 reward for the arrest and conviction of "the murderers." The largest posse in Arizona history, some 3,000 civilians and military scoured the mountains and deserts along both sides of the U.S.-Mexican border for 29 days in the greatest manhunt in the state's history.

Our story begins sometime earlier, when old Jeff Power acquired the rights to a gold mine in Rattlesnake Canyon. The old man and his sons for a time eked out a living from the diggings and raised a few head of livestock. When the war came and young men were being called upon to register for the draft, it was said old Jeff refused to let his sons go. "Let Europe fight her own wars," he protested.

He'd seen enough tragedy for one lifetime. His mother had been killed in a riding accident. He lost his wife when an adobe roof collapsed on her.

The Power cabin where the shootout took place

He became even more embittered when one son, Bud, ran away and joined the Army. His other two boys, John and Tom remained and did not register for the draft. His young daughter Olla May had died recently in a mysterious mishap. The Power family always maintained she had died of food poisoning, yet there were indications her neck had been broken. A reason given for the presence of the county sheriff (McBride) and his chief deputy (Kempton) was to look into the circumstances surrounding Olla May's death.

On February 9, 1918, U.S. Deputy Marshal Frank Haynes, Graham County Sheriff Frank McBride, along with Chief Deputy Martin Kempton, left by automobile from a garage in Pima, apparently with warrants for the arrest of John and Tom Power for refusing to register for the draft. Witnesses later testified that the officers had been drinking bootleg whiskey and when told, "they'd better not go up there drinking," one replied, they didn't intend to bring back any prisoners. The officers drove southwest through the pass that separates the Graham and Santa Teresa Mountains to Klondyke, near Aravaipa Canyon, where they picked up a fourth member, Thomas K. "Kane" Wootan, and exchanged the auto for horses.

* * *

The Galiuros are a rugged, brawny range of mountains, some 50 miles long, that separate the Aravaipa valley from the valley of the San Pedro.

The country, laden with steep-sided canyons, and lofty pinnacles, is some of the most remote in Arizona. During the Apache wars, it was a favorite haunt of Geronimo. It was in one of these canyons that the Power family and Sisson lived. Kane Wootan, the only man in the posse who had been to the cabin, acted as guide.

The posse arrived at the entrance of Kielberg Canyon on the evening of February 9, and decided to wait for morning. A light snow fell throughout the night. Before dawn, the posse mounted and rode to within 75 yards of the cabin. There was an ominous stillness in the air as the four men dismounted and walked towards the dwelling.

Wootan and Kempton picked up a trail leading from the west and south. Haynes and McBride approached the cabin from the north.

Suddenly one of the possemen spooked a belled mare in the open corral. She galloped towards the front of the cabin, the bell tolling the alarm.

The noise made by the frightened horse had aroused the occupants inside. Old Jeff, clad in a pair of long-handled underwear and boots, grabbed his Winchester and stepped through the door. A voice shouted, "Throw up your hands," followed by the sound of rifle fire.

Kane Wootan could just barely see the outline of the old man when he called out. In an instant, he fired, dropping the elder Power in the doorway. He then turned and fired through the window, shattering the glass. Out of the corner of his eye, Martin Kempton saw a figure appear in the doorway with a rifle. Before he could react, the figure fired two quick shots. Kempton saw the flash of fire and felt the shock as the bullet struck him. He dropped his rifle, shuddered, then stumbled to the ground. The man in the doorway then fired twice in the opposite direction and another shadowy figure staggered, then fell. Kane Wootan moved towards a window at the south end of the cabin. Just as he started to level his rifle through the window another flash of fire, then the jarring impact of a rifle bullet knocked him down.

U.S. Deputy Frank Haynes did not see the action at the front of the cabin. He was coming up from behind, heard "two or three" shots and saw Jeff Power fall. He then saw Sheriff McBride lying on his back and decided he wanted no further part of the gunfight. He lit out for Klondyke without knowning that Kempton and Wootan were also dead.

The battle had lasted only three minutes. Another man, Tom Sisson, who worked for the Powers as a ranch hand, weathered the storm by hiding under the bed.

In the grim aftermath of the battle, the boys were confused and angry. They carried their dad inside the cabin and tried to lay him on his bed, but the old man got up, took a few staggering steps outside the cabin, then said, "This is as far as I want to go," then fell to the ground. They took guns and ammunition from the slain men and rode to the camp of a neighbor, Jay Murdock. John and Tom knew the old man was dying and couldn't be helped and they also knew that a posse would arrive shortly. Tom asked Murdock if he would ride over to the cabin and look after his dad. Tom later wrote that the three men originally planned to surrender to Pima County Sheriff Rye Miles. Miles was a friend of their father's and they figured he'd treat them fairly. They rode across the mountains to the hamlet of Reddington where they met a cowboy who told them the posses were not going to bring them in alive. Tom Sisson, fearing for his life, rode along with the Powers. Instead of riding to Tucson, as planned, they turned south towards the Dragoon Mountains and from there east to the Chiricahua Mountains. Most of the time they kept to the high mountain trails and from that vantage point, watched the posses scouring the valleys below. Traveling by night and holing up by day, they crossed into New Mexico near the town of Rodeo and from there into Mexico. Both John and Tom were suffering from wounds inflicted in the fight. (Each would lose the sight of his left eye.) Fatigue from the weary ordeal was beginning to take its toll.

It has been called Arizona's greatest manhunt. The patriotic war fever, along with local prominence of the slain lawmen, generated a great deal of emotion. The newspapers called them draft dodgers and Governor Hunt's official proclamation referred to them as murderers, which no doubt did much to spark the public fire. Three thousand soldiers and civilians joined the chase.

An aerial search might have aided the posses; however, the nearest aeroplane was sitting in El Paso with a flat tire.

The days stretched into weeks as weary possemen and cavalry searched for the "boys." Reports continued to come forth announcing their "imminent capture." Still they eluded their pursuers.

When a cavalry patrol finally caught up with the trio a few miles below the border in Mexico, they were too weak from hunger and thirst to resist or run any further and surrendered without offering any resistance. The prisoners were turned over to civilian authorities only after being given written promises saying they would not be harmed. They were taken to the county jail at Safford and put on public display. It was said people lined up for blocks to catch a glimpse of the notorious trio.

There was no chance of the boys getting the death penalty. Capital punishment had been rescinded in Arizona two years earlier. However, there was talk in Graham County of lynching the three, as it was the only way that "justice would be done." Chance for an impartial trial in Safford was remote at best, so the case was moved to Clifton in Greenlee County. During the seven-day trial, the prosecution insisted that the posse had been ambushed while trying to arrest the Power brothers on charges of draft evasion.

The star witness for the prosecution, Marshal Frank Haynes, admitted that it was so dark, "that you couldn't tell a man from a tree stump at thirty yards." He was behind the cabin and saw none of the action. The Power brothers testified they did not know they had been drafted, and that they never received any official notification to report for duty. If an ambush had been set, they asked, then why were they all still in their underwear? And why did they not remove the windows and cut portholes in the wall for rifles? They claimed the posse never identified themselves as lawmen. "They weren't trying to arrest us. You'd fight back, too, wouldn't you, if they shot down your Pa," John insisted throughout the trial and long afterward.

The slain lawmen were all well-known figures in Graham County. They left behind three widows and 19 children, certainly one of the most unfortunate legacies of the drama. Old Jeff Power's body was tossed into a prospector's hole near the mine and buried. An examination of the bullet hole would have revealed whether or not he was trying to surrender or shoot it out.

The most damaging testimony was given by Jay Murdock who said the boys boasted they would kill anybody who came after them. Frank Haynes, who was there, but did not see the killings, changed his story several times. Interestingly, no record of federal draft charges has ever been found and transcripts from the trial "disappeared" from the Graham County courthouse several years ago. All three were given life sentences. It was not surprising, as they had been previously tried and convicted in the media and by the public before they ever entered the courthouse.

The public outcry was great. Not against the guilty verdict, but that the boys were not hung. A year later, the death penalty was reinstated by initiative petition, a direct result of the shoot-out in the Galiuro mountains.

The trio entered the prison at Florence on May 22, 1918. Tom was 26, John 23 and Sisson was 47. They remained behind bars for more than 34 years before being given a clemency hearing. Still, the boys continued to protest their innocence. The hearing came in December, 1952. Tom and John came well-prepared to defend themselves, not to apologize for their actions. But old hatreds die hard. The embittered survivors of the slain officers successfully blocked their parole applications. The boys declared that they were "railroaded" by the judge and jury and never really got a chance to present their case. Tom Sisson died behind prison walls five years later, leaving $10,000 he had saved from his army pension to John. The Powers always maintained Sisson had not taken part in the fight. Many Arizona legends have been created about the ex-army scout telling how he skillfully led the boys through secret canyons and defiles from his Apache war days. Tom Power said later the only time they followed Sisson's directions they got lost.

But, attitudes change over the years, and new publicity in the case aroused a new wave of public interest in seeking justice for the Power

John and Tom Power as they appeared when they entered prison in May, 1918

brothers. By 1960, the boys had served 42 years behind bars, longer than any other in history of Arizona. The average term for a "lifer" was only seven years. The newspapers which had played such a prominent role in the outcry against them in 1918 now began to muster support for the two survivors. Don Dedera, at the time, a noted columnist for the *Arizona Republic* rallied behind their case. He began a persistent campaign to gain freedom for the two and didn't let up until the brothers were given another clemency hearing.

The second hearing in 42 years came on April 20, 1960. Once more they were allowed to make their plea. Once again they came prepared to make a case for themselves. In 42 years, they had never admitted guilt for their actions. The surviving families were back again to block parole. The attorney opposing parole expressed fear for the survivors of the slain lawmen should the brothers be released. Several people, including three former wardens, spoke out in behalf of the brothers. It began to look like the brothers would be denied parole once more when, in a dramatic moment, former warden Lorenzo Wright jumped to his feet and admonished the brothers for never having expressed remorse for the killings.

Wright looked towards the group who opposed the parole and said: "I spoke for these boys, and you are right when you say they have not shown any forgiveness . . . If they aren't men enough to ask forgiveness and to forgive . . . to walk over to the widows of those men . . . then I withdraw my support." The courtroom became deathly quiet as he turned slowly towards Tom and John. The two brothers, heads bowed, stared quietly at the floor.

"Are you men enough," he shouted. There was silence for a moment, then Tom looked up and said softly, "Yes, we are."

Tom stood up and faced the audience, many of whom were close relatives of the slain lawmen. His voice choked with emotion. "We've got nothing against anybody. There is no hatred. We're not acquainted with any of the families. We didn't know any of the men except Wootan. We're sorry. We would like to be forgiven." He looked down at the floor once again, his voice trailing off, "It was out of control—what happened 42 years ago. We're sorry."

Then it was John's turn. He rose but kept his head bowed. He spoke softly. "We're sorry—we beg forgiveness."

Seldom has there been such an emotional eruption as was seen that day. Amidst applause, foot stomping and shouting, the Power brothers, at long last, had gained their freedom.

After their release, the boys split up for awhile. Tom, now 72, went to Prescott where he worked on a ranch. John, 70, went to Silver City, New Mexico, where he prospected for gold and worked on a cow ranch. In his spare time, he made ornate silver bridles and bits, a skill he had acquired while behind prison bars.

Following their release, they asked for a full pardon, and reinstatment of their civil rights. "We want to vote once before we die," old Tom said. After several delays, they were pardoned in 1969. On September 8, 1970, they cast their ballots and three days later, on John's 79th birthday, Tom passed away.

After Tom's death, John went back to the old mine for a time, then moved to Klondyke where he lived out the rest of his life, dying on April 5, 1976.

The old cabin, nestled in Kielberg Canyon, remains. This writer rode in there three years ago to have a look around. The roof is sagging, part of the chimney has fallen, the walls are weathered and aged. It stands forlorn and silent, a grim monument to that snowy February morning back in 1918 when, for a brief moment, all hell broke loose, and changed forever the destinies not only of those involved, but cast an impact upon Arizona's judicial system that was far-reaching.   149

Tom Sisson as he appeared at age 55 in prison

GAIL GARDNER:
Arizona's "Poet Lariat"

On a cool summer afternoon during the year of our Bicentennial, a large crowd gathered in Payson for the Old Time Country Music Festival held each summer in that mountain community, nestled at the foot of Arizona's Mogollon Rim. A parade of musicians, ranging from country-rock to bluegrass to old-time fiddlers, entertained the throngs, many of whom had driven up from Phoenix to escape the summertime inferno. The audience ran the gamut of age. Tiny tots frolicked in front of the bandstand, young people sucked on cans of beer or pop and the old folks sat around between songs talking about the "good ole days." After the next-to-the-last act had finished, the announcer stepped up to the mike and announced, "and now ladies and gentlemen, Arizona's 'Poet Lariat,' —Gail Gardner."

From out of the crowd stepped a wiry-framed old cowboy with a patch over one eye. He walked with a bowed back on legs shaped like horse collars. His face was full of freckles and sun spots from years spent in the out-of-doors and his grin was effortless. He climbed the stairs to the platform with the help of a couple of friends, took hold of the mike with one hand, pushed his hat back with the other, cast his good eye over the crowd and flashed a wry grin. "I don't use any accompaniment when I sing," he said, "for I've found that the guitar or piano is always off key from my singing." With a wink and another grin, he belted out his doggerel verse masterpiece:

> "Way up high in the Sierry Petes, where the yeller pines grow tall, Old Sandy Bob an' Buster Jig, had a rodeer ramp last fall . . ."

The audience that unforgettable afternoon was given a rare treat. There aren't many real living legends left in the world today. To those who carry fond memories of those "thrilling days of yesteryear," Gail Gardner is that—a living legend. His lyrics have been sung by singers of cowboy songs in the most remote cow camps to the top stars of country music.

It all began back in the early 1900's when Gail and Bob Heckle were running a "greasy sack" outfit in the Sierra Prieta Mountains outside of Prescott. These mountains were known locally as the "Sierry Petes." An old prospector had given them that dubbing some time before the name stuck.

> "Oh, they taken their horses and runnin' irons,
> And maybe a dawg or two,
> An' they 'lowed they'd brand all the long-yered calves
> That come within their view.
> An' any old doggie that flapped long yeres,
> An' didn't bush up by day,
> Got his long yeres whittled an' his old hide scorched,
> In a most artistic way."

In the song, Sandy Bob is Bob Heckle. He is also an uncle of country music star, Marty Robbins. Buster Jig is Gail. He picked up that moniker from his father's initials. His father, James I. Gardner, ran a local general merchandise store and his son Gail was called "Buster J.I.G."

There have been many misinterpretations of Gail's lyrics—mostly from singers and critics who, as Gail says, "didn't know which end of a cow gets up first."

One so-called expert surmised that the two cowboys had to be rustlers since they were carrying "runnin' irons."

"That wasn't the case at all," Gail says. "All cattlemen carried little short runnin' irons in their saddle bags when gathering cows. When we found a neighbor's cow and calf, we put the mama's brand on the calf same as they did when they found one of ours. We worked together that way. Besides, you couldn't carry a branding iron for every outfit in the country in your saddlebag anyway."

"Now one fine day ole' Sandy Bob,
He throwed his seago down,
"I'm sick of the smell of this burnin' hair
And I 'lows I'm a-goin' to town."
So they saddles up an' hits 'em a lope,
Fer it warn't no sight of a ride,
And them was the days when a Buckeroo
Could ile up his inside"

The song, written in doggerel verse and sung to the tune of "Polly Wolly Doodle" tells the true story of two boisterous, devil-may-care cowboys, Gail Gardner and Bob Heckle out on a "whizzer" in Prescott, back before prohibition, when there were some forty saloons lining famed Whiskey Row. Any cowboy worth his salt could start drinking at the Kentucky Bar and down a glass in each saloon, all the way to the Depot House Saloon down near the Santa Fe railroad tracks. Those two irrepressible cowboys had committed just about every vice that Prescott had to offer in those raucous days and were headed back to the Sierra Prietas. Along the way one suggested that the "devil gets after cowboys that act the way we'd been actin'." The other replied in the jaunty manner that typified the breed. "If the devil comes after me, I'll rope'm, mark and brand'm and tie a knot in his tail."

The incident was forgotten until several years later as Gail was going off to World War I. He was riding a Santa Fe train across Kansas when he chanced to see farmers walking among their muley cows afoot and he immediately thought of all the ornery critters he and his friend had choused in Arizona's mountain country. He sat down and on Santa Fe stationery he penned the words to the "Sierry Petes."

Oh, they starts her in at the Kaintucky Bar
At the head to Whiskey Row,
An, they winds up down by the Depot House,
Some forty drinks below.

Then they sets up and turns around,
And goes her the other way,
An' to tell you the Gawd-forsaken truth,
Them boys get stewed that day.

Gail's home on Mount Vernon Street is one of those quaint New England style houses that characterizes the classic, early Prescott architecture. It's full of a hundred years of Gardner family memorabilia. Gail was born there in 1892 and there he remains. The walls are decorated with books, old photographs, paintings, and Navajo rugs. Gail calls the decor, "early Fred Harvey." His western book collection is larger than most public libraries. The whole place lives and breathes Arizona history. In one corner of an upstairs room is an old, high-cantled silver saddle. In the closet hangs a fancy silver concho bridle with an elaborate eight-strand rawhide braided reins and romal.

As they was a-ridin' back to camp
A-packin' a pretty good load,
Who should they meet, but the Devil himself,
A-prancin' down the road.
Sez he, "You ornery cowboy skunks,
You'd better hunt yer holes,
For I've come up from Hell's Rim Rock,
To gather in yer souls."
Sez Sandy Bob, "Old Devil be damned,
We boys is kinda tight,
But you ain't a-goin' to gather no cowboy souls
'thout you has some kind of a fight."

Gail's main "treasure" in this rich cultural setting hangs over the fireplace in the living room. A large painting illustrates two happy-faced cowboys astraddle two skittish, wild-eyed cow ponies. Each has his rope in action. One has thrown a loop over the horns of a diabolical critter that can be none other than the Old Devil himself. He's taken up a dally around his saddle horn while his partner is about to drop a loop around the hind legs of the twisting, scowling Foul Fiend.

So Sandy Bob punched a hole in his rope
And he swang her straight and true,
He lapped it on to the Devil's horns,
An' he taken his dallies too.
Now Buster Jig was a riata man
With his gut-line coiled up neat,
So he shaken her out an' he built him a loop
An' he lassed the Devil's hind feet.

After the war, Gail showed his doggerel verses to a good friend named Billy Simon who put them to music. The two began singing the song at local rodeos. During these years, cow work became scarce and many cowboys got themselves employed as wranglers on dude ranches that were springing up all over Arizona.

The song became quite popular, especially among real working cowboys who recognized the lyrics as having been written by one of their own

Gail Gardner in the 1920's

Gail Gardner and his wife Delia

kind.

They took great pleasure and pride in the fact that it was a couple of cowboys that took the Devil in tow and with some 80 drinks under their belts at that.

Oh, they stretched him out, an' they tailed him down
While the irons was a-gettin' hot,
They cropped and swaller-forked his yeres,
Then they branded him up a lot.
They pruned him up with a de-hornin' saw
An' they knotted his tail fer a joke,
They then rid off and left him there,
Necked to a Black-Jack oak.
If you're ever up high in the Sierry Petes
An' you hear one Hell of a wail,
You'll know it's that Devil a-bellerin' around
About them knots in his tail.

Gail is a kind of an anomaly among old-time cowboys. He left his hometown of Prescott at the tender age of 16 for a year of prep school, thence on to Dartmouth where he was a star athlete. He graduated with a

Bachelor's Degree in Science in 1914 and remained in the east long enough to become romantically involved with a stunningly beautiful New York actress named Marie Carroll. He talked her into coming West and soon they announced their plans to wed. The engagement was announced at the South Rim of the Grand Canyon.

The wedding never took place. She wanted him to live in New York and he wanted no part of that. "That girl I wound up with," he says with a grin, "is worth a hundred New York actresses. You'd never see a one of them out herdin' cows." The girl he wound up with was a lovely, charming lady named Delia Gist.

Gail met Delia while she was visiting at the ranch of a neighbor. She was an Easterner—all the way from New Mexico, but had "wested" and lived in Skull Valley. Her father owned Angora goats and for a time Gail's friends referred to his lady friend as the goat girl. His friends figured he had fallen pretty hard for Delia when they heard he had given her his favorite horse. When Gail and Delia got married in 1924, they kidded him saying he only married her to get his horse back.

A few years later, Gail's friends pressured him into putting the words of his many poems into a book. When the book was ready to be published, Gail rode out to his friend J.R. Williams' ranch on Walnut Creek and asked the famed cartoonist-rancher if he would put one of his drawings on the cover. The book was to be titled the *Orejana Bull.* The title came from an incident that had occurred several years earlier when Gail had locked horns with a particularly intractable wild cow in the mountains near Copper Basin. An Orejana bull is an animal old enough to leave its mama but unbranded and not ear-marked.

Gail bought his first cow ranch in 1914. It was, in his terms, a "greasy sack" outfit, one that is a one or two-man operation. He kept that ranch for 20 years, but remained a cowman until 1960.

Most of the old-time cowboy song writers had their material pirated away because few bothered or even knew anything about copyright laws. Dude ranch cowboy warblers were prone to take any song they might have picked up along the way and if they did not know the author, or didn't care, they just attached their own name to it. One such pirate was a fella named Powder River Jack Lee. Gail tells the story this way. "Powder River Jack came into Arizona with his wife Kitty doin' Hawaii music but that didn't set too well with local folks, so they got themselves some western clothes and began singing cowboy songs. Pretty soon he puts out a songbook that includes *Sierry Petes* and Curley Fletcher's *Strawberry Roan* and claims them for his own."

Curley and Gail got pretty upset about this and decided to take legal action. "It was to no avail, however," Gail says. "Hell, that ole fool didn't even own the clothes he was wearin' and neither one of us wanted Kitty."

Selected Bibliography

Barnes, Will C. *Arizona Place Names*. Ed. Byrd Granger. Tucson: University of Arizona Press, 1960.

Blair, Robert. *Tales of the Superstitions*. Tempe: Arizona Historical Foundation, 1975.

Bourke, John. *On the Border with Crook*. (Reprint) Chicago: Rio Grande Press, 1962.

Boyer, Glenn. *The Suppressed Murder of Wyatt Earp*. San Antonio: Naylor, 1967.

Breakenridge, Billy. *Helldorado*. Boston: Houghton Mifflin Co., 1928.

Burns, Walter Noble. *Tombstone*. Garden City, N.Y.: Doubleday, 1927.

Cleland, Robert C. *This Reckless Breed of Men*. New York: Knopf, 1950.

Dunning, Charles and Edward Peplow. *Rock to Riches*. Phoenix: Southwest Publishing Co., 1959.

Earp, Josephine. *I Married Wyatt Earp*. Ed. Glenn Boyer. Tucson: University of Arizona Press, 1976.

Egerton, Kearney. *Somewhere Out There*. Glendale, Az.: Prickly Pear Press, 1974.

Ely, Sims. *The Lost Dutchman Mine*. New York: William Morrow, 1953.

Forrest, Earle R. *Arizona's Dark and Bloody Ground*. Caldwell, Idaho: Caxton Printers, 1936.

Goff, John, *George W.P. Hunt and His Arizona*. Pasadena: Socio-Technical Pub., 1973.

Gregg, Josiah. *Commerce of the Prairies*. Chicago: R.R. Donnelley Co., 1926

Heatwole, Thelma. *Ghost Towns and Historical Haunts in Arizona*. Phoenix: Golden West Publishers, 1981.

Herner, Charles. *The Arizona Rough Riders*. Tucson: University of Arizona Press, 1970.

Holmes, Kenneth. *Ewing Young: Master Trapper*. Portland: Binfords & Mort, 1967.

Horn, Tom. *The Life of Tom Horn: A Vindication*. (Reprint) New York: Crown Publishers, 1977.

Hunt, Frazier. *Cap Mossman: Last of the Great Cowmen*. New York: Hastings, 1951.

Lake, Stuart. *Wyatt Earp: Frontier Marshal*. Boston: Houghton Mifflin Co., 1931.

Lavender, David. *Bent's Fort*. Los Angeles: Cole-Holmquist, 1955.

Miller, Joseph, ed. *The Arizona Rangers*. New York: Hastings House, 1972.

Mitchell, John D. *Lost Mines of the Great Southwest*. Phoenix: The Journal Co., 1933.

Monaghan, James. *The Last of the Bad Men: The Legend of Tom Horn*. New York: The Bobbs-Merrill Co., 1946.

Myers, John Myers. *Tombstone, The Last Chance*. New York: E.P. Dutton, 1950.

Parsons, George. *The Private Journal of George Parsons*. (Reprint) Tombstone: The Epitaph, 1972.

Pattie, James O. *Narrative*. Ed. Timothy Flint. Cincinnati: John Wood, 1831.

Power, Tom with John Whitlatch. *Shootout at Dawn: An Arizona Tragedy*. Phoenix: Phoenix Books/Publishers, 1981.

Quebbeman, Francis. *Medicine in Territorial Arizona*. Tempe: Arizona Historical Foundation, 1966.

Rynning, Tom. *Gun Notches*. New York: Frederick A. Stokes, 1931.

Schmitt, JoAnn. *Fighting Editors*. San Antonio: Naylor, 1958.

Sherman, James. *Ghost Towns of Arizona*. Norman: University of Oklahoma Press, 1969.

Swanson, James and Tom Kollenborn. *Superstition Mountain: A Ride Through Time*. Phoenix: Arrowhead Press, 1981.

Thrapp, Dan. *The Conquest of Apacheria*. Norman: University of Oklahoma Press, 1967.

Turner, Alford E., ed. *The Earps Talk*. College Station, Texas: Creative Publishing Co., 1980.

Turner, Alford E., ed. *The OK Corral Inquest*. College Station, Texas: Creative Publishing Co., 1981.

Walker, Dale. *Death Was the Black Horse*. Austin: Madrona Press, 1975.

Waters, Frank. *The Earp Brothers of Tombstone*. New York: Clarkson N. Potter, 1960.

Weber, David. *The Taos Trappers: The Fur Trade in the Far Southwest*. Norman: University of Oklahoma Press, 1966.

Woody, Clara and Milton Schwartz. *Globe, Arizona*. Tucson: Arizona Historical Society, 1977.

Young, Otis. *Western Mining*. Norman: University of Oklahoma Press, 1970.

Order these titles from your book dealer

Visit the silver cities of Arizona's golden past. Come along to the towns whose heydays were once wild and wicked. See crumbling adobe walls, old mines, cemeteries, cabins and castles of Arizona's yesteryear. *Ghost Towns in Arizona (by Thelma Heatwole) 144 pages . . . $4.50*

Get acquainted with Arizona's sizzling Indian fry bread, sourdough biscuits, Navajo cake, orange marmalade, Papago beans, beef jerky, prickly pear jelly, cactus candy, chuckwagon steaks, refried beans, salsa, burritos, and much more! *Arizona Cook Book (by Al and Mildred Fischer) 144 pages . . . $3.50*

Take the back roads to Arizona's natural wonders—exotic valleys, natural bridges, idyllic spots, majestic mountains, impassible streams, boxed-in canyons, sparkling lakes—it's all there in *Arizona—Off the beaten path! (by Thelma Heatwole) 144 pages . . . $4.50*

Now, you can prepare these favorite recipes—tacos, tamales, menudo, enchiladas, burros, salsas, frijoles, huevos, almendrado. Home style! Delicious! *Mexican Family Favorites Cook Book (by Maria Teresa Bermudez) 144 pages . . . $5.00*

Follow the daring deeds and exploits of the Earp brothers, Buckey O'Neill, the Rough Riders, Arizona Rangers, cowboys and cattlemen, politicians and miners, shootouts, notorious Tom Horn, Pleasant Valley wars, the "First" American revolution—action-packed true tales of early Arizona! *Arizona Adventure (by Marshall Trimble) 160 pages . . . $5.00*

The lost hopes, the lost lives—the lost gold! Facts, myths and legends of the Lost Dutchman Gold Mine and the Superstition Mountains. Told by a geologist who was there! *Fools' Gold (by Robert Sikorsky) 144 pages . . . $5.00*

Order from your book dealer or direct from publisher.

ORDER BLANK

Golden West Publishers

4113 N. Longview Ave.
Phoenix, AZ 85014

Please ship the following books:

____Ghost Towns in Arizona ($4.50) ____Arizona—off the beaten path ($4.50)
____Arizona Cook Book ($3.50) ____Fools' Gold ($5.00)
____Arizona Adventure ($5.00) ____Mexican Cook Book ($5.00)

I enclose $_____ (Please add $1 per order postage, handling)

Name _____

Address _____

City _____ State _____ Zip_____

This order blank may be photo copied

INDEX

A

Al Ranch, 99, 103
Ajo, 8
Alisos Canyon, 52
Alta California, 19-24
Alvord, Burt, 134, 137
Ames, Frank, 97
Anza, Juan Bautista de, 19-25
Apache Kid, 130
Apache Junction, 113
Apacheria, 21
Apaches, 7, 13, 15, 19, 20, 23, 25,
  30-31, 33-35, 42, 45, 47-55, 60-64,
  92-93, 110, 112-113, 129, 130, 133,
  134, 145
Aravaipa Canyon, 48, 144-145
Aravaipa River, 47
Arizona, 10, 19
Arizona Cattle Co., 95
Arizona Cattle Growers Assn., 100
Arizona Champion, 96
Arizona Historical Society, 46
Arizona Rangers, 134-141
Arizona Republic, 148
Armijo, Manuel, 33
Arnett, George, 141
Arnold, Oren, 112
Ashfork, 34, 40, 95, 105
Ashurst, Henry, 100
Atlantic & Pacific RR, 92, 93, 95, 97,
  101, 103, 125
Awatovi, 17, 18
Aztec Land & Cattle Co., 97
Azul, Chief, 47, 48, 50, 51

B

Babbitt Bros., 99, 100, 101-108
Babbitt, Charles (C.J.), 102-105, 107
Babbitt, David, 101, 102, 107
Babbitt, David, Jr., 102, 104, 105
Babbitt, Edward, 102, 104, 107
Babbitt, George, 102, 104, 105, 107
Babbitt, William (Billy) 101-105, 107
Babocomari River, 52
Baja California, 21
Baldwin, Ephraim, 44
Baron of Arizona, 112-113
Barrett, James, 44, 46
Bascom, George, 51
Baylor, John R., 42
Beadle & Adams, 85
Beale Camel Rd., 93
Beale, "Ned," 92
Bear Springs, 52
Becknell, William, 27
Behan, Johnny, 72-76, 78-79, 82-83
Belden, Charles, 85
Benson, 39, 45, 139-140
Bent's Fort, 30
Big Bug, 8, 37
Bill Williams Mt., 34
Bill Williams River, 32, 63
Bisbee, 8, 39, 40, 57, 58, 109, 137
Blaine, James G., 73
Blevins (Andy, Charlie, Hamp, John,
  Mart, Sam Houston), 116-121
Boom Towns, 56-59
Bourke, John G., 47
Bradshaw Mts., 9, 26, 37, 38, 120
Breakenridge, Billy, 73-74
Brewery Gulch, 58
Bridger, Jim, 26
Brigham City, 93
Brighton, Rawhide Jake, 83
Brocius, Curly Bill, 70, 71, 77, 79-81
Brodie, Alexander, 126, 127, 137

Brunchow, Frederic, 60
Brunchow Mine, 62, 64
Bucareli, Antonio, 21
Buffalo Bill, 85
Buffalo Soldiers, 126
Bullwinkle, B.B., 95, 96
Bumble Bee, 57, 113
Butterfield Stage, 41, 42, 44, 51

C

Cactus, 8
California, 19-24, 34, 35
California Column, 42-46
Calloway, William, 44, 45
Camel Corps, 92
Cameron, Colin, 91
Cameron, Simon, 43
Camino del Diablo, 21
Camino del Real, 24
Camp Grant, 48, 54
Camp Verde, 121
Camp Wallen, 52
Cananea, 138
Canyon Diablo, 102, 123, 125
Carleton, James, 37, 43, 44
Carson, Kit, 26, 33-35
Castaneda, Joe, 39, 40
Cattle-raising, 92-100
Cedar Mesa, 95
Chacon, Augustin, 137
Charleston, 71
Chino Valley, 34
Chiricahua Mts., 146
Cholla, 8
Cienega Ranch, 51
Circle S Brand, 96, 103
Citizens Safety Committee, 72, 74, 76,
  79, 81, 83
Civil War, 41-46, 50
Claiborne, Billy, 77-79
Clanton, Billy, 70, 71, 77, 78, 79, 81
Clanton, Ike, 68, 69, 76-81
Clanton, N.H. "Old Man," 70, 80
Clanton, Phin, 70
Clark, Marion, 6
Clarkdale, 58, 121
Cleopatra Hill, 120
Clifton, 109, 138, 146
Clum, John, 72, 74, 80-81
CO Bar Ranch, 99, 103
Coane, Henry M., 7
Cochise, 42, 51, 54-55
Cochise County War, 67-83, 123, 134
Cochiti Pueblo, 16
Colorado Desert, 21
Colorado Plateau, 125
Colorado River, 21, 24, 26, 29, 32, 37,
  38
Columbia, 56
Colyer, Vincent, 55
Comanches, 13, 15, 25
Congress, 120
Contention, 39, 65
Cooley, Corydon E., 6
Coolidge, Dane, 85
Cooper, Andy (Blevins), 116-119
Copper Basin, 154
Cornville, 7
Coronado, Francisco Vasquez de, 11,
  109
County Ring, 72, 73, 74, 76
Cow Springs, 107
Cowboys, 84-91
Cowboys (Clanton gang), 71, 75-78,
  84-91
Cowlic, 7
Crane, Jim 75, 77, 79
Crawford, Emmett, 129

Crittenden, 39, 51, 54
Crook, George, 55, 129-130
Crown King, 111
Cruz, Florentino, 82
Cuernaverde, 25
Culiacan, 23
Cushing, Howard, 47-55

D - E

Daggs brothers, 100, 114
Dake, Crawley P., 70, 81
Date Creek, 39
Dedera, Don, 148
Desert Land Act, 98
Diamond, Jack, 95, 96
Dilda, Dennis, 123
Dobie, J. Frank, 90, 111
Dons Club, 112
Douglas, 121, 137
Dragoon Mts., 71, 146
Dragoon Springs, 45
Dripping Springs, 48
Dunbar, John, 73, 76
Dunbar, Thomas, 73
Duppa, Darrell, 9, 10
Duran, Manuel, 47, 48
Eager, 92
Earp, James, 69-70, 81
Earp, Josie, 75, 82, 83
Earp, Morgan, 69-71, 77-79, 81-83
Earp, Virgil, 69-79, 81-83
Earp, Warren, 70, 81
Earp, Wyatt, 67-83, 123
Ehrenberg, 38-40
Ehrenberg, Herman, 38
Eixarch, Tomas, 23
El Dorado, 109
El Paso del Norte, 16
Elder, Big Nose Kate, 76
Eloy, 7
Encomienda, 13, 15
Epitaph, 122-123
Espejo, Antonio de, 11

F

Fairbank, 39
Fay, Artemus Emmett, 73
First Mesa, 17
Fish Creek, 8
Fitzpatrick, Tom, 26
Flagstaff, 8, 17, 93-95, 100-108, 125
Flake, Jacob, 7
Fletcher, Curley, 154
Florence, 121, 125
Fly's Boarding House, 78
Font, Pedro, 23, 24
Fort Apache, 8
Fort Lowell, 46, 51
Fort McDowell, 9
Fort Moroni, 93, 95, 97
Fort Rickerson, 95
Fort Rucker, 71
Fort Valley, 93
Fourpaugh, 7
Franciscans, 12-18, 21
Fredonia, 9
Fremont, John C., 72-73
French, Sam, 102-103
Fronteras, 19
Fuller, West, 78, 79
Fur Trade, 26-35

G

Gadsden Purchase, 50, 60, 112
Galiuro Mts., 142-149
Gap, The, 8
Garces, Francisco Tomas, 18, 20, 21,
  23, 24
Gardner, Delia, 154
Gardner, Gail, 150-154